GROOVE, BANG
AND JIVE AROUND

T0021907

Steve Cannon

GROOVE, BANG AND JIVE AROUND

Blank Forms Editions
BROOKLYN, NY

STEVE CANNON (1935–2019) was a writer who shaped the literary history of Manhattan's Lower East Side. He was the founder and executive director of A Gathering of the Tribes, an East Village nonprofit and exhibition space, and the publisher of a magazine of the same name. Tribes, which operated from Cannon's Alphabet City townhouse, functioned as a salon where artists and musicians such as David Hammons, Sun Ra and Butch Morris could reliably be found among a cohort of younger poets emerging from the Nuyorican Poets Café scene. Born to a preacher in New Orleans, Cannon relocated to New York from England in 1962, where, alongside such luminaries as Amiri Baraka and Calvin C. Hernton, Cannon joined the Umbra Workshop, a cornerstone of 1960s African American avant-garde poetry and publishing. In 1973 he, Ishmael Reed, and Joe Johnson cofounded the influential literary and audio/visual imprint Reed, Cannon, and Johnson. As a poet, playwright and professor, Cannon mentored a generation of writers including Eileen Myles and Paul Beatty, and taught across the City University of New York system for more than three decades.

DARIUS JAMES is the author of five books including *Negrophobia* (Citadel, 1992), recently reissued by NYRB Classics. He has worked as a lecturer, spoken-word performer, journalist, theater director and creative writing coach. His documentary *The United States of Hoodoo* was released in 2012.

TRACIE MORRIS is a poet and sound artist. She is the author and editor of several books, most recently *human/ nature poems* (Litmus, 2023), and a professor of poetry at the Iowa Writers' Workshop.

Groove, Bang and Jive Around
by Steve Cannon

Published by Blank Forms Editions;
originally published by Ophelia
Press, 1969; revised for Olympia
Press, 1971.

Blank Forms Editions is produced
with support from Robert
Rauschenberg Foundation, The
Andy Warhol Foundation for the
Visual Arts, Agnes Gund, and the
founding Blank Forms Publisher's
Circle including Olivier Berggruen,
Gisela Gamper, Abigail Goodman
and David Norr, Steven Eckler,
Christian Nyampeta and Mary Wang
and Linden Renz.

Blank Forms would like to thank
Chris Calhoun; Patsy and Evelyn
Cannon; Mary Chen; David Grundy;
Steven Heller and Beth Kleber of the
School of Visual Arts Archive; Amna
Abdus-Salaam; Malia Guyer-Stevens
and Nicholas Martin of New York
University's Special Collections;
Darius James; Patricia Spears Jones;
Jean-Philippe Marcoux; Tracie
Morris; Umar Rashid; Ishmael Reed;
Quincy and Margaret Porter Troupe;
and Tracie Dawn Williams, Chavisa
Woods and the entire staff at
A Gathering of the Tribes.

Cover image © Umar Rashid, 2023
Foreword © Darius James, 2023
Afterword © Tracie Morris, 2024

Artistic and Executive Director
    Lawrence Kumpf
Curator
    Tyler Maxin
Managing Editor
    Ciarán Finlayson
Design
    Alec Mapes-Frances

Printed by Ofset Yapımevi in Turkey

ISBN 978-1-953691-19-4

Blank Forms Editions
468 Grand Avenue
#1D/#3D
Brooklyn, NY 11238
blankforms.org

Editor's Note

This edition of *Groove, Bang and Jive Around* has been lightly corrected and marks the book's return to print for the first time in more than twenty-five years. *Groove* was originally published on Halloween in 1969 by the New York branch of Ophelia Press, a subsidiary of Paris-based Olympia Press, founded in 1954 to publish "the hardcore pornography that helped finance the better writing to be found in the company's Traveller's Companion series of novels."[1] Olympia released a revised and slightly expanded version of *Groove* in 1971—the same year Coward, McCann, and Geoghegan published the first of Cannon's two children's books, *What I Like to Do*, with photographs by Elaine Wickens—changing the closing note, inserting section subheadings, expanding descriptions and introducing several new subplots. Critical attention was limited: it was reviewed only by Michael Perkins in the biweekly pornographic New York paper *Screw*, but became, in the words of Darius James, "an underground classic of such legendary statute that New York's black cognoscenti have transmogrified the work into urban myth."

1   Patrick J. Kearney, *A Bibliography of the New York Olympia Press* (London: Black Spring Press, 1987), i.

Cannon was introduced to Olympia's publisher Maurice Girodias by Clarence Major, a future National Book Award finalist whose *All-Night Visitors*, a gritty novel about sex and violence on the Lower East Side, was released by Olympia in 1969. Cannon and Girodias grew close and became drinking partners, frequenting Max's Kansas City together during the production of the book. On the process of revising, Cannon wrote:

> I had this great editor who was from Idaho. She lived on St. Mark's Place and loved nothing better than sitting around, talking trash and smoking hash. She happened to have her black boyfriend up in jail in Connecticut; she would take him up a pound of reefer to satisfy his needs while he was in the slams. She was a damn good editor and a lot of fun to be around. She was the one who came up with the title of my novel; I wanted to call it *Annette's Blues*, but she decided a better title would be *Groove, Bang and Jive Around* and I agreed.[2]

The updated book was translated and published three times in Frankfurt by the German wing of Olympia under the titles *Sotsch!!* (1970), *Schwarze Haut und weisse Glut* (ca. 1976) and *Nachts in New Orleans* (1987).

Back in New York, in 1996, the Quality Paperback Book Club published a new edition of *Groove*—illustrated by writer, painter and Tijuana Bible collector Richard Merkin and designed by Monica Elias—as part of a series for QPB's parent company, Book of the Month Club, alongside the likes of *Pinktoes* by Chester Himes, *Justine* by Marquis de Sade and *Venus in Furs* by Leopold von Sacher-Masoch. Two years later it was redesigned and reissued to wider distribution by Therion Classics, a short-lived literary imprint devoted to controversial titles from the past, which boasted on the

2 Steve Cannon, "You're Never Too Old to Blush" *Black Renaissance/ Renaissance Noire* 19, no. 1 (Winter/Spring 2019): 53.

rear cover that *Groove* "sold more than 150,000 copies when it first appeared." Therion was a subsidiary of the romance paperback specialists Genesis Press, then the largest independent black publishing house in the United States, founded in 1993 in Lowndes County, Mississippi, by Wilbur Colom, a republican political aspirant and proprietor of a law firm, car dealership and radio station; his wife, Dorothy Colom, a chancery judge; and their business partner James W. Parkinson.

In 2012, *Groove* was reissued as an eBook through Fly By Night Press, a subsidiary of Cannon's nonprofit arts organization A Gathering of the Tribes, "to earn its author some much needed income." Tribes, a gallery, event space and publisher, was founded in 1991 and operated out of an East Village townhouse that Cannon had purchased in 1970 using a combination of money saved by living with friends for a summer and royalties from sales of *Groove*.[3] Cannon sold the 285 East Third Street townhouse in 2004. He and A Gathering of the Tribes remained there until they were evicted ten years later and relocated to an apartment on East Sixth Street. Tribes continues to publish and support emerging and underrepresented writers and memorialize Cannon's life and legacy.

---

3   Sarah Ferguson, "Tribes mounts last-ditch appeal to save iconic East Village arts space," *amNY*, March 20, 2014, https://www.amny.com/news/tribes-exuberant-east-village-arts-space-faces-eviction.

Foreword
by Darius H. James

THE END PROMPTS A NEW BEGINNING

The night I met Steve was also the night I was fired from the Strand bookstore.

Over the loudspeaker, I threatened customers lingering in the basement with the promise that if they didn't vacate immediately, select members of our typing pool would attack them in a blur of claw-wielding depravity. (At the risk of this fine publisher's liability, I dare not repeat specifics.) My announcement was quickly followed by the store manager's voice: "You're fired, Mr. James!"

Upstairs, the security guard, who looked like a toothless warthog with pustuled gums, slowly waddled in my direction with increasing menace, the weight of his belly teetering side to side, fondling the head of his nightstick with an unwarranted excitement. We squinted eye to eye. Then he bounced me through the doors with his buoyant basketball belly.

Boink! Boink! Boink!

This was the summer of 1985. It was also the last time in my life I worked a nine-to-five.

Hallelujah! I'm a bum!

THE NEITHER/NOR STUDIO/STORE

Jobless, I sat outside and considered my options. The plan was to attend an event I saw on a flier thumbtacked to the wall of a rice-n-beans eatery on Avenue C. I stood up, dusted myself off and wandered in the direction of Tompkins Square Park.

Steve's name was on the flier. I knew of Steve through the *Yardbird Reader*, a journal edited by Ishmael Reed, Al Young and others, published out of Berkeley, California. *Yardbird* featured the work of various East and West Coast writers of various hues, continuing the multicultural traditions established in the early '60s by the Society of Umbra, a group of poets and writers cofounded by David Henderson. It was at a dive called the Neither/Nor Studio/Store, located on East Sixth Street between Avenues C and D.

Neither/Nor was the brainchild of Rick van Valkenburg. Beginning somewhere in the American Midwest as a zine; the project took a left turn when Rick decided to pursue a career on the silver screen (he can be seen in *Last Exit to Brooklyn*), evolving into a café, nightclub and raucous shoot-'em-up after-hours spot.

During the day, Neither/Nor was a sedate café. It served coffee and tea. Rick stood guard at the register with a magazine rack at his back specializing in difficult-to-locate print items like George Petro's *Exit* magazine. Contributing to the general atmosphere, musicians who survived the Free Jazz era of the '60s and '70s rehearsed through the daylight hours.

At night, Neither/Nor was another story. It was jazz violinist Billy Bang traveling the Arkestral space ways, his

14

mind illuminated by atomically explosive mushrooms. It was a cantankerous John Farris hosting a weekly reading series and bemoaning the sorry condition of the literary arts in America (or the rhinoceros. Always Del Mundo the rhinoceros with John Farris). It was a completely naked Miguel Piñero spinning out from behind a curtain with torrents of blood pouring out of his veins in tribute to Jean Genet. It was Cecil Taylor snorting a rail of coke off the bar at three a.m. Neither/Nor also held the distinction of accommodating White Zombie's first gig. In a fully lit room, the white, dreadlocked rumored Republican *twanged* to a handful of hippies "skinking" to a strobe light.

I handed over a crumpled five and walked into a warehouse space that once functioned as a mechanic shop for bikers. There was a microphoned platform on the left side of the room. Standing on that was a thalidomide-baby lady with a sheaf of papers in the hand protruding from her left shoulder. She read gracefully, her fingers fluttering with poignancy.

I ordered a beer.

Shortly, the thalidomide-baby lady's reading concluded and Steve Cannon commandeered the mic. Steve surprised me, though he didn't read. He remarked on the literary import of the previous reader to the Lower East Side in the late '60s and early '70s.

* * *

SMUT I WRITE!

Some years passed. I lived in Torino, Italy, occupying that quarter of the city where Nietzsche, compromised by syphilis, spent his final days questioning God's existence with the horses he encountered on the cobblestone streets. After nearly getting my head shot off by an Israeli soldier in Milan's airport (keffiyehs were hip that year), I came back to

15

the US with a taste for heroin (that was hip, *too*). And I left Manhattan for Montreal for the opposite reason. I returned to New York after a year or two for reasons not entirely my own. And I spent a great deal of time at Steve's on East Third Street to escape my suffocating circumstances. Steve's home was filled with his particular brand of Br'er Rabbit humor. It was a welcome respite.

Steve won my affections when he confessed he was a "commie" (many of my friends are "commies," especially in East Germany)—later making for a challenging game of hopscotch in the world of nonprofits. And he told me jet-setting hookers funded the '60s revolution through their Wall Street sugar daddies.

How could you not love a guy like that?

While rereading a back issue of *Yardbird*, I learned Steve had published a novel. Why I hadn't known I can't say. I chalk it up to drunken self-absorption. I called Steve and asked for a copy.

"I ain't got it! I gave them all away!"

Thus began a two-year quest (I'll spare the details since I've recounted my efforts elsewhere. It's enough to know I acquired a copy through my own adventures in *smut*).

When I presented Steve with an edition of *his* book, he was in a particularly depressed period of his life. His sight was slowly fading. His three-story walk-up caught fire. With *Groove, Bang* back, his sense of life renewed. Within months, he began building the organization we know today as A Gathering of the Tribes.

* * *

There are two primary influences on Steve's freshman novel:

1) *New Orleans*. The ghosts of Storyville haunt these pages. The red-light district of the Crescent City in the late nineteenth and early twentieth century was home to prostitutes and jazz, both represented in these pages. It's

likely that bowdlerized rock songs like Little Richard's "Tutti Frutti" had their more salacious beginnings in such places decades earlier. And if Richard Pryor's *Craps (After Hours)* is any indication, high-end brothels were an early home to blue comedians; bolstering my belief that the best in American culture originated in its ho' houses. It's not difficult to imagine the influence these establishments had on bordello songbirds like Lucille "Shave 'Em Dry" Bogan. The musicality and humor of the New Orleans cathouse is clearly reflected in Steve's playful use of language.

2) Not unlike Basquiat, who painted dollar bills into his canvases to assure his paintings' success, Steve Cannon employed Hoodoo trickery in the writing of this novel for good luck. I don't have the space here for an extensive discussion of the very real differences between Vodou and Hoodoo. Simply, Vodou is a living spiritual system (contrary to 1930s Hollywood ooga-booga). I've refrained from providing a brief definition of Hoodoo so as not to foment unnecessary conflict between the two very different traditions.

One aspect of Vodun practice is that one does not rehearse. You practice. You prepare and live in the moment—taking in the transient nature of existence, understanding that all life is like a castle pulverized to sand under the weight of the ocean's crashing waves. It is mutable. *Adaptable.* It is spirit.

According to Steve, Vodou replenishes and renews itself by absorbing new forms. This is one reason why the *loa* are disguised as Catholic Saints in the diasporic expressions of Vodou. The use of these forms in Steve's work became apparent during a discussion we had about *The Set Up*, a play he had written and was producing in 1991. He had this basic structure in mind: the audience would follow the story from point A to point B, while the actor was free to improvise between those two points. The space in-between was a portal. Spirit enters our dimension through these sacred portals.

He compared the process to a jazz solo; citing John Coltrane's "My Favorite Things." This method is very similar to that of a masterful ceremonial Vodou drummer I know.

* * *

Groove, Bang and Jive Around was published in 1971 and received ONE review, in Al Goldstein's highly esteemed *Screw* magazine, getting high marks on the meat-beatable scale. The book sold to jillions of jackoffs. Steve could finally renovate that husk of a brownstone he owned and lived in on the Lower East Side. He held on to that brownstone for most of his life, losing it in his final years. Curiously, the loss of his brownstone only uncloaked the tremendous amount of love the Lower East Side community felt for Steve because of the deeds and support that came out of that brownstone—a love demonstrated by the community as Steve was triumphantly carried through the streets on its shoulders to his new quarters on the corner of East Sixth Street and Avenue D.

In any case, gentle reader, welcome to a very *very* filthy book.

Darius H. James
12/18/2023
7:05 a.m.

THE
NEW
ORLEANS
STOMP

THE GUMBO
HOUSE

It was already late, half-past the cat's ass and getting later, ten back of twelve, and still Annette with her little young fourteen-year-old self wasn't home.

But she didn't care.

She stepped up to the jukebox, dropped two bits in the slot and pressed J-10. The bright hues on the electronic juke changed colors as the records spun and a pulse selected her number. She sensed the eyes of every male in the Gumbo House X-raying her well-stacked ass through her green miniskirt and black panties, down her soft brown thighs and round hairless legs and sandaled feet.

The babe was dynamite. And knew it.

Dip, her partner, grunted approvingly of her shape and form, but mused about the contents as he rubbed her behind. A thrill shot through Annette's asshole to her cunt, up her spine to her head, exploding constellations inside her skull; it returned by the same route, tickling the lips of her pussy and rolling her hams. The pulse passed through Dip's fingers to his head, lighting his eyes with cherries, then down to his swipe—which bulged in his bells, behind the action. Annette dug, but said nothing. Just blinked.

Fenders, snares, basses and twangy guitars vibrated the speakers, sending hot blasting sounds echoing inside her body. Zong! Instantly, her ass began to jump and her shoulders to roll as the music bounced around the room with enough heat to melt diamonds. The whole house rocked. Everybody went into their act.

Some fool yelled: "Let the whole world dance." Another shouted: "Shake it. Don't break it."

Finger-popping and feeling good inside and out, Annette smiled and turned to face the crowd: high-school and college dropouts, ex-Muslims, cons, boppers and bullshit hustlers with their dates and funeral directors' sons out for the night on the make, and sang along with the Tempting Temps.

See . . .
I was born and raised in the slums of the city.
It was a one-room flat we slept in,
Other children beside me.
We hardly had enough food or room to sleep.
It was hard times . . .

She leaned over and looked into Dip's handsome face— her braless titties obvious inside the thin yellow blouse—and whispered: "I'll be back in a sec."

She strolled between the checkered, cloth-covered tables, hearing catcalls and yells, "Oh, yeahs" and "Hey, babes," snapping her fingers, dodging and sidestepping beer bottles and steins that had crashed to the floor as the customers stomped their feet, pounded table tops, laughed, joked, signified and jived, cussing one another in time to the music. She waved and threw kisses to those she knew, but got frightening stares mixed with admiration and hate— ambivalence—from foxes she didn't know. But she was tops, if you let her tell it.

When she reached the bar, five dudes dressed in pink, blue, yellow, green and red pants, plus shirts with matching shoes and socks to boot, gave her the eye as she passed them by.

She massaged her stomach, flashed a shy grin, then patted her love seat. Signifying. Two spooks damn near fell off their stools backwards, grabbing at all that jelly. But Annette eased outasight.

It was a clear summer night: stars, planets, constellations and galaxies, along with astrological signs (Leo, Aries and Sagittarius prominent) and dark unknown Spirits and spacecraft twinkled down on New Orleans, the Gumbo House and Annette. Headlights sculptured her frame in hot white light with the shack as a backdrop. She didn't think twice about it, shaded her eyes with her palm, and opened the door of the ladies' room. A seatless commode occupied the floor.

Dull yellow light from a bare bulb in the ceiling filled the closetsized john. Annette's shadow hovered over the commode where turds floated in piss. She flushed the toilet, glanced around at drawings of people fucking, swollen dicks and giant vaginas on the yellow walls, as roaches, ants and spiders dashed for cover inside the cracks.

Without a care in the world, outside this present natural duty, Annette hummed to herself as she neatly placed two pieces of toilet paper on the bowl's edge. She pulled up her skirt, exposing luscious fine brown thighs, dropped her drawers and got down.

Inside her bowels, the hot sausage and peppers on French played hell pushing the beer, wine and juju seeds to the side so it could duff. Annette belched, grunted and farted; the turds said SWOOSH and shot from hole to bowl. The sound of the Temps still gitting away in the Gumbo House seeped into the shithouse:

You kin be what you wanna be
CLOUD NINE

25

More refreshed, but still slightly dazed, Annette wiped her ass. The green eyes of a black cat peeped through the half-open door. She shooed it away. Her eyes caught the glimpse of a scorched brown hand with dirty fingernails pulling at the door. Her heart skipped a beat, resettled atop her stomach as heat flashed from the tips of her fingers and the edges of her toes to convulse in her womb; her skin felt warm, then cool, as the muscles around her crotch relaxed. Her bladder gave. The beer and wine got out just in time. For days!

The arms, legs and rest of the body entered the small john. A grin wiped away any fear that might have been on Annette's face. She recognized the body as that of Sleepy Willie—eyes half closed, reefer in mouth, the scar on the side of his black face jumping and twisting—staring absently at her seated on the commode. Her mind jumped back to the time he had screwed her in the teachers' lounge . . . on a park bench . . . then to the headlights shinin' outside the Gumbo House. Her eyes grew larger than tensor lamps as she gaped at the purplish, red-headed dick with tight black skin, staring her in the face. But after having relieved herself inside out, so to speak, Annette was ready for anything, even if it had to go down inside the funkhouse. One word escaped her lips, "You . . . " as she grinned.

Not a word, not even a sigh, came from Sleepy Willie even though he was wide awake. He pulled on his johnson with his right hand, and closed the door with his left. From dick head to Annette's face it looked like a well-done, red-hot sausage, 'bout twice the size of a salami, but umpteen times as potent. And alive! A clear liquid oozed from its lips. Sweat broke out on her forehead, under her armpits, between her thighs, and her insteps felt hot too as saliva formed in her mouth and the adrenalin drained.

Like a baton twirler with lots of practice, Annette grabbed Willie's pipe, puckered her lips, blew small breaths on the head, kissed it, then rubbed it around her lips, her ears, creating a kind of suction with sound, rouged it with her cheeks, and over her eyelids. Dark passages became real; then she rubbed it against her titties. Willie moved along with her, without a word of praise. Annette let his hang hang. "Didn't that feel good?" she popped, repeating the actions previously mentioned: re-wiping her behind and drying her hole.

Willie grunted something incoherently. Something 'bout "Sho' do, but don't stop naw." He grabbed the back of her head and pulled it towards his johnson which was jumping as if he had the aches.

"Hold it, sweetie. We've got to do this thing right." Annette stood, coming up to his chin. Pulling his hand from behind her head, and thinking maybe she'd kick him in his balls if he fucked around.

Realizing she wasn't high enough, in more ways than one, she stood up on the commode, grabbed Willie's joint and rubbed it against her ankles, legs and over her thighs. She bent slightly forward and let it play around the outer edges of her cunt. Willie started getting excited. Annette was still in control. She jerked him off slowly, letting the liquids paste and dry on her tender young thighs.

Instinctively, like acting out some unknown ritual a trillion billion years old, Ole Sleepy Willie stuck his head between her thighs and began sucking Annette's love like someone gone wild. She snickered a bit, feeling good inside, as he kissed her clit, sucked her lips, and stuck his tongue all inside against the walls, with his nose running interference.

Annette took her right thigh, placed it on his left shoulder, then holding him by his burr head, she placed her left thigh on his right shoulder. His johnson was aimed directly at the commode, jumping and jiving in thin air. Annette held on, with both hands clasped behind his neck. Willie's hands pushed into the soft flesh of her ass. Holding her up, he kissed and licked her cunt, between her thighs, and checked out her ass. Thrills shot from one end of Annette's body to the other, as his tongue ran circles around her behind, giving her a rim job.

She started to come, jerked his head forward and made him georgia her some more: pulling his head forward, and feeling her stomach muscles tighten, laughing and panting something awful, looking down, then up at the bare light bulb and over at the walls; seeing the drawings of people sucking and fucking, she came in his mouth—on his tongue—while he emptied some of his seeds in the commode below. She climbed down.

She stood on the commode with her skirt up above her waist, drawers hanging down around her left ankle and her blouse completely opened. She let him feel up her breast and kiss her on the stomach and the navel, while his hand played up between the fat cheeks of her ass and rubbed her cunt. She rubbed it against his chest for a minute, panting and groaning, feeling all hot, wanting to spend again. While trying to think of a position, his dick slapped her against the legs.

She got further down, sat on the commode and took his ripe joint—limp and fallen—in her mouth, and sucked it hard and hot, rubbing the head all back on her tongue, her cheeks bulging like Diz blowing trumpet; she unsnapped the top of his pants, squeezed his balls with one hand and finger-fucked herself with the other. It started feeling so good, she chafed it against her face, faster and slower, slower faster, and kissed the black wiry hairs around his balls, letting her fingers pierce his ass, sending chills up his spine, down his legs, causing him to jerk and twist, push and pull. She opened her lips and clamped down on it, the head in the roof of her mouth, rubbing her clit, kissing the lips of his joint, her tongue so hot it felt to Willie his joint was in a barrel of hot molten steel as the salivated tongue souped his prick! His balls tightened, the blood drained into his joint swelling it bigger and bigger; he felt it coming. Annette worked like a pro in Martha's White House, sending the thrills, chills up and down his spine, causing his head to spin. He felt like he was gonna let loose. She stopped abruptly. Sat down on the back of the commode, watching his dick jerk up and down under its own steam, ready to spout and spill his seed. He got down and sat at the other end of the commode. She wrapped her legs over his thighs, and he sent his dick up her cunt. Her uterus felt like it was gonna burst open. She stuck her hot tongue down his throat, bit him on the neck, wrapped her arms around him, and started jumping up and down, slowly and fast, fast slowly, clamping his dick with the muscles of her cunt, squeezing it and releasing it. He finally gave it up!

He panted and swooned and damn near fell over backwards off the commode. She held him around the waist, her cunt muscles squeezing his dick, draining his drops and looking at his half-closed eyes as she felt the hot juices spurt up into her, round the side of his dick, down into the commode.

"Damn, baby," Willie started, gasping for breath, and trying to grin, "I mean, damn!!!" Remembering that it wasn't this good the last time.

"You liked it?" The question didn't mean anything—she knew she had turned his ass round.

"Liked it?" He kissed her on her round firm tits, stuck his head down below her neck and kissed her rich golden-brown shoulders and let his fingers play around the bottom of her ass, tickling her asshole as his dick slipped out.

Suddenly, without giving him a chance to say another word, Annette started kissing him passionately on the neck and eyelids, running her tongue over his ears, down his throat; working, working it like his joint had worked inside her cunt, laying it on him hard and good, solid and final. He felt the blood throbbing at his temples, at the pressure points between his thighs; and felt his insteps rise, trying to climb up into his ass, and his dick got harder than when he had been sitting out in his car thinking about her and his chances of a good fuck. She reached down behind and under her ass, grabbed his joint and slipped it in her well-juiced young, not-over-fourteen, dripping-come-all-over-the-commode cunt, squeezing with her muscles, and looking in his eyes as she shook her ass up and down, sideways front and backwards, both of them moving now, their lips glued together, tongues fighting inside their mouths, and feeling transport like Onassis and Jackie on a love seat instead of this dirty-assed commode. Working and working, him going up, she coming down, Willie ran his hands up and down her spine and images of chickens and dogs and bulls and cows fucking ran through his mind as she grabbed his asshole and made him push his dick further up her snatch, closed her eyes and started screaming and yelling, "Come, motherfucker! It sure is good. Damn, you really got what it takes."

They both exploded at the same time.

"Shit! You sure do know where it's at." She smiled and kissed him on his bloodshot eyes. He got off the stool, his joint going limp, but his mind still on fucking. He caressed her nice soft round ass, let his hands run down her thighs, up inside her thighs, grabbed hold of her cunt and started finger-fucking. She jumped, squirmed, wiggled and panted, "Ah . . . Ah . . . Ah gotta go naw. Dip . . . Dip is waiting for me." But the intensity of Willie's finger movement, swirling round and round inside her, his thumb and forefinger squeezing and releasing their hold on her clitoris, was too much for her to resist. "Wait! Wait, Willie! Let me get it together."

He took his hand away and rubbed her stomach, between her thighs, her juicy hole—his dick harder now than when he had walked into the john, since the smells of beer, vomit and menstrual blood had been camouflaged temporarily by the smell of their bodies secreting odors from their pores.

She turned and leaned over the toilet, grabbed the back of the bowl, her brown-skinned ass sticking up in his face. She spread her round thighs, then reached behind and grabbed hold of his stiff dick. Still slippery and covered with jism, he eased it into her from behind, her feeling it all the way up to the tip of her womb, bending down even further and pushing back. "OOH, damn, OOOh, damn, uh uh, uh, uh, ah, ah, ah, ah, ah, come on, come on, give it to me. Shit, man, all the way." Willie shoving for all he's worth, feeling the insteps of his feet blood hot, like firecrackers exploding under them; the veins of his legs tightened like four-ply rope. Him, feeling the blood moving throughout his body, like liquid oxygen being converted into raw energy, from the tips of his fingers, the edges of his toes, centering again around his groin as he slipped his stiff, bouncing-like-a-motherfucker dick in and out of her juicy cunt.

Annette continued to grasp the back edge of the commode, took one hand and flushed it, feeling hot and sweaty, her blood at the boiling point, her skin feeling like a trillion cunts prickling under his touch, joy juice oozing down her legs. In and up, both getting hot, moving unconsciously *and* consciously to the rhythms of the music—inside the Gumbo House—that filtered through the walls. Willie felt his balls tighten like an iron vise, the muscles contract inside Annette's warm juicy cunt. He slid it out, out, around her ass, inside her cunt, around her ass, pushed, tried to drive it into her small asshole—which was sucking air like a Kent commercial sucking smoke. He can't get it in, slipped it back into her cunt, getting hotter and hotter, squeezing his own balls with one hand, the other hand playing around her stomach and her pointed tits under the opened blouse. Shaking his ass, she shaking hers to his counter-motions, he slipped it out, covered with come, and tried again at her asshole.

She squirmed, stooped further down, sending her ass riding higher off the ground. On the balls of her feet, her knees round the middle of the commode, her hands grabbing the back of the toilet, her head down, almost inside the commode, her eyes looking at its rim as she shook her ass up and down, sideways and round and round, feeling the weight of his body as he charged her—like a bull behind some Spanish Fly, sailing into a cow. She let out a scream that could be heard for two blocks around.

The sound reverberated inside the close walls of the john like a thousand women giving birth at once, bouncing out into the night air—shocking people on front porches, children playing hide-and-seek, fucking for toys, their words stuck in their mouths as they searched for its origin.

To Dip—inside the Gumbo House, finishing his Oyster Loaf and wondering what the hell was taking Annette so long anyway, listening to the Temptations finishing *Cloud Nine*—it sounded like Satchmo blowing at the Gates of Hell. Immediately his mind went to Annette and the ladies' room. He followed his mind, the dudes in pink, blue, yellow, green and red followed *him,* and the night cook with a meat cleaver in his hand followed *them.* They all ran out the back door, behind the bar, from the kitchen to the john. Some joker unplugged the jukebox so everyone could hear!

Dip's eyes bucked. Willie was standing with his head thrown back, his hands on either side of the walls; while Annette moved her ass backwards and forwards, sucking the last drops from his sacs as he emptied them into her hole. If you could have seen the looks on Willie's and Annette's faces you wouldn't have to be told twice it felt good to 'em both. Take my word for it. To Dip: all he could see was a black ass with green silk pants down around the ankles, a conked head shining beneath the light bulb, a black cat meowing around some nigger's legs, blocking the view of the commode. "Wha . . . what the fuck is this?" Annette's hands climbed the walls as she pulled herself up, feeling all groovy. Her skirt dropped down over her behind. She reached down, taking her time, and pulled up her drawers, carefully stepping inside the right hole. She pulled them halfway up her thighs, twisting her hips, paused, got two small pieces of shit paper and placed one inside her burned out asshole, the other inside the lips of her cunt. Then she pulled her drawers up around her hips and dropped her skirt. Willie leaned against the wall and began pulling up his trousers, still breathing hard.

For a minute, Dip stood frozen in his tracks. He refused to believe what he perceived. His imagination said: "Yeah, all things are possible." But his schoolbook mind rejected it. De Sade and Henry Miller fought inside his skull with Jacqueline Susann and Harold Robbins, while images of Dirt, Grime, Smut and Hitler's demise flashed images of dead nuns being screwed by Jews. A world of strange notions took possession of him—all at the same time. "Not Annette," he blurted. "Can't be."

He rushed up, grabbed Willie by his red silk shirt and pulled him out of the way. Willie was feeling so good, no blame, no pain, he shrugged his shoulders and laughed. "Sorry, Bro."

Annette looked right past Dip strugglin' with Willie—at the dudes in pink, blue, yellow, green and red shirts, pants and shoes and socks; pop eyes peering at her fine brown frame seated on the shitcan, buttoning up her blouse and smiling, knowing inside herself this must be some kind of Bad Joke!

Outside. The Jive Five grabbed Willie as he stopped to pull up his pants. His sacs might have been drained, but his strength hadn't stopped. He could still waltz. And he did.

Dip, with his long lanky self, came inside the john, and hovered over Annette: "What . . . what's going down?"

Annette flushed the toilet, then jumped self-righteous. Looking him dead in the eye she screamed, "You kin see what's going down, or what *went* down for that matter. We got it together, that's all. He wanted a little bit, so I gave him a little bit. Anything wrong with that?"

"But . . . " he stammered. But, hell, let's face it, Dip's mind was blown. Gone. Suddenly remembering Annette when she was still in diapers tipping around her ol' man's house when Dip was going with her sister, both being in their early teens—and seeing her fine round thighs now down on the john, the look of impudence on her face, and those eyes? Wow! Saying something. He thought to himself, Why not? But said out loud: "But, baby . . . I mean . . . you know . . . better." That's just the way the words came out, short, quick and disconnected. Like as if he was really trying to say: Baby, you know I'm better. Or something to that effect, as his jones got harder just gazing at her face, titties and thighs.

But Annette let that one slide. She looked past him outside to check what was happening with Sleepy Willie.

Stompin' Sam, the night cook, moved around the outer circle as the Jive Five swung on Willie, trying to crash his skull with the meat cleaver. Willie was in the midst of trying to be Muhammad Ali and the world's heavyweight wrestling champ all at the same time: He swung on Blue, he hit the ground, kicked at Red, he collapsed in a bundle, elbowed Yellow, his face was cut up. This left Pink and Green, who were afraid to get their clothes mussed up. They moved back, left Willie shadowboxing by himself, dodging the cleaver Stompin' Sam swung. Swiissh! He sliced the air every trip. Willie backed up. The crowd gave them room. Pink and Green went over to the curb and picked up bricks.

When Annette spotted this action, she jumped off the stool and flatfooted it on outside, yelling at the top of her voice, screaming, "Leave him alone. Leave my man alone. He ain't done nuttin' but what you niggers sit around and signify, jive and lie about." She pounced on Stompin' Sam.

Shocked out of his skull, Stompin' Sam brought the cleaver down to his hip, shrugged his shoulders as he looked into her blazing eyes—remembering the face from somewhere but not able to exactly place it—and slipped through the crowd, back inside.

The Jive Five let their heads hang low. Blue, Yellow and Red slipped behind the crowd of onlookers. Pink and Green disappeared outasight.

Steaming, Annette strolled through the crowd of neighbors, door poppers, minding-other-people's-business ol' timers who sanged bop choruses of *Ain't That a Shame, Lawd Today, These Young'uns, Don't Know What's Gon Become Uv Um,* as the little kids on the block, male and female, looked on the scene with Awe, wondering if Annette was some kind of *Queen,* a Hoo Doo with mystic charms. But Annette didn't care what who thought. She knew who she was, how bad her thing was, and what was happening. Inside.

Hence: Let the people talk. They talked about Damballah, Tit Albert, Papa La Bas, and the late J. C. of biblical days. Some claimed *he* was a faggot, so she knew they would talk about her. Word has it that even Erzulie wasn't free from their slanderous good-for-nothing-but-old-folks' entertainment. Rubbish, but if they'd reach down and look into their own bags, somebody sure wasn't wearing clean underwear. But, like I said, Annette didn't care. The juju seeds had gone to her head.

Willie flexed his muscles a couple of times, finished pulling up his pants, and brushed himself off.

"You're all right?" Annette walked him to his car. The headlights were still on.

He got into the car, lit up a bush, looked sleepily out the window at her, and smiled. "Yeah. Fine." He passed her the joint.

Annette took a whiff, passed it back. "When'm I going to see you again?"

Willie snickered, looked out at the putdown crowd, shadows in the foreground, at Dip still in the john, silhouetted by the bare light bulb, then back at Annette. "Sometimes."

He kicked the car in reverse, backed out of Daneel, put it in drive and barely missed a bus as he turned the corner of Daneel and Louisiana Avenue. An old woman was hopping across the Avenue and he barely missed hitting a brat pushing a baby elephant in a carriage as he stepped down on the gas and headed towards the river. Gone.

Annette felt a cold chill sweep up her crotch. A slight dizziness spun her head around and an emptiness hit the pit of her stomach as she felt the eyes, ears, nostrils of everyone in the block, like the ol' time crowds in Congo Square—making up legendary tales, on the spot, of what had taken place that night.

But proudly she turned and walked back to Dip, still standing in the door of the john, as the crowd, the shadows, slowly dispersed, going their separate ways in ones, twos, threes and fours, the children still stunned, finding all this hard to believe, but mystified and on her side. "Let me finish my beer, then you kin take me home."

Dip nodded and followed her back into the Gumbo House. Not a word did he say. Nothing. But his thoughts were going zing zang zoom. It shoulda been me. And all that jazz.

Miss Inez, the owner, came over to the table, told Annette her presence was not wanted. "Besides, you're under age," she said.

Annette's mind, into the putdown she had received from Willie anyway, jumped salty as a dog and dropped the blues on Miss Inez, began telling her 'bout herself. "Lissen, you ol' flat-chested, halfwhite, two-timing, good-for-nothing, following-after-young-boys *hag,* you kin kiss my sweet pink ass. Kiss it till the moon comes out to shine and the clouds become mine. Hear me? You ain't nothing anyway. Who are you to talk? You ol' dried up yella cunt, go sell your ass down to City Hall, maybe it will get you outa your misery. Don't be trying to tell me all that stuff 'bout my presence ain't wanted."

Annette got up and pranced.

"Come on, Dip, let's get outa this double-talking, two-timing bar!"

36

Flaming red eyes, knowing her own background, and not about to be loud-talked by no fourteen-year-old, without another word Miss Inez went back into the kitchen and grabbed her snub-nosed thirty-eight.

As Annette hit the door, Dip following like Nixon following Ike, Miss Inez put three rockets around the door frame; customers hit the floor and Stompin' Sam among others grabbed Miss Inez' hand. The other three shots went wild, breaking window panes and hitting the juke, as the Temptin' Temps took *Cloud Nine* on a second go-round. "I'll kill that bitch. That little yella whore. She ain't got no business talking to me thataway. I'm old enough to be her grandmother, damn her. Bitch! Don't you ever bring your dirty, funky butt back in this place! Let me go, Sam. Let me go."

But luckily for Annette and Dip, Sam held on.

Dip ducked, beat Annette to the car. Huffing and puffing, his heart going ten miles a minute. Annette gave Miss Inez the finger, making signifying noises with her tongue, saying in so many words, "Suck my . . . you know what. Whore! Suck it. You two-timing lessie, Catholic bitch."

Dip got the car started in less than two seconds, backed up onto Daneel, stuck the car in drive, burned rubber gettin' around the neutral ground on Louisiana Avenue, bouncing off the curb, passed Holy Ghost Church with candles burning inside like it was the Witches' Sabbath, headed towards Bayou while Annette fumed, relaxed, then laughed to herself, listening to Miles' *Bitches'Brew* on the FM.

Feeling Sassy.

It was much later, quarter to the cat's hole, but not that late—half-past twelve—and still Annette wasn't home. And she wasn't even thinking 'bout *going* either. That's the gist . . .

THE HOUSE OF BLUE LIGHTS

DIP PUSHED THE LITTLE CAR hard—past china-berry trees, their branches forming an archway above the four-lane Avenue with neon-lit bars in the background: The Monkey Bar, Cotillion, Brown Derby, Club De Lisa, Chez Black, Brunhilde's Last Stand, Tosca's Lament, and the God Damn Rungk; past hospitals with bodies being surreptitiously sneaked out the rear and shipped to medical research centers; past housing projects, stray dogs, cats and brats, and stone-cold ofays hidden behind draperies, afraid to come out (the night belonging to the Infidels)—till he was at the corner of Claiborne and Louisiana Avenue, ten blocks away from the Gumbo House. Then he got the message that his headlights weren't on.

The fact is, some dude crossing the intersection had to drop the news on him, adding: "Lucky *they* didn't see you; you'd be in a whole woop of trouble by naw." The spook eyed

Annette through the windshield, wondering, Who's this fine sister?

Dip smiled, coming back to his senses, gave him a clenched fist salute and turned on the headlights at the same time.

The traffic light changed. The informer waited on the corner, still eyeing Annette, like he knew her or something, and commented dryly: "You got it naw, man. Your world."

Annette watched him, stare for stare, checking out his clothes—black and red jumpsuit, golden tam on his head, shades, and gold, diamond-studded teeth in his mouth. He was doing The Slop down the street, singing:

Down the road, come a junko partner
Man he was as loaded as can be . . .

as Dip dropped the car in gear, burned rubber turning the corner, headed cross town.

Annette shook her head, but still didn't say a word. Dip was cruising at about forty miles an hour, listening to Miles' rendition of "Pharoah's Dance" on the FM and watching cars, zip, pow, flash by. Annette's asshole and slit began to itch. She uncrossed her legs, relaxed a little bit, and moved closer to Dip. He put his arm around her, steering with his left.

Suddenly Dip swerved to the right, touching the brakes lightly to avoid an accident (tires screeching, horns blowing and people yelling) that was in the process of happening in the left lane at the corner. Two cars, a Volkswagen bus, two bicycles and a cop car went crashing head-on into each other sideways and from the rear, with bodies being flung out windows onto the neutral ground, atop hoods of cars, through windshields, mangled in the carnage of plastic and steel—gas fumes and outright funk filling the night air. Blood, bones and flesh all over the place. Two drunks staggered up from nowhere, each grabbing an arm of a cyclist whose body was hinged between the bus and the hood of a car. A woman holding a headless baby crashed through the bus's rear window. Under the flashing red light of the police car, a cop's head, streaked in blood, looked out through the broken windshield, while a kid, apparently the other bicyclist, ran down the street, holding his guts. Others sitting on the side, moaning low.

"Wow! Will you look at that?" Dip shouted. Annette looked. "Some accident." Dip slowed the car down to about ten miles an hour, and had to drive over the curb to get past the rubble and the people who had sprung up out of nowhere, rushing towards the scene, mostly to watch, with one or two trying to offer some sort of assistance. "That shit's really outside."

Annette turned in her seat while Miles wailed on the FM, looking at the people gathering from blocks around to get a good look—staring, describing to one another how the accident had taken place. Jumping-up-and-down kids running around the crowds, eyes big as saucers, sneaking between adults' legs, anything to get a peep. "Damn . . . Shame." She resettled in her seat, watching flashing lights, ambulances, fire engines, police cars and wrecking crews speeding in the opposite direction, going to the scene of the accident, shaking her head. "What a crazy world. Sure you didn't make it all up?"

Dip let that one pass, not sure that it meant anything; driving the car more carefully now, conscious of his every move.

Annette hummed softly along with Miles, not a care in the world, and kissed Dip softly on the cheek. "Sorry I got you so upset."

"Huh?" Butterflies wavered in his stomach behind the accident, especially the boy running down the street; then back to Annette in the shithouse. Willie's black ass in the light. He linked up, answered: "I was wrong, you were right."

"I don't understand. *You* were wrong?" Hot air blew in through the car's side windows. Annette snuggled up next to Dip. Her ass and slit still itched. She uncrossed her legs and casually dropped her left hand between his legs.

"After all, it's *your* body." Still the images in the john were playing hell with his mind. Comparing those to the scenes of the accident, he was getting kind of mixed up. He stopped for the light. Signaled for a left turn.

Annette squeezed between his legs. No reaction. Cold and limp downstairs. She kissed him on the neck. He pulled away.

Something was bugging him, but he couldn't quite put his finger on it.

Miles blared. "Pharoah's Dance." Annette slipped her right hand underneath her skirt, exposing her brownish-black thighs, and pulled the toilet paper from her slit, said "Ugh" then threw it out the window.

The light turned yellow. Annette tried again. She felt a slight movement, a swelling sensation between his legs; this time when she kissed him he hadn't pulled back. He turned and looked at her. The light rested on red and yellow. Miles flared. Blared. Wailed. Pranced and danced. Suddenly she recognized the neighborhood, her immediate surroundings. A ball park, gym, the overpass, the railroad tracks. To her right, housing projects, to her left, shacks. "Hey, you're not taking me home, are you? I'm not going home. Listen."

"Gotta, baby, it's getting late. It's almost one o'clock." The light turned green. Dip started to turn.

Annette squeezed. "Oh, sweetheart, you know I'm going to look out for you . . . that's why I asked you to take me out tonight. I mean, I know you dig my sister, that you're going out with her and everything, but come on, I know this great place. Besides, I'm not staying there tonight anyway." She grabbed him around the waist, pulled him towards her, rubbed her breasts against his arms, and kissed him on the lips, the nose, the cheeks, the chin and the eyes. He started breathing hard, remembering his own comments in the john, and the ideas which had gone through his mind.

42

Dip momentarily put the car in neutral. Two cars whizzed through the green light. A cop car prowled and slowed; two red faces looked in their direction. "Something's the matter there, johnny?" a hard metallic voice with a slight drawl inquired.

"No, officer. Jes trying ta make up my mind which way I'm going."

"Well, don't stay there all night. You're blocking the streets." The red face disappeared back into the car, the prowl car prowled across the tracks.

As if nothing had happened, Annette kept her hand between Dip's legs, massaging him ever so slightly, feeling him swell inside his trousers. His dick was getting harder. She talked: "I know this great place right on the other side of Canal Street, opposite the cemetery—white, trimmed in green with an iron-laced fence around it. The House of Blue Lights. Let's go there for a minute."

The light had turned red. "What kind of place is it?" Dip had lived in New Orleans all his life, but still he didn't know all the ends and outs, outs and ins—have it your way.

Annette laughed—she couldn't help it—as she unzipped his fly, wrapped her hands around his long slender joint, and looked up in his eyes. "Just a place, silly. Let's check it out."

Dip didn't get it, but he decided he'd let it slide. Lots of houses served liquor and had music in the back, sometimes gamblin'. So went his thoughts.

Without a conscious break Jimi Hendrix's "VooDoo Child" replaced Miles' "Pharoah's Dance" as the light changed. Dip stepped on it, and headed towards the House of Blue Lights.

Annette was down on her knees now, working him over easy and slow; salivating his joint, massaging his balls. The head of his joint swelling. His midsection hot. He was trying desperately not to discharge, wanting to save it for when they got to the place. But it was a hard nut not to crack. So to speak.

But nature being nature and instincts being what they are, Dip felt himself losing control. He grabbed Annette's head, pushing her further down on his power pack, guiding the car with one hand towards Canal and Claiborne, glancing out the window at three neon-lit bars: The Dirty Boogie, The Funky Butt, and the Bucket of Blood. Annette downtown going for broke, while Chicanos and bloods outside the bars beat the nightlight out of po' trash from across the way, driving them out their territory. For New Orleans, it was just another same old Saturday night. For the trash it was a helluva mash.

At the corner of Canal and Claiborne—the meeting of neutral grounds (with streetcar tracks intersecting Claiborne, dividing the city into black and white, left and right, the grounds remaining neutral)—Dip made the light and was traveling parallel to the greys' burial grounds surrounded by a high grey-bricked fence keeping outsiders out. Suddenly his legs stiffened, his asshole closed, and the joy-juice shot. Annette swallowed, "Gulp," and Dip's joint continued to bounce up and down like it had a heart and mind all its own. Dip slowed the car down, mad with himself because of having shot his load, and started looking all around for the House of Blue Lights. Three words blurted from his mouth, without really knowing he was saying them: "Where is it?"

Annette gulped a second time, releasing her hold on his cock, watching it go limp, and sat up. She pulled out a handkerchief, wiped her mouth, then his thing, and threw the rag out the window. Hendrix's "VooDoo Child" became persistent on the FM.

"There, fool. See?" She pointed to a white frame house, trimmed in green, on the other side of the street, between trees on the neutral ground.

They both laughed. Dip self-consciously. Annette outright *at* Dip.

Dip signaled for a left turn and waited until the lane was clear, as Annette put his plaything back in his pants. He turned, barely missing two cats—one white and the other black—being chased by a toothless hound dog. Annette zipped him up and Hendrix's "Child" had her last fling; the announcer's voice was running down the details concerning the traffic accident. To Annette and Dip it sounded like something that had happened in another space age, possibly on another planet. Before you could think Bozo and Dolly, Dip had pulled the car in front of the house. Parked. They both were out.

A pale yellow moon hung over the Southern sky, showering its light down on the grey cemetery, the trees, the house *and* Annette and Dip walking hand-in-hand towards the gate.

"This is a nutty place," Annette smiled, remembering the first time she'd been there, and the treatment she'd received. "They don't ask any questions, just give you the key if you got the bread."

Nutty place. The words stuck in Dip's mind like bubble gum on the brain, and slowly worked their way down to his jones. And only fourteen, Dip thought. How in the hell did she know so much? But he let the thought slide as the root meaning of the words, nutty place, got down.

Annette released his hand, opened the gate, and led the way down the gravel path, sea shells crunching underneath their feet. They stood at the side entrance.

A bare light bulb glared from the porch. Gnats swarmed around it like space capsules around Earth.

Annette recognized a couple seated at the table in the rear of the courtyard. She waved. The girl giggled, then waved back. The guy nodded. Moss from the Weeping Willow touched the girl's shoulders, giving them a sinister appearance back in the shadows. Dip never noticed.

"You go in and sign the register. I'll wait here."

Dip was confused. He was busted. And for some strange reason he'd assumed it was free. "Do what?"

A wry grin crossed Annette's lips. She hesitated, then whispered. "You got any money?" Looking up into his eyes, Annette rubbed her cunt against his thigh and fingered his nutty place while Dip patted her soft behind.

"We ain't *gotta* go in. I mean, we kin do what we gotta do in my 'chine, dig?"

Annette smiled, tiptoed and kissed him on the lips, he was so tall and silly, all at the same time. And twenty years old too. Wow! She reached in her bag and slipped him her allowance—two crumpled dollar bills. "Sign the register. I'll wait. Okay?"

Dip looked down at her, puzzled for a moment; he flattened out the singles, then slipped them in his pocket. He lit up a cigarette, then trudged up the wooden steps.

Annette took a seat near the couple under the Weeping Willow, brushing the moss back off her back. The girl's name was Mary, her date's name was Hank.

"Ah saw Miz Perkins and Fess Williams sneaking out jes 'fore yawl arrived," Mary giggled, then twitched. Hank nodded and turned in his sleep.

Annette laughed. "I heard they been making it together for quite some time, like since the beginning of the semester."

They both laughed, then swapped lies 'bout who was screwing who back at the school, brought it down home, talking 'bout people in the neighborhood, grinning all the time; took it out to cover presidents, state heads, nuts, and sports figures too. Even went so far as to talk about the people on TV, and a woop of movie stars. Making up tales as they went along.

"You know Miss Inez at the Gumbo House? The bitch threw me out."

"Child, you don't say?"

"Yeah. Told me never to come back." Then Annette took it from the top and ran the whole story.

Meanwhile, Dip was having his troubles in the kitchen.

A long, lanky blond—big wide hips and breasts the size of honeydew melons, coffee-colored skin and muddy brown eyes, explained: "Sign you and yore wife's name in the book."

A blue-lined notebook with names scribbled in pencil lay open on the enamel table.

Dip signed his name but had to think about the wife thing for a second.

"Your girlfriend, fool. I know you didn't come here by yourself, or with some man. Sign her name." She poured herself another shot from the pint of Old Crow on the table. "And be sure you put down how long you gon be here."

"About fifteen minutes," Dip blurted, carefully writing Annette's name underneath his own.

The woman let out a crackling laugh. "Fifteen minutes?" She guffawed again, louder this time, covering her mouth with her hand. "Lawd, chile, you cain't be that fast, les' your name be Speedo. Put down an hour. That's the shortest we's allow." She leaned way back from the waist, putting her hands on her hips and laughed again. "Here. Lemme see what you dun wrote in this here book." The woman leaned over, resting her bony fingers on the table, squinting her eyes. Dip was standing over her looking uncomfortably at her grey hair streaked with blackening and smelling tobacco juice blended with bourbon emanating from her. He waited. And Annette had said this was a nutty place. In more ways than one, he thought to himself.

She made him scratch out Annette's name, and wrote Mr. and Mrs. before *his* name. "The police see that, the way you had it there, we's all going to jail."

Feeling low and square, bashful as a faggot at a bull-dagger's ball, Dip pulled his bills out of his pocket and threw them on the table. "That's what you told me to write . . . her name 'neath mine." The woman laughed again, shaking her head. Another woman walked into the kitchen, big, burly and fat, and just as black. "What's going on, Bea?"

The first woman was still cackling, holding one hand over her mouth, the other pointing at Dip. Dip glanced at the two women, down at the register, then headed out the door. The first woman began, through peals of laughter, to explain to the other what had gone down. Dip mumbled to himself as he hit the screen door: "But I still say it's only gon' take fifteen minutes."

A couple came out the side door as he was going down the steps, the guy straightening out his stingy brim, the girl her Afro-blue wig and purple hot-pants. They disappeared down the gravel path. Sea shells crunching. Crunch. Crunch.

Dip's jaws were so tight, he'd lost his erection. That is, until he heard Annette call his name. She sat on the bench, her legs crossed, brown thighs smooth and round all the way up to her fine behind. Her little mini-skirt damn near up to her waist.

She'd finished running down the scene at the Gumbo House, the mess with the Jive Five, Stompin' Sam, the traffic accident, the cops, Miles' *Bitches Brew,* the dude in the monkey suit. She was exhausting Mary, getting her mind confused.

The tall lanky woman come out the door behind Dip and yelled, "Next!" jingling keys in his ears. Again she couldn't help but laugh.

Mary slapped Hank slightly on the cheek. He stretched, looked around and started to leave. Mary grabbed his hand, mumbled something to Annette and vanished behind the woman, inside the House of Blue Lights.

Being lost for words, but wanting to make conversation, and all the while trying to forget the matron with the keys—the madam if you please—Dip found himself talking to Annette about her sister whom he'd never laid. He had a cunt collar around his neck bigger than this galaxy—just out there somewhere on the other side of HERE.

But Annette, who knew what was happening—that her sister wasn't shit—didn't pay him the least bit of mind; she continued to slobber on his ears, his neck and cheeks, rubbing his joint around inside his trousers and placing his right hand between her legs.

"I mean, I really go for the broad. It's not the leg so much, getting laid and all, but she acts kind of funny, like she don't really want me around."

Talkin' 'bout jive, Annette thought. She dropped it on him. "Forget about her, man. She's in love with some fool what's in the Nam. Some childhood sweetheart. She's holding her aces while you play your trumps." She squeezed his pipe. "Gives her something to do. That's all. Dig?"

Flabbergasted, fucked up and confused, that's where Dip's mental processes took him, bordering on insanity: mad beyond repair, and almost left him there, if it wasn't for the woman named Bea crunching sea shells bringing them the key.

"Hey." Again she laughed. "Yawl's room's ready . . . Speedo." She dropped the key into Dip's hand. It hit the ground. The woman laughed again, then added: "Second door on the left. You got a *whole* hour." She cracked, trudging back into the house.

"What was that all about?" Annette asked, taking her hand from between his legs, his hand from between *her* legs, standing up, and brushing off her skirt. "Let's get inside, these 'squitoes 'bout to drive me nuts."

"Nuts," Dip echoed. "The bitch's nuts. Both of them."

Annette crunched the shells. Dip followed.

"Both of them? Who's the other?" Annette was holding his hand, leading the way up the stairs, through the screen door and down the hall.

"Your sister's the other."

"Ha. I coulda told you that . . . a trillion years ago. Plus she's still a virgin. Ever met a virgin nineteen years old?"

Dip thought, as their footsteps echoed down the narrow hall, red and blue lights shining above the doors on either side, "Not even a nun."

"Or even a cantor's son," Annette let fly. She stood before the door. The light above was blue. Red was for those rooms which were occupied. "Give me the key."

"Huh?" He had left it on the ground. "Who's the dude?"

"Man, *damn her,* where's the key? I'll tell you later on . . . he's some fool who's making a career in the war . . . a soldier. Some half-white, Creole nigger what ain't got good sense. Now where's the key?"

"I forgot to pick it up." It was more than just a dumb look on his face; it was actually super silly—out THERE. His nose had been open so wide you could fly a flight of SSTs wingtip to wingtip next to a flight of 747s through it—and still have room for a whole battalion of Cong guerrillas. And he still wouldn't know what happened. That's how turned around he'd been behind Annette's older sister. Miss Virgin Spring. Talkin' 'bout a mind blower? Whew!

"Well?" She didn't know why, but even after all this she was still gonna give him the drawers. She lifted up her skirt, dug down in her behind, got out the toilet paper, smelled it, UGH, and threw it in the air.

He turned and went to get the key.

Annette took the key out of his hand and unlocked the door. The room was in total darkness, save for a candle, which burned on the night table near the bed.

Annette locked the door, grabbed Dip's long frame and stuck her hands behind his back, rubbed her cunt against his thighs real slow and easy, and her breasts against his chest, backed him up against the door while she secured the lock and put the key in her purse.

He reached down and fondled her breasts, letting his hands tear down through her blouse, breaking the buttons and ripping the button holes to shreds. They panted and groaned and moaned for a couple of minutes while Annette stripped off her skirt in the middle of the floor, still holding him close to her, and unsnapped his pants. His joint jumped out like a rabbit out of a hat. She went down on her knees and sent thrills shooting up and down his spine, causing his thighs to ache. She grabbed his balls, crawled backwards towards the bed on her hands and knees, jerking her head; she massaged his joint with her tongue, lips and bottom teeth. Dip had never felt this good in all his life. He grabbed her head and held on for the ride, letting his shins move in and out between her thighs as they staggered towards the bed. He hung his elbows on the bed and got down on his knees.

Annette released her hold on his penis, let it slip over her breast as she got off her knees, and clutched his balls with her right hand, running her left up and down his spine, in his ear and through his hair. Dip climbed up on the bed with his joint sticking up in the air, pulsating up and down inside the rhythms of his pulse and heart, as images of ofay chicks with great big titties and extra-large hips flashed through his mind. Annette climbed on the bed, grinning from ear to ear. The candle slanted long shadows across her breasts; they looked larger and firmer than they actually were. Dip looked up and cupped them in his hands, pulling her towards him. She wrestled her legs over his midsection, sat down on his joint, slipping it in with the ease of fingers into a fine leather glove, her muscle contracting around the bottom of it as she leaned forward and let him milk her breast.

She panted some more and grinned silently in his ear, breathing hard, and rolled over on her side. Dip got up on his right knee, rolled over as she grabbed a pillow and stuck it under her ass. They started going like astronauts screwing on a trip to the moon. She pulled him down on her, sending his stiff, slippery joint pounding back to the tip of her womb as her muscles relaxed.

Dip continued to work over her, shoving his hips down to slap against hers as they worked up a sweat. She would meet his delivery halfway, bounce and turn from side to side as he worked her across the bed, sending the pillow slipping from beneath her ass, behind her back, her legs going up in the air as he relentlessly greased her fat juicy cunt, slipping it in and out.

"Come on, baby, do it to me hard!" Annette murmured in her little girl's voice. She grabbed his balls and pushed— with her one hundred and two pounds—Dip over to the right. This lessened the burden of his weight. She locked her legs around his backside, and wrapped her arms around his neck while he stuck his fingers down on her stomach. They moved from side to side on the bed, panting and moaning, grunting even, like mismatched wrestlers down on the canvas.

Annette kept her eyes closed, shoved her tongue down Dip's throat, then slipped it in his ear, kissing him inside his earlobes. She started crying like a baby—it felt so good, all down around her crotch, inside her stomach and bowels. Her whole body felt like a flame, bursting with energy, his prick a torch. Dip continued to pound her in silence, grabbing the pillow and sliding it back under her twat, and getting back atop her without missing a stroke. The sweet smell of jism enveloped the room. Dip closed his eyes, working her over and sucking her hardened nipples, squeezing one with his large palms and kissing the other alternately, while she wiggled and shifted her bottom delightedly. Annette screamed in passion, tears rolling down her cheeks, kicking up her legs and clenching his neck, then lying back helpless on the bed. His joint slipped out; he looked down and watched as her cunt moved up and down, squished out the juices, awaiting his return. She reached down and grabbed it, helped him to guide it back in. He mounted her a second time, grabbing the cheeks of her ass and controlling the movements of her hips, nuts ready to explode.

She closed her thighs, making him spread his knees on either side of her hips and go into her like a groundhog burrowing its hole, working up and down frantically now, his joint tight against her clit. She imagined she was being screwed by a ten-foot pole on an overcharged electric blanket as shock waves shot through her cunt, down her asshole, up her spine to her head and back down to her titties, causing the nipples to harden, while Dip continued to rack her cunt for all she was worth. He exploded inside her as though his joint was the nozzle of a hose, moaned right along with her as she wrapped her legs tight around his bottom and they both rolled from side to side. She twisted her ass up and down and her vaginal muscles clamped down on his joint as they rolled off the bed in cosmic climax.

It took about three minutes before Dip's head stopped spinning and he was again able to recognize the room. Annette climbed on top of him and dripped on his stomach; it felt warm and gooey, sticky like paste.

Annette laughed. "Was that a trip or wasn't it a trip?" She got up, folded her legs under her, her bronzed body glimmering in the candlelight, giving a soft roundness to her form as her eyes smiled down. Her body was completely relaxed.

He couldn't keep his eyes off her. Suddenly he felt younger, like a kid of ten, having just been laid by the madame of the house.

Annette caught the change of expression in his eyes. "What are you thinking about?" She leaned over and put her head on his chest. Her fingers toyed with his limp member, his balls and pubic hair.

"Huh?" Again he didn't know what to say. His mind had skipped past the Gumbo House, the guy holding his guts, and pounced on the theme of Annette's sister: Goot-n-tight! For some strange reason he was thinking about fucking her in the butt, nose, eyes, ears, mouth, but he was powerless to act. "Nothin'."

"I know what you're thinkin' about." She got up, lit a cigarette and put her hand on her hips. Her backbone slipped.

"What?" Did she really know? He sat up on his haunches, kissed her thighs, smelled her cunt and kissed the lower curve of her belly. A cynical smile crossed her lips.

But her eyes refused to dance. They became old, hard and stone sober. "How a nice, young girl like me could ever . . . Forget it, man, I know what I'm all about. Besides . . . " She broke off, turned and tipped towards the bathroom. " . . . I've heard it all before." Her voice trailed off, her ass shaking like jelly on lamb, as she disappeared into the shadows. A door opened, then shut, somewhere in the general direction she'd gone.

Dip shook his head. That one, he couldn't figure out. He gave up. The good parts, only the good parts (fuck the rest of tonight) stayed in his mind. He closed his eyes, dreaming for a second. He heard water running in the bathroom. A couple moaning and groaning; a girl softly crying somewhere else in the house. He got up off the floor, climbed onto the bed, the tension gone out of his body. In less than five minutes, he was sound asleep.

FRONT GAME: Beneath the House

ANNETTE UNPLUGGED THE TUB and watched the water drain out. Scum floated to the top, rushed to the whirlpool that had formed near the front and was summarily sucked down the drain. She stood and observed the full length of her body—the full thighs, the slightly curved stomach, her breasts like peaches in the sun and the squared shoulders. She laughed to herself as images of Willie with his joint in his hand came to mind, and smiled cynically thinking about Dip outside the house. No money. Her sister. The witch!

Silence weighed down on her ears. The water faucet dripped a two-beat rhythm into the tub. Somewhere in the distance a dog barked. A girl giggled. A man wailed, moaned, then sighed. Footsteps shuffled down the hall. A door opened and closed.

Annette finished drying herself, noticing how her flesh had turned reddish-brown, with goose pimples forming on her thighs. Her buttocks felt like twenty-five-pound sacks of sugar, but were as soft as ever. Anxiety wavered over her body. Was she gonna be fat when she got old? She dreaded the thought. Running the towel between her soft thighs, the crack of her ass and the lips of her cunt, her mind drifted back to the first time she got laid, as she cupped her breasts in her hands, checking herself out in the mirror.

She, her brother and a dude from the neighborhood were playing a game of hide-and-seek. They were hiding beneath the house. Three years ago to this day. Night, if you wish. Sonny, her brother, was ten. The other boy, twelve. Seems like centuries ago. Now.

She had lay back on an old wooden plank, slipped her panties off her bottom, pulled her dress up around her shoulders and looked over at the other boy, then at Sonny, saying with a sigh: Come on.

Junior pulled out his thing. It looked like a horse's cock—black, long and fat, with a huge pink head. He chafed it, pulling the skin back and forth, as if working some sort of mad magic, staring at her seat of sweet delights. A slit like a healed wound—pink, fat, and hairless. Annette lay there, her eyes slivers, her legs stretched out, her body straight as the plank, confused because he was taking so long, whispering: "Come on, hurry up."

Sonny was on the other side of her, his dick in hand, sweat beads on his forehead, eyes big as saucers, saying in a heavy-breathing, muffled voice: "Go 'head, Junior. You go first."

Annette began getting impatient. Here she was stretched out on the board, two big dicks on either side, with scared faces gazing on her body. It's finding out . . . what's it like.

So ran her thoughts. This was an only chance. No one really knew their hiding place. "Come on," she whispered again.

"Hurry up, Junior," Sonny urged. "We ain't got all day."

Junior didn't move. He looked bug-eyed and scared stiff, like Eddie Cantor in blackface. Screwed!

He stared at her coffee-and-cream tanned body, the long slender curves, the boyish limbs and almost totally flat breasts, the innocent face and her eyes. Annette was neither smiling nor frowning, but looking curiously at him, as if her whole body were egging him on.

Sonny's whole face was covered with perspiration now; he looked as if he were crying. Really, I'm not making this up. It actually happened. The blood looked like he had tears in his eyes! "Joog her, man. Joog her, she wants to be jooged," he pleaded.

Annette opened her thighs. Junior, feeling a strange tightness in his chest, breathing heavy, mounted her. She clasped his biceps. He touched her cunt with his prick. Annette squirmed, then pulled back. Then spread her legs wider.

Perspiration oozing out his pores, Junior got down, sat casually aside the plank and unbuttoned his pants. He dropped them down below his knees.

He remounted her. Sonny moved closer to them, pulled on her arm and made her play with his thing. She smiled and looked into his eyes. No one knows, even to this day, what Sonny saw there. In her eyes.

Junior spread her legs even further apart, grabbed his rod with his other hand, and heaved. Annette issued a muffled "Ooouuucch . . . !" Nothing happened. He hadn't penetrated.

Junior's heart, temples and pressure points were beating a wicked tempo throughout his body, feeling like a thousand Voo Doo drums at Damballah's rites, while pictures of mothers calling, eyes peering underneath the house, gossipers spreading the tale all over the South, flashed through his skull.

His long fat black thingamajig was harder now than even he could ever remember, in spite of the fact that he'd been playing with it since he was five. "You've got to push harder." Water logged her eyes. She continued to play with her brother's prick.

"Hurry up, man. You go first. I'll take sloppy seconds, anytime." Annette's warm hand was making him cream.

Annette felt her nerves outside her skin. Any small prick would send thrills tinglin' through her entire being. Like the universe being all fire.

Annette began getting nervous, impatient. Junior held his penis around the base, knelt down between her legs, closed his eyes and pushed with all his might. Annette screamed, jerked her legs together and they ended up around his hips; she squeezed her brother's joint with her small hand and let go. She tried to push Junior back off her. But she was too late, his prick had entered. Blood trickled down around her asshole and onto the plank. Tears rolled down her cheeks. Her entire body, from the waist down, felt as though it was on fire. Junior's penis felt like a log stuck up her tight hole. He moved it slowly up and down, backwards, slowly, and forwards, looking at her with tears in his eyes. She whimpered, sighed, panted and sensed the feeling down around her thighs. Slowly the initial pain subsided, ever so slowly, then it started slowly feeling good as the dog watered in her nest. He leaned forward, kissed her nipples, held her around the hips, and let tears roll down on her neck. "Feel good, baby?" Junior asked.

Through sobs, Annette had answered, still stroking her brother's penis with her left hand. "Yes, YES!" Junior continued to work; he did not know when to take it out, worked longer and slowly. Then, kissing her on the cheeks, eyebrows and neck, "We gon' make babies and get married, Annette?"

"YES!"

She closed her eyes, trying to remember his face. Her mother shouted, called her name after that. Junior had jumped off, almost injuring her tight vagina with his sudden movement, slipped his pants on and helped her pull down her dress. Her brother knelt before her, yelling, "Suck it, Annette. Just for a minute, suck it." She grabbed it in her small mouth and kissed the head, licking the lips with her tongue. He closed his eyes and sighed; it dripped a clear liquid, then subsided. He put it back in his pants and kissed his sister on the mouth.

Her mother's legs, body, then face peered under the house. The three of them were crawling from under, towards the light, on hands and knees.

"Come on, Sonny, you and Annette come on and get in the house. What ya'll doin' under there? I'm gon' beat the livin' daylights out of both of you. What ch'all doin'?"

"We're just playing hide-and-seek, Mama," Sonny whined.

Annette merely looked at her, said not a word.

Junior was too embarrassed to say anything; he was afraid that Sonny would tell his mother, then he would get it. Little and young as he was, he still felt somehow funny about making love to Sonny's sister right before his eyes. He did not know why, but he did.

"And you, Junior, you go home right this minute. Sonny and Annette have to eat their lunch and I know your mother's gon' be calling you. So you just go home."

Annette smiled at herself in the mirror. Somehow it all seemed like it was such a long time ago. She had learned so much. She rubbed the towel over her face, the high forehead, the long eyelashes, large brown eyes. Her nose was small, so were her lips, which had a natural reddish-brown color to them. She wondered to herself how many joints she had sucked over the last three years. She smiled at her image in the mirror. She was a pretty young chick. Must admit that. Really together, and damned, so fine. Too much.

She made a turban of the towel and wrapped it around her head.

A low soft moaning came from the adjacent room. She knitted her brow, ran her hands rapidly over her body—from the ankles to the breasts—around her neck and rubbed her cheeks. Then she perked up her ears to listen again. She heard the same low moan, but could not tell if it was a man or a woman.

BIG BERTHA: Teaching the Kids A Lesson

LIKE COMING OUT OF A TRANCE, refocusing her eyes and looking at the image reflected in the mirror. Old, haggard, fucked around and down—like some ancient hooker on the banks of the Nile (really the Mississloppy, but she'd never know the difference)—Annette tried to break the mirror with her bare hands. It didn't work. Refusing to look again, she wet a bar of soap and smudged the mirror's surface. Still the inkling of an ugly face grinned back.

She turned, coming out of her dream world, remembering slowly, the consciousness returning to her, where she was at and how she'd gotten there in the first place. The Gumbo House. The trip through the City. Even outside with Dip. But it all seemed so long ago. Like eons. As distant as X-rays in Space. She glanced around the bathroom again: the tub with its ring. The sink with the silver faucets and a golden ring. The john. No turds this time. Clean. The mirror. A little girl smiled at her, not over fourteen, bright eyes and all. She recognized herself and smiled back. She knew. It was the House of Blue Lights.

Turning out the lights in the john, Annette opened the door and peered into the darkness. A cold draft swept up her backside. Her teeth chattered and her knees buckled. At the far end of the room, near the window, two fiery red and black shadows danced on the wall, reflected the light of moonbeams coming in through the window panes, and the candle on the stand. Sighs and low moans of good loving came from the bed. Still Annette could not distinguish the figures. Softly she stepped further into the room. Some huge amorphous form was atop the bed. A gorilla? A grizzly bear? She didn't know.

Annette didn't know from nothing. Frightened out of her wits, but not to be put off, Annette figured it had to be some of Dip's funny shit. Puzzled, she dropped the towel and barefooted it across the floor. She stood before the bed. A slight feeling of horror mixed with a strange feeling of desire fought for possession of her body.

Before her on the bed sat a big, burly, fat black broad, legs straddled across Dip's hips, ass hanging down and her black nappy hair sticking out in all directions—like some African mask—giving Dip the works.

After the initial shock, Annette recognized her. Big Bertha. (The woman who had come into the kitchen when Dip was having his troubles with Bea.)

Her huge legs were folded under enormous thighs, gobs of flesh hung low around Dip's thighs, touching the bed; her body was bent at the waist, her massive hands deep into Dip's shoulders, as she shook her ass, working him over. Breasts the size of honeydew melons were partially hidden by her juggler's-sized arms. She rocked back and forth, up and down; the bed heaved a sigh, the springs gave a whistle, and Bertha shook the bed like an elephant's cradle.

Dip lay on his back, Bertha astraddle his hips, working his joint around the walls of her cunt. Annette was so taken aback, turned around by what she dug, she ran her hands sensuously over her body, signifying, implying that she wanted to join in the fun.

Bertha, rocking back and forth, side to side, answered, shouting out loud, "Sure, child, what you think I'm here for, but to teach you younguns a lesson." She gave a toothless grin, purple gums all over.

Looking at Bertha's big black thighs, roly-poly stomach and volleyball breasts, Annette's mouth began to water, her cunt to quiver, and the sudden sensation of wanting to make it with a broad swept over her body. She flushed when the thought hit dead center and blushed when she looked down at Dip, his eyes shut tight, off in the fog. Gritting his teeth, his hands felt up Bertha's fat round thighs and fondled her behind. Gone!

Annette crawled over Dip's face, dropping her asshole on his nose, the bottom of her cunt over his mouth, as he in turn ran his hands around her behind, her waist, and in between her thighs, feeling the soft, fresh flesh, sticking his tongue inside her core.

Hot and cold chills pulsated through her body as she leaned forward and hugged Bertha's big tits and bit her lips. After a moment they began to swop spit.

Bertha's hot tongue shot up her mouth, Dip's lips and tongue played around her hole, his nose up her ass. Combined with the sounds they were making and the smell of success, catapulted in a unity of three. DISCHARGE!

Dip worked his joint up and down, in and around Bertha's big hole, while Bertha shook her big ass, kissed Annette on the cheeks, squeezed her firm breasts, and Annette eased her fingers down around Bertha's cunt, rubbing her clit every now and then.

The three were working so hard. (Really, I thought the bed was gonna collapse.) Dip was on the bottom, concentrating on Annette's juicy cunt with his tongue and lips, rubbing his nose all up and in her asshole, and his joint felt hot, then cold, and was rapidly becoming numb from the hard work that Bertha was putting on him, her soft fat thighs covering his hips and her pussy tightening and squeezing his joint, and both of them growing hotter and stronger at each stroke, as Annette felt it coming—and caught a discharge.

She threw her body forward and let out a scream. Bertha clutched the little girl's head on her breast, leaned backwards herself, as Dip busted his nuts, his joint slipping out, and Annette felt it shoot up around her stomach, sperm wetting her navel and making her discharge some more. She felt his tongue lapping it up, and every now and then working her asshole over.

Bertha lay back on the bed, still moving her hips, pushed Annette's head further down, down around her stomach, rubbed her shoulders, her arms, and felt her young breasts down on her thighs. Annette slowly got the word and moved further down, easing her thighs, cunt and ass back over Dip's forehead, and grabbed his member in the palm of her hand, rubbed it over her cheeks and her nose, letting out soft cries, sobs and closing her eyes, opening her mouth and taking it in, licking off the joy-juice and dreaming of coming as she felt his fingers working up her cunt.

Bertha grunted and relaxed her big body back on the bed, kissing Dip's feet, while Annette stuck two fingers up her squishing cunt and sucked Dip's joint, squeezing his balls until it was all over. They lay exhausted in the bed.

Annette rolled over to the other side of the bed, panted a couple of times, then sat up Indian-fashion. Bertha got up, smiled, strolled across the room, picked up the towel and rubbed it rapidly over her body. She came back and sat on the side of the bed, leaned over and kissed Annette on the arm, thighs and belly button.

Annette rubbed her shoulders, felt her huge breasts, felt herself getting warm again, and looked over at Dip. He had had it.

Too tired to say anything, he got up off the bed and went into the john.

Bertha explained to Annette that she had seen them come in and had decided to teach them a few tricks; she said that she loved to watch and help young folks just getting started to make love. She liked to do it, see them do it, and have something to do with them doing it too. Annette giggled, said, "That's nice."

Dip sat on the commode and took a long shit. He tried to get it straight in his mind who was this Bertha, and what was Annette's bit. He was twenty, and Annette only fourteen, but Bertha was damn near old enough to be grandma to both of them. It just didn't make any sense; all this screwing, fucking and sucking, three generations, in the same room.

(You see, Dip was the son of a preacher man. That was part of *his* problem.)

He glanced at the ring Annette had left around the tub, got a good feeling as the brown, black, green turds slid out his hole into the bowl, and felt the muscles doing their job, tightening, then relaxin', as his thoughts filtered down to ride back to town. Goot-n-tight! Annette's sister. Would he bring it up again?

Fuck her, he thought, and all the other lesbian virgins cluttered in the box. He wiped his ass with a face rag, climbed into the tub to take a bath. That's where they all were at, playing with their clits, not giving him a bit.

When he got back into the room, two dark shadows were dancing on the walls, dark bodies wrestling on the bed, Annette and Bertha sat next to each other, getting the whole trip straight in their heads. The candle was out. Pale blue moonlight shone in through the white curtains.

Annette spoke in a soft, murmuring voice, her arms wrapped around Bertha's massive body, caressing her breasts, kissing one, then the other, and resting her head between Bertha's jolly fat thighs—licking the hairs around her cunt.

Bertha lay back and let her work out. It felt good to be loved by someone so young. She picked up on Dip's vibrations the moment he stepped into the room.

Dip reached down near the edge of the bed and grabbed the towel, walked over to the window and stood looking out at the night, bats flying overhead, rabbits jumping to and fro, snakes slithering past—listening to the sounds of loving coming from the various rooms.

Directly behind him Annette and Bertha went into a sixty-nine that'd make Mighty Dyke frown.

Annette had crouched down on Bertha's chin and her thighs were in Bertha's arms, but the movement was vice versa. Annette's arms were around Bertha's thighs and her nose played around with the bottom of her ass, along with her fingers, as her tongue worked inside that sloppy, juicy, greasy hole, as if Jordan had rolled.

Their bellies were wet, their holes and mouths were well juiced and they were enjoying themselves; in spite of the world's damnation.

Dip felt his body tense, his balls a sack of cement; he felt like some fool watching erotic film strips on Channel 13. (NET!)

He took his rod in his hand, pulling it around once or twice, then trudged over to the bed and got over Annette's head.

He grabbed Bertha's ass while Annette, at the bottom, held on to his ass. He felt her backside hit his stomach, and a muffled voice yell out, as he went sailing off the bed and landed on the floor. "Naw, you young buck, I dun' play that there; that's for faggots and sissies, lessies and dykes. When it comes to that kind of carrying-on, you better count me out. Fact is, I'll cut your throat, you little motherfucker, iffen you try that shit again." Bertha went back to work on Annette's little-girl cunt, licking up around the edge of her hole, slipping her tongue down to her asshole, and squeezing her well-shaped thighs around her ears.

Annette let go of Dip's balls, rubbed Bertha's thighs and pulled, with her right hand, Dip's joint with her fingers wrapped around it. He held on to the side of the bed.

He was becoming so depressed, although his joint was still hard, behind what Bertha had run on his ass, he wanted to leave the premises. But he had to take Annette back to her house.

Bertha ran her tongue over Annette's stomach, and moved slowly forward, her cunt out of Annette's mouth, kissed her all over her thighs, her hips, her backside and breasts, and stuck two fingers in her cunt as it bounced around on her hand.

Dip was on his feet, naked as a jaybird, his rod in his hand, looking at those two lovely creatures working out on the bed.

When Annette got her rocks, Bertha was getting close to getting hers; she bent down and kissed Annette smack on the mouth. Dip couldn't hold back any longer, he stuck his joint between both their lips, and emptied his sacs against their tongues.

HOME

AROUND FOUR-THIRTY THAT morning, Annette strolled through the projects. She was headed for home. Dip had driven her all the way back from Claiborne and Canal, silent the whole trip, dropped her on the corner, then drove off. The ritual dance of a bitch in heat acting out dreams with Willie and Bertha, then Dip at her side, filled Annette's adolescent mind. She dismissed it with a sigh. She was into gitting into the house, sneaking in silently if possible and facing her mother's wrath in the morning.

Monday morning would be different. Back to school.

To Annette home wasn't where her heart laid; home was where she slept and took her meals, changed clothes until she was old enough to git in the wind. She walked between the wired fences behind the four-storied brick buildings of the housing projects, listening to the sounds of her sandaled feet scraping against the pavement. She heard blues drifting out of the rooms, along with the sounds of people snoring and fucking behind closed curtains, along with trains, buses, streetcars, and planes overhead, or somewhere in the distance.

When she got to her building, a man was seated on the back doorsteps. He was in a dark felt hat, dark suit, white shirt and red tie—with a bottle beside him. Immediately her mind went right past being raped or robbed or mugged in back alleyways to the idea of a drunk being the barrier between her and her pad. She got a slight pain in the ass.

As she went to sidestep him, a hand shot up her dress, rubbed her soft, drum-majorette thighs, massaged her cunt, then patted her belly. Outrage and panic shot through her body, but subsided into a childish passion mixed with grief and despair. She jerked her body away from his grasp and looked down, clutching her pocketbook under her arm.

It was her father. Drunk. With the Monday morning blues.

"Annette," his hoarse voice called in what sounded like a pleading voice. "Sit down, I wanna talk ta ya."

A sense of guilt flashed through her body, exploded in her head, dropped down to her stomach and vanished through her asshole. Came out a fart. Her head pounded like a jackhammer slipping in mud, blood shot to her temples as hot anger crimsoned her bronzed skin; she was madder than a straight chick at a lesbians' ball. Images of him and her mother fussing and fighting over a lousy coupla bucks, threatening to cut one another; then balling in the kitchen, the hallways and down on the couch in the living room, flashed through her mind like a film being rewound. Her little brother, sucking his finger and caught beating his meat in a corner to "playmates of the month" mixed with the images of her mother and father making it, and her rendezvous tonight brought to consciousness a feeling of despair. But it was gone as fast as it had come.

A sudden sense of superiority mixed with rage caused her throat muscles to contract. She felt strong, grown, independent, as if she wasn't even *in* their shit. Her eyes became as cold as the most distant rocket floating in space and her face froze in a copper frown which would take a blowtorch

70

to unmask. "Whatchou want?" she asked defensively, trying to sound lowdown.

Silence.

Pops dropped his hand back down to his side, then reached for his bottle. He unscrewed the top, took a long swig of Southern Comfort and offered her a drink.

She refused, stood over him for a second, breathing hard. Slowly her pulse returned to normal.

Meanwhile Pops didn't pay her no mind. He reached slowly into his pocket and pulled out a rumpled pack of butts, lit one and took another slug from the bottle. He started talking, addressing the four winds. "Gitting home late like this got your mother all worried. I know where you been, ain't no use for you ta be denying it. It ain't that I care about you screwing and fucking these young dudes, but you gotta have enough sense to keep yourself clean."

"I'm clean," she blurted out, thinking 'bout the shower over at the house, dismissing the john from her mind.

Slowly Annette felt her body getting hot for no apparent reason, the blood shooting back up to her temples, a certain lawlessness invading her consciousness. She grabbed the bottle, took a long swig, bent down and started kissing her dad's throat, his face, and shoved her hot tongue down his throat. He kneeled over backwards and Annette unzipped his pants and started jerking at his dick. She was panting and moaning with tears in her eyes, trying to get her drawers down, his pants down, and get it in. "C'mon, c'mon, I know this is what you want." Her brown thighs looked ashy in the distant streetlights as she straddled his body on the back stairs, her ass facing up to the moon, her cunt down on his joint, pushing with all her might till she felt it up against her womb.

Pops was just drunk enough where he didn't care who cared or what they cared. He fucked that cunt like it was brand-new, like this was something that he had been hoping for since the first day she had been born, socking it in her hole, slipping it back to her ass, grabbing and squeezing her titties and kissing those lips. They both lay there, moving and grooving, feeling the hot juices drip down inside Annette's well-used hole. He threw her off the steps, down on the grass, and Annette moved her ass like a thousand mosquitoes were under her ass.

Something had exploded inside both their brains. Pops closed his eyes and thought he was a boy of twelve, gitting his first piece on the Levee, while Annette's mind was still inside Dip and Bertha and sneaking Sleepy Willie. Pops shot off in her cunt, exploding like a bomb; she reached over and held him tight around the ass, squeezing the muscles of her vagina to keep him from slipping. Without a word, and without wasting time, she slipped from under him, turned him over on his back, went down on him, cupped his balls in her small palms and sucked his dick like a mistress turning tricks. She rested her cunt on the instep of his right leg, ran her free hand under his shirt and over his scrawny chest and squeezed on his balls till he shot a second wad. She held it in her mouth, tried to smile up at the stars, kissed him with it in it and they both got a charge.

He ran his hands over her sacks-of-sugar for an ass, feeling the meat with both hands, ran a hand up her spine, got a third hard-on and slipped his dick back in her as she sprawled on top of him, yelling and screaming, "Damn, damn, Pops, make me come." She knew she was better than Moms, who was too tight and frigid, and only gave him drawers on payday—which was once every two weeks.

She worked that poor old man damned near to hell and back, had him panting and groaning and tossing his ass on that grass, like a young phys-ed student fucking the teacher.

She felt him getting exhausted, but she was still hotter than hell; she stuck her tongue behind his ears, gave him the chills, ran her fingers up his ass and squeezed his balls, worked her muscles until his rod got harder and worked the sides of her pussy till she got a discharge. She fell face down on his stomach, ran her hands up his arms, caressed him like a baby one month out of the cradle. They laid there panting for a second, then her eyes got soft and watery.

Their features were similar—same nose, same eyes, same lips, saving one was older and their sexes were different. She felt totally relaxed, like one who had survived a bout of paralysis and was now recuperating. She laid her head down on his chest. He watched the stars fulfill their missions, the greyish-black night, the moon dropping below the horizon and wanted to dream like a kid, about what the fuck *is* man if he ain't allowed to fuck his daughter.

She looked up into his eyes, tears rained down her cheeks and on his lips, softly asking, "You did like it, didn't you?"

He let out a grunt. "If I didn't," he smelt like jism, Southern Comfort and cigarette butts, "you'd known about it before this." Suddenly the feeling that they were the only two people on the face of the globe overpowered them.

Pops felt a fourth erection starting down around his crotch, felt Annette's mound down on his thighs, her stomach covering part of his joint, her firm soft breast on his stomach. He ran his hand over her well-shaped ass, up her spine to her shoulder blades. He kissed her fully on the lips, shoving his tongue down her throat, closing his eyes, dreaming he was transported to the far reaches of the universe, on the outside of the planet Earth, looking back on a long-lost dream which had been a nightmare of blues, troubles, worries and cares.

They started again as he slipped it in, Annette laying on top of him, moving her ass to meet his jabs—slowly at first, then faster and faster, then slow, and fast, each feeling the other like a second rebirth.

Annette tossed her hips from side to side, working them up and down slowly and slower, like a bass player walking the blues. Pops shoved it inside on the sides of her hole, worked the bottom for a while, then rubbed hard against her clit. She felt it coming, her crotch got hotter and hotter, and started squeezing of its own accord. She flattened her palms on the grass and breathed slowly in and out, her breasts enlarging on her chest like hamburger hills as he moved forward, kissing the nipples, shoving his dick all the way in. She let out a sigh, closed her eyes, the walls of her cunt tightened, then relaxed and she came round the sides of his joint. His joint felt hypersensitive, and when it felt the hot blast it shook and throttled and let go its last load. They laid there again, panting in each other's arms, his member limp in her hole, her moving her ass to keep it from getting cold.

After about ten minutes they got up and went and sat back down on the back steps. Both were tired and exhausted, trying to recuperate from their fantasies which had been dutifully and ritualistically carried out.

The sky turned purplish red on the eastern horizon, grey clouds of dawn like almonds hung there, Venus shined like a silver ball; and the projects looked brighter, the grass a blue green, as that part of the world tossed and turned in bed, getting ready to meet the dawn.

Annette and her father didn't say anything to one another for a while. They finished the bottle of Southern Comfort and Annette, being resourceful, found a weed in her purse; they smoked it, and exchanged tales of mirth. He told her about the first time he had gotten laid, back on the sugar plantation where he had grown up, and about when he first got to New Orleans, square as he could be, and how he got a job working in a cat house over on Rampart Street, breakin' in whores and running errands for the mistress. He was so relaxed and cool in telling his tales, like he was talking to some dude about his own age. She confessed the night's visitations, from the john to the car, and then to the house and big Bertha.

He knew Bertha, so he told her, from a long time ago, when he was living uptown and she ran a house for runaways.

74

They laughed and joked and continued to exchange stories till the sun was five minutes past the horizon and noises in the city increased its beat. Then they got themselves together—the liquor was all gone, the reefer all smoked, and they had enjoyed each other's arms, legs, thighs and members. So they went into the house.

They crept in silently, like snakes slithering through a rose garden. Pops went directly to the living room and lay back on the couch. Annette brought up the rear, dragging her handbag and scraping her feet on the rug.

"I think . . . " she yawned and put a balled fist to her mouth, "I'm going to bed." She squeezed her left breast, then rubbed her stomach. She wanted to screw.

Pops looked up from unlacing his shoes. He thought he was looking at some two-bit whore on the block. Then he mistook her for his ole lady when he first cut into her at a bar, backatown. As his eyes focused in on his child, he swore up and down that he was looking at her when she was two months old, three years old, seven, twelve, now standing before him like a stand-in for Raquel Welch, a fourteen-year-old sex fiend, ready for some more action. But he didn't say a word, merely nodded. A feeling of eternal spring eased through his body and was communicated through his eyes.

Annette picked up the vibrations, but she knew, deep down behind his eyes, having done wrong caused his heart to ache, saw the sense of the tragic that invaded his face, and knew right away that this cat was lost. Forget about him being her father, he was strung out.

She wanted to soothe his mind, tell him that it was no big thing, their screwing on the lawn, but said instead—"I'm turning in."

MOM'S OFFSPRING

THUNDER RUMBLED OVER THE east like bombs dropping over Hamburger Hill. A grey mist filled the room. It was three o'clock in the evening. Annette lay in bed next to her twelve-year-old brother, who was ill with spring fever.

In her sleep she grabbed her brother's joint, squeezed it softly, jerked it, kissed its head and ran it between her huge mounds of flesh, her breasts. She cupped his balls in her hand, sucked his joint like a drunk licking mustard off a hot sausage and rolled it around in her mouth.

Red, blue and yellow streaks of lightning flashed across the window pane, flickering on and off like multicolored strobes. The apartment house shook and rocked on its foundations as though the planet itself had been knocked out of orbit.

Nightmare images of the night before scrambled rapidly through her mind with such speed that she got Dip confused with Bertha, Bertha confused with her father and herself confused with Willie. She dreamt she had a penis instead of a cunt, looked down and saw a big black snake shooting out her bottom hard as a piece of ebony wood.

She woke up and gave a start. Her little brother was still asleep, rolling his body from side to side, moaning and half talking to himself. Annette felt hot all over. She cupped his balls in her hands and sucked his nuts, working his member up and down, over her cheeks and ears, then stuck it back in her mouth.

He grabbed her head, pushed down, moaned in his sleep like Namath crying the blues on TV; he was still fast asleep.

Time passed and the room grew lighter. Jet planes, trains, cars and buses passed overhead and outside the apartment. The rain still fell like it was the second diluvian and thunder roared as if the core of the earth had cracked, shattering the fragments to the four corners of the universe.

Annette laid between her little brother's legs, working his penis up and down with her hands like some distant flutemaker on the Lower East Side smoothing a parched limb of pine.

The radio downstairs was turned on to the news somewhere. A TV explained the dating game. She heard someone calling her name as if in a dream. The background noise of the storm still brewing outside, mixed with the noise of the radio and TV, sent images of ambushes and dogfights in Vietnam flashing through her mind.

"Goddamnit, you little whore, git outa that bed and leave your brother alone." Her mother pulled the covers off the both of them, and was standing over her with a strap in her hand. Cold sweat popped out on Annette's forehead, under her arms, and between her thighs. She was caught—black-handed. When she looked and woke up to the facts of what was happening, the edge of the strap—her father's belt—came down on her backside. She yelped and scrambled to pull the covers up.

Her mother stood at the foot of the bed with pincurlers and rollers on her head, cracking down with the belt like the Zorro kid, dressed in a long black robe, nothing underneath, her teats shaking in the wind like the udders of a cow, looking like St. Theresa's double turned blacker than soot, shouting obscenities at her, cursing up a storm.

"Damn you, damn you," Annette shouted, grabbing for the belt and jumping out of bed.

In all the racket that was being made, her little brother woke up, dick harder than times in the Eisenhower years or in the middle of a recession, sperm oozing out his cock—which was nine inches long—jumping up and down, and he couldn't keep it down. He felt like Portnoy caught jerking off. He looked at his sister, naked as a jaybird, fine as could be, but his mother looked like some intruding witch, Cinderella's stepmother, come to do him in. He charged out the room, images flying through his mind, getting himself confused with Adam when caught jiving with Eve, pounded his pud up and down, shot his wad in the toilet bowl.

Her mother raced her around the room. Annette dodged and kicked, then stood over in a corner and started yelling, "Shit! What the fuck do you *want*?" Obviously she was madder than General Abrams when questioned 'bout Hamburger Hill. Her mother had caught her stone in a trick, fornicating with her little brother, actually blowing his dick.

"Listen, you little heifer, you little incestuous bitch," her mother started off, letting the black robe drop off her body, showing a midriff bulge and sagging hips, greyish black hairs round her pussy with big pink lips. "I got the word from a neighbor that you and your ol' man was out fucking on the lawn, that you didn't get here till dawn and had been out screwing all night. I saw that nigger downstairs, asleep on the couch, started to cut his throat; 'stead I threw his ass out."

She slashed again at Annette with the strap, like the slavemaster's wife. Annette ducked, turned, ran out of the way, still cursing up a storm, while the rain came down. Without another word Annette charged out the room.

Annette was talking to herself, words bubbling out her mouth as she packed her bookbag, grabbing this and that. She threw red, pink and black flowered bell-bottoms and multicolored blouses in her bag, along with some drawers, got her Afro wig off the black head form—a blonde Afro at that—and put it on her head. She decided right then and there she didn't want to have anything to do with her mother—in fact, with anyone in the house. "All these people are crazy!" Her mother, don't even mention it; her brother, really out to lunch. And her father, "Poor fool was really in a rut. Bitch runs the place and is trying to run me. I might be *only* fourteen and all that shit, but I know one thing; I'm gitting the fuck out of here before I end up dead, crazy as a loon with the rest of these fools."

While she was talking to herself, her mother came in and stood in the doorway. Annette ain't paid her the least bit of mind. "Hell, yes, I like to fuck, screw and jive around, plus I'm tired of all this shit about the Church, the School and these fucked-up rules."

Meanwhile her little brother, after he finished jerking off, took a long shit and let it all hang out. Then he went back to his room and had diurnal dreams of white and black bitches dancing before him, a couple sucking his dick. He creamed in the sheets, then went out like a light. Last heard of him, he was dreamin' of eight-pages with *Blondie and Dagwood* and *I Love Lucy* doing a jig of the five assholes in a ring. It was called the Tynan bounce. Mama came on like Mae West in a Pearl Bailey stunt. "Let me have the pleasure, Clyde, of telling you to leave, to git the hell outa this house 'fore I call the cops."

Annette continued to pack her bag, throwing all kinds of shit in—panties and Kotex, snake rings and charms. She smiled cynically at her mother, but didn't feel any harm.

"You don't have to have the pleasure of putting me out, lady, I'm leaving as it is. You got Pops so fucked up he don't know his ass from a hole, and you and your girlfriend down the way, you both turning tricks, and my little brother's turning into a jerk-off queen, watching people fucking on *The Late Show*, reading sex magazines, too shy to talk to girls and won't play with boys. The whole family should be put away in some kind of institution."

Moms was so mad she damned near fainted. Blood rushed to her temples and her heart started pounding as if the President had been shot and the Pope had made the supreme sacrifice, given up faggots and turned back to bitches. She held the tears in check and came on hard, but she couldn't hold it. "You . . . you . . . you suppose to be my daughter. Lissen, you little hussy, you ain't nothing but a whore, a two-bit hustler who ain't even learned all the rules. You little devil, you! You're the one who got us all fucked up, trying to take care of you and all your crazy dreams. Why, I thought that you would turn into my pride and joy, bring life to me in my old age, instead of all this suffering."

Trying to get her point across, Moms came all the way into the room, stood before the mirror and dropped the recovered black housecoat onto the floor.

Annette looked at her and lifted her eyebrows. Cold shivers went down her back as she thought that she might look like that one day, when and if she ever got old. Her mother's big baggy tits looked like elephant bladders dried up and parched, the big ass and hips looked like a black cow's behind and the gray hair on her pussy came damn near down to her knees. Annette wanted to puke. Her jaws ballooned as she charged out of the room.

Her mother humfed after, pouting and frowning.

Annette went into the medicine cabinet, grabbed the root oil, pulled down the three packs of birth control pills that belonged to her mother, took two of them, leaving the third—thinking her mother might still want to screw.

"Put those things back." Her mother stood in the doorway, naked, hands over her pussy and yelling.

"I'm not putting anything back."

Frustration and despair fought each other inside her mother's chest. She took one step forward and slapped at Annette. Annette ducked, rabbit-punched her behind the neck. Her mother hit the ground.

Madder than hell, she went to her mother's room, got down her pocketbook, robbed her of her coins, five twenty-dollar bills, then went back to her room.

She put on her red dress, which came up above her knees. Looked at herself in the mirror. Satisfied. Left.

Moms got off her knees when she heard the downstairs door slam and knew that Annette had split. She went back to her son's bedroom and climbed in with him. He opened his eyes and cuddled up close. She whimpered and cried, feeling alone and forsaken, lost in a sea of strange situations. She rubbed his balls and kissed him on the cheek, asked, "You love me, don't you? Don't you love your mammy?" She squeezed his joint and guided it into her ghost-ridden pussy, grabbing his ass with her hands and making him shove it in and out.

He whimpered and cried like a two-year-old, nodded his head and kissed her gums, played with her flat breast and screwed her as best he could—first time he ever had a woman, too bad it had to be his old lady. They fell asleep cuddled up next to one another, Eros had descended causing them to spin. [Editor's note: For those of you who want to know, Annette's sister, Virgin-Spring Goot-n-Tight, had eloped with The Priest from Holy Ghost.]

FLATTOP'S
BABY DOLL

LESS THAN AN HOUR LATER Annette was standing on the corner of Louisiana Avenue and LaSalle waiting for the light to change. Rain mixed with hailstones the size of golfballs roared down from the sky. Clouds exploded in the vicinity, telegraphing streaks of bluewhiteyellowredpurple lightning, igniting power lines, sparking along rooftops and freaking off down the street. Cold sweat broke out on Annette's forehead as she dug the action while standing under a live oak tree, bookbag in hand and pocketbook overhead, on her way away from home.

The light turned green. Rush-hour traffic jammed bumper to bumper, honked horns (as if in defiance of the thunder clattering overhead, sending shock waves through the city like the Earth was about to crack), stalled in this mild deluge.

Cartoon characters from Sambo to Shine (AngelFood McSpade, hobblin' along) ambled along the street. Annette dodged them, the cars and puddles of water as she zigzagged across the street, making it to the nearest bar.

Dark red and blue light inside the joint illuminated her body, giving it an exotic glow: like some mystical dream image shooting down a Hoo Doo trail—her red dress reflecting lavender hues, tan thighs, brownish hues, her face an Indian red, and Afro-blonde wig appearing greenish orange.

But still she was TOPS. This time she *was* telling *it*.

She wiped her sandalled feet on the sawdust. "Hey, what's happenin'?" she asked of the Jive Five seated directly inside the door at a side booth. She put on her mod rose-colored sunglasses. It was the same dudes that had grabbed at her in the Gumbo House, dressed in red, blue, yellow, green and purple pants, shirts, shoes and socks. Yellow, gold and white teeth, marceled hair and black faces glistened at her, mirror sunglasses reflected her image.

"Everything is everything, baby," the five answered in unison. "What's happening with you?"

"You got it," a fifth voice bellowed, sounding like a trombone playing the bottom of a dirge. The voice belonged to Blue. He was a small-time hustler and numbers man, who pimped on the side. The Jive Five were his boys, merely because he had a car and kept a pocketful of bread.

Annette figured at last she had found some people who wouldn't put her down. She sat down.

The place smelled of gumbo, red beans, chitterlings; a mixed bag of soul food. Stale beer, cigarette smoke and liquor lingered in the air. Blues from the jukebox cut through the thick odors and brought the atmosphere back home. The food made her hungry, the liquor made her glad, but the music went down to the bottom of her entrails, making her hotter than hell.

Flattop the bartender, a football-head spade if there ever was one, teed-up on weed, with a red scarf around his neck, came over to the table to take her order. He spotted her as a delinquent, but his thoughts were way out in front of his words, and he forgot to say anything about it.

They ordered drinks all around. Annette ordered an oyster loaf, potato salad and a Jax beer, giving Flattop the eye.

Like it was some everyday conversation, Annette told the Jive Five about Dip after they had left the Gumbo House, and the sudden appearance that Bertha put in, describing the action down to the last details, then about her father and her little brother, then the final scene with her mother, adding: "I gotta have some place to stay for the night."

They had listened attentively, laughing about Dip getting horny behind Bertha, growing weary and confused about her father and mother and the news about her brother; they didn't know if they were supposed to agree, or put her actions down. They thought it was some strange shit, but glanced at one another, realizing she liked to fuck.

Blue remained cool, then added his bit, "Wow, baby, that's really some other shit!" He crossed his legs, reached down in his pocket and pulled out a snort rag filled with cocaine. He snorted, passed the rag around. Flattop brought the drinks and Annette's food.

Annette glanced up at him. His eyes were sunk way back in his head. She looked around the bar.

The place was comparatively empty, considering the hour—Happy Hour. But you could blame that on the deluge taking place outside. Two middle-aged broads in tight-fitting dresses were seated at a table near the jukebox eating fried chicken, yakkating away and guzzling down beers. A guy in his early forties in a well-tailored Edwardian-cut suit, with enough jewelry on to invest in Fort Knox, sat talking to a broad in a white dress, who couldn't have been a year past sixteen. They sat idly at the bar. Annette got paranoid; she thought it was the man. Then she realized it couldn't be, not dressed like that. More than likely a gambler, the goods being his bankroll.

She got busy with the food. The others were quiet for a while sipping their drinks, snorting from the rag.

Blue thought for a minute. "Where's your old man?"

Annette laughed. "He probably went back to his mother's pad; that's what he always does when he has fights with his ol' lady. Probably in some bar in Girt Town."

"You hang around here you're subject to get put in the slammers," Blue said, not blowing his cool. He passed the snort rag to Annette.

She held it for a minute, said: "I know, that's why I'm thinkin' 'bout splitting," adding through mouthfuls of oysters, hot stuff and beer. "Maybe going out to the coast, or to Chicago, or even to the Big City. I got some bread."

Annette knew that had been a slip. Her immediate reaction was to get away from these po'-assed niggers.

"How much you got?" the five asked in unison. Blue maintained his cool, arms folded, legs crossed, looking at her.

"Enough to get me a ride on a Greyhound bus." She finished the sandwich and sipped the beer. She took a snort out of the handkerchief. The hairs inside her nostrils felt as though they were afire. A slight dizziness overcame her, then she felt relaxed, cooled.

They were silent for a while, the Jive Five staring at her, Blue sizing her up, her face looking back at her through their sunglasses. She started feeling paranoid again, plus dizzy at the same time, thinking either they were going to rob her, rape her or kill her and take her bread.

Blue ordered a couple more rounds of drinks. They passed around the snort rag. Annette inhaled a long while on the rag, saw daggers sticking out at her from behind their eyes and her heart started pounding like a conga drum. The palms of her hands began to perspire.

The storm outside the joint had subsided, moving over Lake Pontchartrain with heat lightning glowing in the distance, leaving a track of neon signs, billboards, trees, wrecked cars and two downed jet transports destroyed in its path. The bar began filling up with Blue Monday party-timers.

Annette started feeling dizzier and dizzier, with cold sweat breaking out on her forehead, and the seat of her dress soaking wet. She had to walk.

Blue followed after her. She glided somehow over to the jukebox, moving slowly past blurring faces, tried to focus on the red, white and blue lights. She dropped a coin in the slot and picked a tune. The records looked like they were going round and round, the lights spinning up and down, the faces of the people looked like a whole woop of media freaks out of television sets, comic books and movies. She started cracking up; this was really some funny shit.

"I got a place over on Washington Street; I kin put you up there." Blue started in behind her, feeling up her hips, her soft, smooth, round ass. She leaned her fat juicy cunt against the jukebox and the heat shot between her thighs; the touch of his hands sent chills down her spine as the muscles of her vagina contracted. He smelt like reefer smoke and cocaine, blended with port wine. Thoughts of Willie flashed through her mind.

"Good," she started, "but let's have one more drink, then we'll go." She smiled back at him, flashing little girl's eyes.

He looked hornier than the Pope at a lesbian nuns' orgy. But he cooled it, going back to the booth, fingering his drink.

A middle-aged dude came over, the one that had been standing at the bar, and grabbed her by the breast. She let his hand squeeze. She pressed 1-3, then turned around.

"You, you wanna dance?" His voice sounded like he had sandpaper and rusty nails stuck in his lungs.

"Soon as the record starts." Behind the three beers, the food in her stomach, the coke in her lungs, she had floated out past the promised land, on the other side of "Cloud Nine."

Guitars filled the air, sound broke loose from the box, dropped down between Annette's thighs, quivered the lips of her cunt and caused her belly button to jump. A male voice shouted out through the speakers, the sound bounced around the room, wrapped Annette's body in guitars plucking as she dropped her red dress on the floor and began dancing in her drawers.

You played hookey from school and you cant go out to play.
Mama said, for the rest of the week, when you come home,
* you gotta stay.*
Now you feel like the whole world's picking on you,
But deep down inside, you know it ain't true.

The hip, big-time New Orleans gangster in the well-tailored Edwardian suit didn't know what to do. He started to dance with her, but she was moving her body so wantonly, so easily around the floor, like it was some amorphous form instead of a solid mass, he simply stood in the middle of the floor, kind of snapping his fingers. With the blonde wig on her head, turned green in the blue lights, the mod rose-colored sunglasses covering her eyes, bare-assed to the four corners of the room, and her sandals cutting a rug, it was even too much for the crowd of teasers.

Annette moved her ass to the rhythms of the beat, shaking her thighs with her pinkish-brown pussy quivering in the heat. Folks at the bar, around the tables and standing near the booths, looked on and started to cheer. Broads jumped salty and called attention to their ol' man's ears. The Jive Five jumped up, Blue in the lead, formed a circle around her as she did the knee bend, moving from a squat to a jump, shaking up and down.

She bent backwards on her haunches, exposing her cunt to the moon, letting it all hang out, as some Smiling Jack character came over and started feeding her candy—dropping jelly beans on her stomach; she bounced them up in the air, caught them in her mouth, still shaking her ass.

Annette stood up slowly, wiggling like a cobra, stepped out of her drawers and threw them in the air. A fart smeller, way over in the corner, grabbed them, started sniffing, getting his cookies. Flattop dug what was happening and went and locked the front door. He passed the hat around to the customers, then set up a table and started charging admission.

All up and down the street, the word was out about what was happening in the bar. People started leaving other places to come down and see the fun.

Annette hit her stride, started really getting away, shaking her ass like jelly, her tits like balloons, causing the crowd to rock, cheer, laugh and swoon. While she shook her flesh down to the core.

Blue was getting eager, but he didn't want to blow his cool. This was his hangout, but not his copout. Nature was telling on him as his dick got harder than the rock of Gibraltar, and sweat popped out on his face the size of speed balls. He held on as much as he could. The other four Jives danced around a circle watching Annette's moves.

Dudes could be seen all over the place, one hand between their old ladies' thighs, the other running wild.

Annette was going wild, shaking her ass all over the room, shaking her titties, her ass in the wind and pussy moving up and down like a Voo Doo queen in some kind of trance. She grabbed her breasts and squeezed them real hard, dropped her hands down and started rubbing her thighs, ran her hand over her mound and up on her stomach, then back to her breast, then she shouted. The Jive Five kept the circle tight, moving in and out, dancing around her, they too somewhat still in a fright. Hands, arms and legs tried to break through the circle, but they held all comers back.

Annette danced around in circles inside the ring, then climbed up on a red-and-white checkercloth table and really got into her thing.

Some joker threw a twenty-five-dollar bottle of pink champagne all over her body. She lapped up what she could, rubbed the rest of it on her belly, her ass and down around

89

her cunt. She danced around the edge of the table doing an astronaut's spin, bending her ass backwards doing an Afro-grin.

Dudes got carried away, some parted from their old ladies, lined up near the table getting ready to go in.

Annette sat on the edge of the table, spreading her legs wide enough for a bulldozer to get through, called on the brothers to take a spin.

Women hollered and screamed, and a couple of studs creamed. Blue couldn't hold back anymore; the wine, the coke, and Annette's behind, all had gone to his head. He got down on his knees and clamped his lips over her cunt, running his tongue over her clit, feeling his balls getting hotter and hotter, as she came in his mouth. Two studs kissed her titties while she lay on her back, Blue down between her legs. She bounced her ass way up in the air, shouting like a sister hit by the Spirit.

Candles were brought to the center of the room, the lights were turned off. People were trying to break down the doors, climb in through the windows; old men and women, from bygone days, remembering the mulatto balls from ages past, were shocked back into adolescence as they peeped through the windows. Annette was standing up on the table circling the candles all around her, passing them near her titties, down around her cunt, up between her legs and back under her rump.

The Jive Five started taking turns, going down on her pussy. She greased their lips good, shoving cunt in their faces—more than the day they were born. Other studs got carried away and started jostling for a place. Brothers with dicks in hand, and broads squeezing their cunts screamed and hollered while some called on Jesus.

Flattop tried to call the whole thing off as a fight broke out right near the table, knocking Annette off the top, back down in the sawdust, down on her knees.

A big black stud broke loose from his wife, got down on Annette dog fashion, riding her up and down the place.

Annette screamed and yelled along with the crowd, enjoying every minute of it, yelling over and over, "Give it to me, honey, make me come, one more once."

"Ah'll see to that, baby." He continued to ride her ass, slipping his pudgy dick inside her hole, screwing her like the bomb had fallen and this was the Day of the Locust.

Annette slipped down to the floor, the dude's dick came out, jerked in the air, started coughing and spitting as his seed dropped on her back. Annette turned over, catching the sperm on her stomach, wiggled up and down like a snake about to strike.

The Jive Five jumped salty, and tried to pull the big fella off. He was back down on his knees trying for a second time. Realizing that things weren't happening the way he had planned, Blue pulled his thirty-eight and told the man to run.

Flattop charged through the crowd, his *forty-five* in his hand, told Blue to grab a cloud and drop his piece or he'd never see the sun.

The crowd got quiet, everyone was frightened, save for Blue and Flattop and the stud standing over Annette beating his meat.

Somebody unplugged the jukebox, and then out went the lights.

Annette felt hands all over her body; she started crawling in the sawdust, trying to get out of the way.

Lips were kissing her titties, hands were up her ass. She struggled and hollered, "Let go, let go," as loud as she could. By some miracle, she got out just in time.

The cops showed up five cars full, guns drawn and ready for action as the place went up in flames.

Fist fights had broken out, and shooting was taking place all over the bar, people running for cover, away from this dive. By the time the cops got ready to charge the place, most of the people were gone. Flattop was standing in the doorway, his gun still drawn. A trigger-happy cop shot it out of his hand. The only one arrested was Flattop and the big black stud who had been standing over Annette. Blue and his boys were lucky; they got away without a scratch.

When it was all over and the fire put out, two lay dead on the barroom floor. Some jive-time pimp, his dick in his hand, and a mean old lesbian. No one knew who to blame.

They took Flattop down to the station and booked him on suspicion, running a striptease and charging admission.

He pleaded not guilty to the first, second and third counts, got out on bail the next day. Word has it that he's running 'round the city crazy, looking for Annette. He wants to get her head.

When the fist fights started, the lights had gone out and the shooting began. Annette had crawled on the floor all the way back to the booth, and climbed through a window in the ladies' room, with her bookbag and purse. She couldn't find her dress nor her underwear; they had got lost somewhere in the bar.

People in the streets, on buses, and in cars, yelled and screamed when they saw her making it down the street just in her skin. She ran back towards LaSalle and Louisiana Avenue, turned left and headed up towards Holy Ghost Church, passed kids on bicycles, women sitting on their front porches, with a whole crowd following after her, trying to get her to stop.

Fear encompassed her face like she had seen the Virgin Mary standing before her without a stitch. She ran past live oak trees, ignoring as best she could the cars and buses and people climbing out of them, joining in the chase, the kids charging after her, some fool trying to grab her arm, trying to get her thoughts ahead of her body; wondering to herself what all that shit had been about. The way she had originally planned it, she was going to stay with Blue, but that fool had got in the fight, that was the last she'd see of that. When she got to the corner of Louisiana Avenue and Daneel in front of Holy Ghost Church, diagonally across from the Gumbo House, she saw the door of a car fly open, and a head sticking out.

By this time at least forty people were charging towards her, coming from every which way; she couldn't think of no other choice than to charge for the car.

"Hey, come, git in here," a voice yelled out, a dark hole in a white face.

She went for it. The car took off, burned rubber, got up to sixty, headed for the French Quarter.

The crowd at the corner stood around for a few minutes, swapped lies, told tall tales, then went home and waited for the late news reports, sure they had something to talk about for a week.

DA DA
VOO DOO
HOO DOO
SUR REAL
LISTS II

MARIE'S SECRET CEREMONY

DURING THE TRIP FROM HOLY Ghost Church to St. Ann Street, Annette and the driver, a blond kid wearing a white space suit, exchanged less than a dozen words. Marie had sent for her. *His* name was Charles, his job to pick her up on that corner.

A light feeling of suspicion shot through Annette's mind, like a dagger up the ass. She lifted her eyebrows, but decided to play it by ear. Besides she was still ruffled behind the hassle at Flattop's bar; images of dicks coming up and down at her from all over the place were still spinning round in her head.

Charles drove through the city—racing through the streets, passing houses on the right, barely missing pedestrians—like being chased by phantom bloodhounds in the Mekong Delta. He pulled up to a curb, and parked under an oak.

A white duplex with red shutters loomed in the fore-ground. A pale yellow moon hung low in the eastern sky. Sycamore trees, rose bushes and white camellias surrounded the house.

Charles got out of the car, saying to Annette, "This is it," and went up the front steps. Wrapping a blouse around her waist, grabbing her bookbag and purse, Annette followed after him.

Off at a distance, hounds began to howl, owls were heard to hoot and cats meowed.

Looking through the screen door, Annette could not believe what she saw was real. She blinked her eyes a couple of times, blamed it on her head being into something else, looked again. It was real. The sight she peeped would make the devil go straight.

A tall mama with huge eyes, a straight nose, full ripe breasts and a round stomach underneath a red bandana bikini, and great big juicy-looking thighs, a nice round ass and well-shaped legs stood in the middle of the floor before a black altar, holding a black snake coiled around her neck. This was Marie.

She had a peach complexion, rich smooth skin, weighed about a hundred and twenty, age about thirty-eight. She was so together, so fine and stacked, gigolos on the corner—or squares in the john—would eat a mile of her shit just to slip her some dick. The broad was dynamite.

Annette's first reaction was to get *uptight*—she was already thinking of herself as the *one:* especially after the ruckus she had caused at Flattop's bar. But one look at Marie changed all that. This woman was so sensual, beautiful and clean—the animus of old men's dreams, young boys' schemes—she would make the world's great whores beg to bow down at her *door.*

Annette stepped inside, eased over near the wall and looked around the room. People of all colors sat around naked. Two brothers in red fezzes and red handkerchiefs around their necks sat in one corner beating out a poly-rhythmic cadence on conga drums.

Charles slipped past and prostrated himself on the floor before this creature.

Marie looked down at him. A black altar crowded with stuffed cats, alligators, lions, tigers and wolves covered one wall of the room. Four candles flickered on high stands over the crowd.

Charles slithered forward on his stomach, like some space-age lizard, and kissed the floor upon which she walked. Marie picked up a black snake out of a black box on the altar and swung it up in the air. Flames shot from plates of *congres,* black-eyed peas and rice cooked in sugar, on the altar. Charles went to kiss her foot. Marie looked down, frowned, jackknifed her right leg and kicked him dead in the face.

He rolled over on his back, came up on his knees, crawled on all fours, yelping like a dog mad with rabies. He disappeared into the next room.

The drummers began to beat a slow even rhythm on the conga drums, being joined by others with rings around their knees, bells on their ankles—women mostly—black and white, people playing tambourines and castanets, while Blind Man Willie in a corner, two big gorgeous blondes at his side, wailed on clarinet.

Marie danced around in a small circle with the black snake in her arms, let it kiss her lips, slide down her crotch and drop to the floor. She picked it up, swung it around over the heads of the others, wrapped it around her neck, its tail eating into her stomach, then dropped it back into the black box. Like in a trance, she yelled and screamed. Her eyes glazed, she wiggled down to the floor, shaking her body from hips to ankles, swaying like a cobra, and turned cartwheels before the altar.

Four women danced around Marie, candles balanced on their heads. Others, men and women, joined in the ritual.

They swayed bare asses, shook thighs, tits moving round like shaking off flies, and clapped their hands to the pulsating rhythms emanating from the drums. Chants and shouts in Creole and Angolese escaped from their mouths. The mood was contagious.

The brothers on the drums pounded even harder, mixing rim shots with shouts, egging the dancers on; they now moved around the room, the entire place was caught up in the act, forming one long line moving in and out of circles and shaking their behinds. Annette got the feeling deep down in her bones, forgot all about being uptight, dropped her blouse to the floor, and joined the commotion. She felt free, complete, on her own. The line broke. The male dancers paired off with females, one on each arm. Annette was grabbed by a big tall soul brother who could have easily passed for Jack Johnson's double. He had a short redhead on the other arm. A freckle-faced girl with green eyes, stoned on speed. The clarinet wailed blue notes, the bells, castanets and tambourines clanged, clinked and banged as the drummers underneath paced the beat. Marie's voice broke over the crowd, shouting high octaves and chords in a low contralto voice. The crowd continued to buck and grind, clapping their hands, shouting divines, calling up demons from under the deep.

The redhead went wild, got frenzied and started shouting, fell down on her knees, dead into a trance. She crawled around on the floor, shouting insults and curses, her eyes wild and strange, her body exuding demiurges and exotic desires. She clasped Annette's partner around his thighs, grabbed his member and stuck it in her mouth, squeezed his nuts and worked his member from head to stem. He stood straight up, looked down at her head working his twelve inches without an iota of shame and got HOT. He dropped his hands on her red head and helped her out.

Annette moved off to the side. She danced near the altar where Marie was mumbling words in the unknown tongue, giving out mojos and passing along black candles. Annette glanced back at the redhead. She was still into her thing, down on her knees sucking the brother's ebony rod. Others in the joint were too busy into their own thing to give very much thought to the redhead's passions.

Annette bowed as she received the candle from Marie and moved back around the floor. A strong sensation of desire had swept over her as she caught the fragrance of Marie's body.

A grey-haired old codger burst through the dancers, came up near the altar, grabbed at Annette's breasts with both hands, missed and fell flat on his face.

He pulled himself up slowly and came back in the circle, grabbed at her arms, swung around on the floor. She danced with him for the rest of the set until the drums slowed down their beat to an almost silent whisper.

She led the old cat over to the corner where her blouse lay on the floor. Others had paired off. They drank rum and anisette, passed the reefer and the coke. Everybody got high, mellow, together. A groove.

Marie disappeared from the altar, candles flickered around the room, strange sounds could be heard coming from inside the walls. Ha'nts and ghosts made this their abode.

"What weird sounds," Annette commented, wrapping the blouse back around her midsection and sitting down on a black cushion.

"Oh, that's nothing. Happens all the time," the old man answered, crossing his legs, hiding his privates as his midriff bulge drooped to his thighs. His pink skin had red splotches all over it as though he had been beaten with a whip, his toes were covered with corns, his face was flat as a pancake and he looked like he had been beaten with an ugly stick.

Someone passed Annette the reefer; she inhaled, passed it to the old man and asked, "Do you come here often? I mean, what sort of place is this?"

"Yeah." He took the reefer, inhaled like a dope addict dying for a fix, inhaled a second time, getting just as stoned as he could, and passed it back to her. His head was as tight as Dick's hatband. "To relax, that's why I come here. What's your name? I mean, I'm Max. Who are you?" He dropped his hand down on Annette's fine brown thigh.

She let it rest. "Annette."

"How would you like to go to New York?" He wasn't wasting time. His hand slid up under the blouse, tickled the hairs of her cunt. She spread her legs, giving him room to work. The reefer was taking effect. Another hand passed her a glass of anisette.

Max did not waste a second. He got down on his belly, crawled between her thighs, wrapped his arms around her hips, squeezed her ass with his open palms and sucked her cunt with his lips and tongue. Annette lay back, sipped the anisette, wrapped her legs around his shoulders, dropped her legs over his back, felt a little embarrassed, so she covered his head with her blouse. Someone spread the word so the others came over to find out what was happening. A tall spade cat whose only comment was "Like, *WOW!*" stood over them with a stiff dick, waiting his turn. A young college professor from New York's Lower East Side, with his wife—a short broad with wide hips and black hair—came over and stood next to tall Larry, exchanging comments.

"You like him?" Larry asked, his eyes half closed, his joint real hard.

"It's all right," Annette started, feeling Max working out, his nose all down in her clit, his tongue touching the bottom of her asshole, while she held him by the ears, still under the blouse. "But you look like a head man; when he finishes, you too can get down."

Larry grinned at the college professor and his wife, and then looked back at Annette. Judy, the college professor's wife, started getting agitated just watching. She dropped down on a cushion and spread her legs. Before the professor

102

could say a word about where this was at, Larry was down on her ass, screwing her for all she was worth. He slipped his joint right down in her, she wrapped her legs around his back, kissed him on the ear, on the chin, then bit his lips. She began yelling and screaming and scratching him all over his back, looking up at her husband, tears streaming down her cheeks, yelling, "Honey, honey! Oh, oh, oh, baby, it's so good, I really can't stop it!"

Floyd did not know what to say; he watched Larry fucking his old lady and felt kind of silly. He couldn't get his joint up in public, he wasn't one of those kind, he had to wait till they got to the hotel, or home, or somewhere else, all he could do was watch the action, feeling sorry for himself.

Max was still working out inside Annette's cunt. She had pulled the blouse off his head to give him some air. He licked the lips of her pussy, rolled his tongue around her ass, stuck it into the top of her hole, and tickled her clitoris. She jerked up and down, dropping the anisette out of her hands, rubbing his head and all over his shoulders. She hadn't at first believed a grey-haired old white man really had it in him, but seeing is believing and now she was feeling fine. She squeezed his head with her thighs, while he stuck his fingers up her ass, working his tongue like it was a joint, squeezing her hole harder and harder. She dropped her palms to the floor, shoved her ass in the air, covered him with pussy, feeling the balls of her feet getting hotter and hotter as her stomach contracted and her titties became firm and stiff, watching his head as it bobbed up and down, down between her luscious thighs.

Larry and Judy were still working right next to them. He was on the bottom now. She rode him like a pony. Her palms on his shoulders, his dick slipping in and out as her ass and white thighs moved up and down, turned from side to side, up and down, side to side, and both began to come. She let out a scream, dropped down on his chest, he jackknifed his legs, grabbed her by the ass, started shoving it in and out so

103

hard they both shot a blast. She tongue-kissed him on the eyes and lips, shoved her red-hot tongue down his throat, moved her thighs off his hips, slid down over his stomach, grabbed his joint and ran it between her big creamy white breasts, eased further down and took it in her mouth. Larry lay back with his eyes closed, worked his hips up and down, down and up, as she shoved a finger up his ass and made him shoot off some more.

Judy's husband shook his head; he didn't know what to do, looking down at his wife's fine rubbery-fleshed ass sprawled on the floor, and watching her head jumping over Larry's brown stomach. He left the corner and went and stood out on the porch, wondering and thinking, should he get a divorce?

The redheaded girl who had grabbed Annette's partner earlier was standing next to one of the blondes, trying to shake her down. The blonde told her "No," said she didn't swing that way. Red jumped salty, grabbed a young dude in the corner. He was just sitting there talking to his old lady, a colored broad, long and lanky, who had a nice body on her, real nice skin and great big eyes.

Red got down on her knees, grabbed his joint, chafed it up and down while looking in his eyes, then kissed him on the lips, her hot breath blowing in his nostrils. His member got so hard he couldn't hold back. The spade chick who had been sitting there started feeling Red's behind, sending thrills up her spine, causing her mind to become entwined. She couldn't decide whether she wanted to fuck the guy or suck the girl. She decided on the former, leaving the latter till last. She mounted him in the sitting position as the spade chick continued to finger her cunt, slipped her fingers out of the way just in time, grabbed his dick with her hand. She squeezed the head of his joint, looked over at Red and asked: "You want it right naw, all eight inches up your crotch?"

Red looked around with tears in her eyes, said, "Give it to me, honey, don't be that way." So the spade chick let it slip up into Red's greasy hole and they both began to roll. They were hugging one another, going back and forth, she hugging him, he kissing her titties, both hotter than a June night down in Hell. As the spade chick sat watching, her imagination flew every which way. She stood up and straddled Red, making her suck her cunt, and her boy friend kiss her ass. It was a threesome that just wouldn't quit. Judy's old man walked back in the door, and when he saw this he damned near had a fit.

He rushed right by them, went over where Larry and Judy were sprawled out on the floor, her big white thighs around his neck, red-lipped black-haired cunt in his mouth, she working his balls and joint while he blew her cunt.

Max was finished. He sat next to Annette and watched Larry and Judy working out, and had a sip of rum. Annette stood up, joy-juice dripping from her snatch, patted Max on the head and asked, "Where is the john?"

"You're coming back?"

She smiled. "Yeah, you old codger, it was good, enjoyed it for what it was worth. I'll be back."

He ran his hands up and down her fine thighs, patted her on her big ass, and kissed her cunt. He looked up over her mound, feeling his balls getting tighter. Dreamy-eyed and pathetic, he asked in a rusty voice. "I . . . I wantcha to come to New York wid me, please."

"Wait'll I come back from the john; we kin toss it around." She smiled coquettishly and walked around the altar. She felt a chill coming on.

PAS DE HOO DOO

SHE PRESSED THE PLUNGER ON the john. The water drained down. She reached in her bookbag, pulled out her sunglasses, checked to make sure the roots were still there, rubbed some on her cunt, dug down again and got a pair of sky-blue-trimmed-in-yellow-dayglo drawers and slipped them on. They had a red circle in the middle that covered her cunt. She then checked herself out in the mirror. She still looked young, pretty and sexy. She turned the lights out, the panties glowed in the dark, her body becoming a terrific elongated shadow. She flipped the light back on and was about to depart when she saw the door open. It was Marie—nude.

Annette's heart pounded in her chest like a conga drum working by itself. She felt her pulse rise, blood shoot to her head, and had strange feelings of desire crawling up her thighs.

Talk about a broad who was really something else! Man, baby, Marie was more than just another woman, she was the dream of a thousand men in any part of the world.

The black hairs over her cunt were at least an inch long, the mound protruded outward, like a good bulldagger's trick, her breasts were soft, round and firm, the nipples stuck out, and she had a recess running down between them, which stopped at her navel, where her stomach balled over, just enough to want to hold it. The blue-black hair flowed down over her shoulders and settled over her ass, and when she walked her hips jogged, accentuating her body as if she were balling. She moved over towards Annette and, like the first time, Annette's immediate reaction was to get uptight. But one look into Marie's hazel eyes, and her head was off into a trip. Annette couldn't figure out what had come over her. There was a certain mysteriousness about this woman which she really couldn't begin to get to. Some rare quality, as if the inner beauty was ten times as potent as the flesh which met the eye. Marie's soul seemed to glow through, pierce to the back of Annette's skull, dropped down inside her nipples, bounced around in her stomach, entered her womb, shot down to her feet like particles of light, backed up around her hole, cunt, stomach, breast, inside her arms, shooting out on her fingers, through her neck, through her mouth, nostrils, coming out her eyes as tears. Annette felt strange, magnetized towards her, all over.

"I sent for you," Marie stated, and placed a hand on Annette's shoulder. Triple thrills shot through the surface of her skin, she could feel the touch in her bones. Outside, the conga drums, castanets, bells, rings and clarinet started up in song. Marie continued, looking down into Annette's eyes like a mother, "I've got a message from your mother; you were seen in the john. I know what you've been through."

Have you ever seen magic work, fascination take a spin? Well, Annette hadn't either, but looking at Marie, she just couldn't help herself. She didn't swing with broads normally—that wasn't her stick—but somehow being next to this broad, she knew it meant luck.

She dropped down on her knees, kissed Marie's luscious creamy white thighs, the soft silky hairs around her cunt, while Marie spread her legs, moved over and sat on the edge of the commode, doused the lights so Annette could work in the dark, as she stuck her tongue up that sweet cunt. It was a nice-sized crack, none too large, none too small, smelled like the essence of roses, the pure taste of camellias. Annette hugged her round thighs, squeezed her round buttocks, and worked her nose on her clitoris, her tongue up her hole, and let her hands ramble through her hair and fondle her breasts.

Marie leaned back in the darkness, looking down at her lover, sweet tears of gladness running down her cheeks as that young chick gave her a loving which she wasn't gonna forget. Annette kissed the inner parts of her thighs, ran her tongue over her belly, kissed her navel and her breasts, leaned further down, took her foot to her face and licked her ankles, her feet, then stood up and kissed her face. They held one another in a passionate embrace, then Annette got back down on her knees, eyes closed, nostrils filled with the sweet smell of roses, jism, saliva and fish, worked her tongue inside Marie's hole, tickling the clit with her teeth and made her cream in her mouth, wrapping her big shapely thighs around her shoulders. When she tasted the liquids oozing out of Marie's snatch, she dropped her hand down inside her own panties and masturbated her cunt, working harder on Marie, giving her another charge—three in succession—not letting up until she too had shot her load. They sat there in the dark for the next five minutes, listening to each other breathing, silent. Then Marie got up off the stool, turned on the lights, and stood before the child.

Annette stood up, head down, embarrassed. She hadn't known what had caused her to act like some pervert, this wasn't her nature. "I'm sorry," the words slipped through her lips.

"There's nothing to be sorry about." Marie came forward and wrapped her arms around Annette's shoulders. Her breasts rubbed softly against her cheeks. Another thrill shot through Annette's body. This time she controlled it.

They stood in front of the mirror, looking at one another.

For some strange reason, although Annette had never noticed it before, there was a striking likeness between the two. Even now, Annette didn't really notice it; she was watching Marie's image.

Marie saw it, but only said, "Come."

Annette put on a pair of yellow bell-bottoms and a yellow blouse and followed Marie—who had thrown a long black robe over her sensuous body—up a spiral staircase. The room they entered had the most amazing color combination imaginable. A deep black ceiling, a dense red floor, three white walls and a deep blue reversing mirror covering the fourth wall. The room was lit by five black candles on a chandelier.

A bed sat in the middle of the room, and an altar, similar to the one downstairs, but instead of one black box it had three, with pythons in them, and *gris-gris* was laid out all over the floor. The bed had white silk sheets and on it, an old woman with a pasty complexion and white hair, wearing sunglasses and reading a comic book, lay—resting silently.

Annette was completely turned around. She followed Marie into the room, and sat in a soft white chair near the bed. Marie sat opposite the old woman, calling, "Mother, guess who's here?"

The old woman looked up, smiled, showing purple gums and black rotten teeth. In her sockets were two glass eyes, which stared through sunglasses at Marie.

"Did you find her?"

"Charles brought her, right after the mess at Flattop's bar." Marie smiled, crossed her legs, exposing a fine thigh.

Annette was still puzzled. She didn't know why she had been brought here or to what purpose, and really didn't know who these people were—Marie, Charles, the old woman. Becoming impatient, she put the question to Marie, before her mother.

The old woman pressed a buzzer next to the bed. An Indian squaw walked into the room. She looked as if she could pass for Marie's sister; the only difference was that she was a little heavier, but just as beautiful. She also wore sunglasses. "Yes, Madam?"

She leaned down and listened for the old woman to speak. "Send Jeanne in here with some sassafras tea. We have a guest." Her voice was squeaky as an old cane rocker and she spoke with great strain.

The Indian vanished from the room. Annette felt her hands perspire. Looked in the mirror and saw the three of them reflected. Candles burned above her head. The room smelled of African incense, roses and camellia—like Marie's cunt. The dead smell of feces emanated from under the old woman's bed. Somewhere a bullfrog croaked.

A black cat stretched itself and jumped off the bed.

Annette gave a start. She hadn't seen the cat when she walked in.

"Come back here, Sapphire!" Marie yelled at the yellow-eyed cat. He meowed and jumped into her lap, staring at Annette.

A girl about her own age, white as the Queen of England, walked into the room. She carried a tray with three silver goblets and a carved silver pitcher of hot smoldering sassafras tea. She set it on a nearby table.

"There's some people downstairs inquiring about an Annette."

She spoke perfect English without a trace of French, addressing herself to Marie.

"What are their names?" Marie stared harshly at the girl.

The girl looked over at Annette, at the mother who was still hidden behind the glasses, and then, finally, she spoke again to Marie.

"Dip and the Jive Five." Question marks rattled through her brain.

Annette's and Marie's eyes met. Annette felt a twitch at her temples. Her hand itched.

"Tell them to wait. I'll be down in a few minutes."

The girl tiptoed out of the room. Marie poured the tea, addressing her mother. "Annette just got here, and she has guests already. I'm afraid we will have to get rid of them."

"Too bad." The old woman raised up, took off the glasses, rubbed her eyes with a handkerchief. They stared blankly out into empty space and she put the glasses back on, taking the cup of tea in her scrawny hand.

"Well, my dear. It sure is nice to see my granddaughter after all these years. I was afraid that I would done passed away before I had a chance to see ya. Soon as I got wind of you was planning on leaving I had Charles to go and git ya, was so worried about ya." She sipped the tea, cackled, showing the purple gums and black teeth again, then leaned back on the pillow.

HOW LONG BLEW ANNETTE'S MOTHER TOO

ANNETTE FELT WARM, HER HANDS and feet began to sweat. She sipped sassafras tea, glanced at Marie, the old woman—then at their images in the mirror, which sent her head into a spin. The candles burning overhead melted, dripping black wax to the floor.

"Your real mother died a long time ago," the old woman's voice cracked. She coughed and continued talking like one possessed. "She put a curse on the Governor which drove him insane. They came here and picked her up. She died while in jail."

Annette was definitely shook. Things weren't jiving, lining up nor making sense; this did not explain anything. She figured the old lady was lying. "That being the case, who is the woman whom I've been living with, *and* my father?"

The old woman reached over and grabbed a marijuana-loaded cigar off the coffee table. Marie gave her a light. She inhaled deeply, coughed a couple of times, then continued, staring straight up at the ceiling as if seeing ghosts.

She cackled like a hen laying a rotten egg, lifted her hand for silence, then went on.

The beat of the conga drums pounded through the floor.

Charles stepped into the room, still wearing the white space suit, and stood in a corner. His eyes gleamed, as if he had been smoking weed.

"Back in the days before the civil rights movements, cries for freedom and all the other rebellions, the Governor used to visit this house along with mayors and senators, writers and artists. He used to come here saying he was seeking advice. Your mother was running the show; she was the one in charge. She read his palm a couple of times, gave him good advice, told him to free the coloreds, let everybody go. He got so excited he didn't know what to do. So she fixed him a plate of gumbo, lit candles at the table, set the altar for him, then danced with the snake. She got a pot of hot water, just as hot as could be imagined, dropped a black cat in it, skinned it alive. She tore it apart, scattering the pieces all over, got down to the bones, gave him one as a charm. He put it in his pocket, smiled graciously, then he went away."

The old lady paused. "Yes, Charles, I heard you come in. What do you want?"

Charles' face turned red as a beet; he knew she was blind but always failed to remember that her hearing was so sensitive.

"There's a woman downstairs claiming to be Annette's mother, saying something about she ran away from home." He bowed, looked at Annette, at Marie, and stared at the old woman. The cat jumped down out of Marie's lap, raced across the floor, and tore at his throat. He screamed like a woman gone wild. Marie called the cat off: "Get down, Sapphire, and behave yourself." The cat dropped to the floor, leaving claw marks on Charles' neck. It drifted back to the bed, sat on its hind legs, its yellow eyes glowing.

Annette felt chilled to the bone. She wanted to leave, to jump out of the window, but there wasn't any; she thought about cracking the mirror, going through it, out the back of the house. But it seemed irrational. Dumb.

"Bring her on up," the old woman answered Charles. "She

might as well hear it along with everyone else." Her voice rattled like a sack of bones. Charles walked nimbly out the room.

Marie stood up, her robe flew open. "Do you really . . . ?"

"It's all right," her mother cut her short. Marie's mother was possessed, had had a connaissance two hours previously, and spoke presently through her *loa*.

Annette massaged her palms; strange events seemed to be taking place in this house. She glanced at Marie as she eased back into the chair, wrapping the robe around her thighs.

"'Tis Marie's sister," the old lady informed Annette. She inhaled on the reefer, sipped the tea and continued: "You wuz born back in Parish Prison. I was called in to be the midwife. Fact is, I know my daughter never told ya, but you had a caul over your face."

Annette sat quietly; suddenly her eyes flashed, fright covered her face. She could have sworn she had seen a figure move on the other side of the mirror. She jumped out of the chair, the wig flew off her head, the tight curls on her head made her look like Topsy; her mouth flew open, and a shriek choked in her throat. The figure, or apparition, was gone. Her heart pounded in her chest like the knock in *Inner Sanctum;* her breathing came slowly, in gulps.

The old woman sat up in bed and motioned for her to be seated. Annette had never believed in ha'nts, poltergeists, none of that way-out shit, but in this house—well, everything seemed part of the scenery.

Marie, who had stood up when Annette got up out of her chair, returned to her seat. They stared at the old woman. The black cat purred, jumped off the bed, meowed before the mirror.

The old woman explained the curse. "After the Governor left that day, your mother scrubbed the front steps for a solid week with red brick, washed it down with scalding hot water, danced before the altar eating shrimp covered with hot cayenne pepper and prayed in isolation. She even

115

went so far—she was seven months pregnant by him, the Governor that is, when this went down—to burn two black candles upside down, bury the remains of the black cat in the yard by an old sycamore tree in the back of the house and sleep on her stomach in the coffin for seven days, laying on her face.

"When the news hit the papers that the Governor was on TV cussing out everybody, saying the niggers was right, and then when he stole that plane and took off to Texas, she knew the curse had worked. She was so happy she didn't know what to say, just sat there silent the whole time, till they came and got her. They put her in prison, just like I said, then you were born with the veil over your face."

Annette heard noises in the walls, sounding like snakes, rats, something . . . She saw an image flash through the mirror; at that instant, four of the candles went out. She couldn't hold it back. She screamed, "MOOOTHER! MOOTHER! MOOOTHER!" at the top of her voice. She prostrated herself on the floor, crawled around like a snake, whimpered and cried, cried and whimpered, felt the presence of another in the room, someone she couldn't see.

No one said a word. Marie stared with cold black eyes. The old woman sat up in bed, took off the glasses. The glass balls for eyes reflected the one lit candle. The black cat was in her arms, the red tip of the cigar shone.

The beating of the drums downstairs continued, the chanting increased, sounding like another ritual had started and was working inside the beat as the handclapping began. Feet could be heard pounding on the floor. Annette's heart was pounding inside her chest, her eyes were closed tightly, her muscles felt loose, her skin drawn, the fucking and sucking she had been doing caused her to moan.

The mood lasted for at least five minutes, but to Annette it felt like an eternity. Then neon lights came on all around the room. The old woman was sitting up in the bed, she had gone into a trance.

Marie lifted Annette from the floor. Her whole body trembled and tears filled her eyes; the fright was still on her face. The noise downstairs had ceased. The whole house was quiet.

Marie led Annette to a room opposite. It was laid out in purple and blue with a large bed in the middle. The mirror was there, she could look into the old lady's room. She sat up in bed, staring at the altar, eyes glassed, false, transfixed: as if listening.

After Annette was nestled all snug on the bed, and had gotten over her scare, Marie sat beside her on the bed exposing her cunt. Marie ran her hand over her face, rubbed her stomach, massaged her back, and told her, "It's all true. All of it.

"Your mother is my sister. We got along fine, she was such a beautiful woman—smart and hip. The only trouble was, she couldn't stand white folks. I don't know where she picked that up from, probably from your great-grandfather, Doctor John—he called them all devils."

Annette had heard of Doctor John, the legend around that name. She couldn't believe it was the same one, the Voo Doo Priest. Marie confirmed this, and told her about the other sister.

"After he died, the family split up. Our mother, she was his disciple, lover for a while, Doctor John's. We moved into this house and mother ran the whole thing. She had another friend who used to come around—Zozo Labrique. But they had a falling out. She stole my other sister, the one you call mother, took her to a house somewhere uptown, and when she got to be the right age set her up in a whorehouse, had her turning tricks for anyone with a dick.

"We looked high and low for her, but couldn't find a trace, so when your mother died she showed up for the funeral. Mother told her what had happened, how worried we had been, but when she found out about our practices she wanted to turn us in. That other woman had filled her

117

head with lies: in return she went to the officials and told them she would take care of the child, meaning you. She got the permission; after all she was your mother's sister too, and she's had you all the while. That guy you call your father—he was a pimp on the Ramp, had a job breaking in girls but had gotten too old. She married him, took care of him, gave him pocket money.

"But we knew about you anyway, knew how you were doing in school, the whole bit. Stompin' Sam at the Gumbo House, he's one of us. He knew us way back then, recognized you from a picture mother had. And when he saw what happened at the Gumbo House, he came over and ran it. That's when we sent Charles to pick you up. He's really your uncle you know, your grandmother's mulatto son. He's deep into a spell, but you ain't got nothing to worry 'bout. Really he's harmless."

Annette was too upset to say anything. She sat on the side of the bed and looked Marie in the eyes. What she heard she knew to be the truth, never doubted one word; it made her feel better, not as ridiculous as before. The only question which still gnawed at her brain was why had it been kept from her for so long.

She began to get sleepy. She yawned, thinking about what had been told her tonight, the story about her birth, her mother and the Governor, and Marie's sister. She looked down at her own skin—brown, smooth, somewhat red. Marie's skin was peach, her mother's white as a sheet, the same with Charles, he looked like an ofay. The coke she had snorted, the changes at Flattop's bar, the rum she had drunk, all were taking effect. She yawned again, looked over at Marie, popped the question: "Can I sleep here tonight?"

"Of course," Marie answered. They got up off the bed. Marie pulled the covers back. A rattlesnake's vertebrae lay in the middle of the bed.

Annette fainted.

CONGO DUN REEL

DAWN BURST OVER THE MISSISSIPPI *as if John Henry had cracked it with his hammer. A red, yellow bluish-green sky covered the earth. People hurried up and down the streets inside metal machines, entranced like zombies, frowning on their way to work. Ants, roaches, spiders and snakes crawled out of their way, going to sleep for the day. The electronic city had turned on.*

Annette tossed and turned in the purple bed, sweat pouring off her like a thousand pricks discharging at once as her naked body went through changes in her sleep. She opened her eyes and her head shot straight up in the air as she stared through the mirror. The old woman was standing before the altar, not a stitch of clothing on, doing some weird dance, as Charles crawled on all fours around on the floor.

Marie stood in a corner with a black snake wrapped around her head, nude, fingering her cunt. Charles moved forward towards the skeleton-like frame of the old woman, clasped his hands around her thighs, stuck his mouth inside her snatch, and sucked that cunt solid and dry. The old woman, who was too old to come, dropped a turd on the floor. Annette fell back on the bed, her head spinning around, tossed and turned, laid flat on her stomach.

She saw her mother standing before her, feeling up her flat breast, her father in another corner, jerking himself off. He stopped his motions, came forward towards the bed, grabbed his wife around the legs and kissed her thighs, her legs, her feet. About his head, she played with his ears, kissed him hard in the mouth, then sprawled out on the floor. He mounted her, his dick damned near hard as stone, jerking and jumping up and down as he skinned it back. His eyes were wide open, his face grinned from ear to ear, his wife's thighs looked so enticing he thought he would die. He scrambled down on the pussy, slipped his stiff joint right in, grabbed her around the waist; she threw her big thighs around his back as they moaned and groaned and bounced around on the floor.

Annette turned over and laid on her back, spread her legs wide open, tossed the covers off her body, and fingered her hole. Dip, the Jive Five and Sleepy Willie were in the room. Her mother stood straight up, next to Annette. It wasn't her real mother but the broad who had raised her. She clasped her arms about Marie, rubbed her shoulders, her ass, felt her big thighs, and rubbed her belly against the others. Dip, the Jive Five and Sleepy Willie stood over the bed. Each had his dick drawn, hard as stone. Sleepy Willie left the bed and went over to Marie and the other. He rubbed Marie's ass, squeezing the fat mounds with his hands, grabbed her right hand and made her pull his prick. She milked it up and down, backwards and forwards, working slowly at first and grinning all around. The other woman went down, got on her knees, took his dick in her mouth while Willie and Marie kissed with their lips, him feeling her big firm titties, running his hands up her behind, playing with her pussy, while the other was down on her knees.

Dip couldn't stand it much longer. He started playing with his prick, and was just about to discharge when Bertha charged into the room. She grabbed him by his penis, pulling him around the room, laid back on a couch and spread her thighs. He tried to mount her. Bertha didn't want anything to do with it. She pushed him forward, he turned on his back, she mounted him. She lifted big shiny thighs and her big soft ass, and had her titties pointing straight up in the air.

Dip was so excited, his joint was standing straight up. Bertha bent down and chafed it. She licked it with her tongue, rubbed it over her breasts then directed it towards her hole.

She sprawled over his body, her hand on her fat hips, while he lost his hands in the cheeks of her ass and stuck his head between her thighs. They rolled over on the bed, Bertha collapsing on top of a pillow, shoving her legs around his shoulders and beating him on the back as he worked on her hole. One arm was around a big fat thigh while with the other he pulled on his pecker, getting a charge in this peculiar manner.

The Jive Five stood stock-still, their eyes riveted on Annette. She lay in bed fingering her pussy, sucking air through her teeth, her eyes closed, legs tossing around on the bed.

Blue was pulling on his joint, rubbing Red's ass. Green was down on the floor with his ass sticking up.

Just then the door opened and in walked the two blondes who had been standing near the clarinetist when Annette first walked into the pad. Blue stopped what he was doing and ran directly over towards them, dick in hand, not waiting for an introduction. He had often had dreams of fucking white women, long time ago, when he used to hang out in movies, watching TV shows. The tallest one grabbed him, her nipples looking hard, strong and straight, her breast extra large, big hips shaking and thighs real fine. She got down on her knees, kissed him around the balls. His head went back, his tongue stuck out, rubbing his member over her hair. He mounted her from behind, feeling her soft thighs, slipped his joint into her hole, and started really working out. She bounced back and forth, moved it around some more— big black dick, going in and out that white pussy, integrating sexes. She moaned, groaned and shouted, holding herself up, while the other four studs left the side of Annette's bed, and charged over towards the other girl. She stood in a corner all by herself, sunglasses covering her eyes, a G-string covering her cunt. Her body was big and fine, with a nice soft ass (but somewhat flat), big shapely thighs; and her cunt protruded like Marie's, covered with

121

*brown hairs. Red knelt down and kissed the hairs, Green went for
her titties, Yellow kissed her mouth while Purple grabbed her from
behind. She spread her legs as best she could, leaned back on Purple.
He slipped his member in her ass, working up a sweat. Red continued to suck her cunt, his hands wrapped around Purple's balls. Green
kissed her stomach, grabbed her hand and made her jerk him off.*

*The redhead from downstairs danced in with Max. She held
him by his arm, and pulled him across the room. They came over
and stood before Annette's bed, looked down at her for a second,
both laughing their asses off (Annette couldn't hear a sound), and
started doing the jerk. Flattop charged in with a knife in his hand;
it flashed in the sunlight that poured in through the window. He ran
up to Blue who was down on the floor working the first blonde over
something awful. The knife sliced air. Blue ducked his head just in
time, and jumped up off the broad. The broad jumped up, grabbed
Flattop's arm, let him feel her titties; he dropped the knife on the
ground, grinned and got hot between the thighs. She walked right up
to him, stuck her tongue out teasingly, rubbed her juicy snatch over
his member and tickled his spine. He shot his wad between her thighs,
exhausting himself, and stretched out on the floor. The redhead and
Max danced around in circles, then they were down on the floor, he
was in between her legs, sucking her cunt, working on her twat, while
she held his head and laughed out loud.*

*The room was filled with couples fucking; even Judy and her
husband were there. She and Larry started screwing, the professor
watching as before. Not knowing what to make of it all, he started
taking notes.*

*Everyone was screaming and yelling, a few moaning low, I mean,
really going for broke; the room smelled like a burlesque house, or
some of your underground—surfaced—dirty shows when the lights
are turned out.*

Annette woke up. Her head ached. She couldn't figure out
where she was. Charles stood before her, wearing the same
suit and tennis shoes. He spoke in the same soft voice. "I was
sent to tell you that . . . " He drifted off, glancing around the
room. It was neat and tidy, everything in place; the mirror

gave off a blue light. It appeared opaque. Charles continued: " . . . Max sent a car for you; it's to be here in an hour."

Annette was still a little drowsy. She batted her eyes and felt for the blonde wig. It was gone. She batted her eyes a couple of times, images of people fucking, screaming and yelling, laughing and balling reeled through her mind.

She opened her eyes again. Charles was still standing there, like, waiting for an answer. "Max?" Confusion cluttered her childish mind. "Max?" She tossed, turned and twisted the name around in her brain, trying to conjure up an image. Dip, Willie, the Jive Five and Pops collaged inside her mind. She shook her head, trying to think. "Max? Who's Max?"

"The Right Reverend Max, whom you allowed to perform cunnilingus on you last night, after the ceremony." His voice sounded like a soprano sax, riffing on a Bach fugue.

"Cunnin . . . *Who?*"

"Excuse me, mademoiselle, to give you some *head.*"

A head job? Annette was still trying to get herself together. "Last night? Shit." It seemed like ages ago. "Last night?" She couldn't remember anything, save for some old lady telling her tales—and Marie. She was as sober as Lieutenant Calley being tried for war crimes.

She looked around the room. Outside it was dark. A candle burned on the nightstand near her bed. The mirror looked dark blue, almost black. Everything was in place. Spic and Span danced a jig in the corner, two little rats made of plastic. She was trying to get straight in her head how she'd arrived there, in the bed.

Max? Max? The name bounced around in her skull like it was the name of some Mad Arab working with America to keep Israel in her place. "You said he has a car waiting for me?"

Charles was getting impatient too: his job was merely to deliver messages, not to play twenty questions. "Yes." He bit his bottom lip. "It will be here in *one* hour."

Annette scratched her ear. Then the bridge of her nose (like she'd seen politicians do on TV, when about to lie). She looked at the creature standing before her: white space suit, tennis shoes, blond nappy hair. What a sight! Slowly the mosaic took shape and formed a singular image. Yeah, he was the driver Marie had sent to pick her up, and whom she had kicked in the face. Then it was all there. "Oh, that *fool*." She slapped her forehead. "The old codger," as the image began to solidify inside her head. "He sent a *car for* me?"

"Yes. At midnight the car will be here." From out of nowhere a towel and a bar of lye soap appeared in his hands. He placed them at the foot of the bed, pointed to a door on the right, saying: "That is the bathroom." And vacated the room.

"Hey, wait a minute." But it was too late. Charles had vanished.

Slowly Annette climbed out of the bed. A wet spot was in the middle of the sheet where her body had lain. She leaned over and smelt it. Perspiration. She sighed, sitting on the side of the bed, still trying to clear her head.

Marie, Flattop's bar, home, the fight with Moms, her brother, Dip and Bertha, and Sleepy Willie in the john—it all came back to her like the clanging of bells. Each turned on another light.

Her bell-bottom trousers, the yellow blouse, the blue panties with the red circle in the middle were all scattered on the floor. The room. Still, she couldn't remember how she had gotten here. She assumed that she must have been stoned. Ripped. Just out of it. She shook her head. It felt like rocks inside. The ache endured. Her bookbag and purse for her bread—five twenties (thank God or five other white men for *that,* she thought). The roots, charms and snake ring! It was all there.

She stood up, naked as a jaybird, and stretched herself. Her body appeared bluish brown in the mirror. She rubbed her thighs, her round behind, her stomach; then squeezed her breast. She was all there—physically, at least. Echoes of the night before slowly fragmentized and gained some sort of cohesiveness in her consciousness.

She took Charles' advice, grabbed the blue towel and lye soap, disappeared behind the door and turned on the shower.

Drums, castanets, tambourines and the wail of a clarinet filled her eardrums as she walked down the spiral staircase. She smelt gumbo coming from the rear of the house. Instinct took her in that direction. She headed for the kitchen. A pot-bellied stove sat in the middle of the room. A black coffin was in the far corner; a candle burned over it. A body lay in state. Annette's heart increased its beat. Slowly Annette crept towards it. A bat flew through the window and settled on the ceiling. It was Marie.

Annette let out a scream that encircled the house; she dropped to her knees and crawled out of the room, down the halls and towards the living room. Her heart was pounding, her chest was like sticks of dynamite exploding, cold sweat popped off her skin the size of tennis balls; she felt cold and warm at the same time as she hurried through the house trying to catch her breath. She couldn't believe nothing any more. Nothing. She was gasping for air when she got to the front room. The crowd, which was just beginning to dance around the redheaded girl, stopped in the middle of the ceremony and charged towards her. Charles picked her up off her knees. "What is it? What's the trouble?" His eyes were pale green, his face red and tortured; he looked like a devil.

Annette could hardly keep her eyes open. She was damned near frightened beyond all comprehension. All she could think of was leaving; she didn't care how, why, what for—just leaving. A hollowness filled her stomach, the blood pounded at her temples, she felt weak, humble, helpless as an astronaut lost on a moonshot. "Marie, Marie," she panted. As the crowd moved back, a big black man came over, grabbing her in his arms, sticking smelling salts to her nostrils and settling her down on a cushion before the candles—near the black altar covered with snakes, stuffed cats and a red-eyed bear. The conga drums continued with their beat, slow and rhythmic, the castanets dinged, the tambourines kept up a constant sound and the clarinet moaned the blues. The women looked at her, shaking their heads, white powder covering their faces, their eyes circled with black mascara.

The big black man kept the smelling salts to her nostrils until she slowly returned to full consciousness. She heard people chanting softly around her, a few asking questions about her—Charles and the big black man answering them in low whispers. Yes, she was the girl who had been found running through the street naked. Yes, Marie's mother had sent for her, she was her granddaughter. Yes, she was to leave, go with Max to New York a few minutes from now. Yes, she would be all right. Yes, her mother had come by and had had it out with Marie's mother. The Jive Five and Dip had come by looking for her, but had been ousted from the house. Yes, this was Annette, the girl who was born with a caul over her face. Her father, yes, had been the Governor.

She slowly came back. A girl with a warm smile on her face, hair done up in braids, gave her a cup of sassafras tea. She sipped it slowly. The black man cradled her head in his strong arms.

She looked up at him. "Is . . . is she dead? Marie?"

"No, little girl. She's in a trance. She placed a curse on someone. Who it is is a secret, and won't be known unless the curse works." He smiled a broad smile, then let her sit up. She leaned against the wall, trying to get herself together. She still felt weak.

She breathed deeply; slowly she began feeling better . . . strong, much stronger. Charles came over and held her hand. He seemed strange, distant, preoccupied. She looked into his pale green eyes. "Has the car gotten here yet?" She was ready to leave. She had had enough.

"It shall be here in a quarter of an hour. Half past the cat's ass." He look quite seriously at her. "How do you feel?"

"Better. Much better. I think I understand it all now . . . or some of it." A faint smile crossed her lips.

"Good." He pressed a red handkerchief in her hand. "Marie told me to give you this. You must keep it with you at all times."

She squeezed the tight-balled handkerchief in her hand, and felt something hard inside. "Thanks. Tell her thanks— Granny too." She got the words out, "Granny too."

"I'll get your things." Charles smiled, disappearing into the back of the house and getting her bookbag and purse where she had dropped them to the floor when running out of the kitchen. Two black candles burned upside down near the coffin; they looked as if they were going out.

A tall brown-skinned man dressed like a naval lieutenant in *Madama Butterfly* stepped into the house. He wore white gloves, shoes and spats, dark green sunglasses.

Charles exchanged a few words with him and pointed to Annette. She stood up, smiled at all who were present, wished them good luck and followed the black naval officer out the door. He was the chauffeur. He escorted her to a black Rolls Royce which was parked under an oak tree. Charles came out to the car.

Annette wrapped her arms around him; down below it felt as though he had been castrated or something—she felt strange and an eerie feeling crept through her body. She released her hold, got into the back seat of the limousine and pulled the curtains closed. She tossed her bookbag and pocketbook on the seat next to her, held tight to the red handkerchief and thought again about Marie in the coffin, the four black candles and her trip to the madhouse. Wow!

The car sped through the dark city, siren blasting, radio blaring blues and rock, while Miles wailed in the background. The driver remained silent, strictly business during the entire trip. Annette was asleep, having bad dreams when the car pulled up beside the curb at the airport.

JUMBO JET INVERTED DIVERSIONS or How Two Unknowns Beat the Bones

ANNETTE DUFFS: But, Oh, What a Nutty Trip

SEVENTY-TWO HOURS AFTER having dropped the coins in the juke at the Gumbo House, excusing herself from Dip and heading for the john, Annette was further away from home than she'd ever been before. Fine, dandy, together and down, so ran her feelings; she was ready to take on the world, the whole universe, give love a chance and do her own thing.

Bookbag in hand, purse thrown over her shoulder and clutching the red handkerchief tight in her fist, she tipped up the ramp on her way away from home.

Images of Marie lying in the coffin filtered through her mind as she felt something hard inside the handkerchief. But she never gave it a second thought.

She hurried through the cardboard and plastic passengers with frowns on their faces, their children, little monsters, and headed for the gate.

A sign overhead screamed out to be read:

GATE TWELVE . . . *12* . . . STRAIGHT AHEAD

She hurried underneath the sign. A pink face, grey hair, eyes and dull grey teeth in a reversed collar, black shirt and suit waved at her. Max. He was back into his priest's bag.

"I was so worried," he started, grabbing her bookbag and kissing her embarrassingly on the cheek. "I thought you weren't going to make it."

"What's this?" She pulled back away from him, wiping the saliva off her cheek. He smelled like garlic bread blended with King Bee tobacco. "Some kind of super-sad joke?" His rags turned her around.

"Sssssh!" He put his index finger to his lips, blew air through his teeth and glanced around to see who was listening.

Two brats in harnesses slapped palms, got their jollies; one cupped a hand over its mouth, the other to the ear and pointed to Max.

He felt like two cents. "No, this is what I do for a living," he whispered. He was really scared she was going to put him down. Real hard. Call him a no-count, faggoty, pussy-sucking toothless Jesuit with a bad case for black eyes and vampire plans—a scheme-less sissy who didn't know where dick was at.

Annette dug it. The words flowed through her mind, but she kept her thoughts under wraps. Her head was into duffing, getting away from New Orleans, she had had it. All of it!

Max hurriedly led her through the swinging doors into the cool air–filled night. A burning star turned red, then black—vanishing into the darkness as they mounted the portable steps, leading to the plane.

Annette saw a dead bird on the plane's wing—a hawk.

Max was so busy talking he saw nothing but her. "I was lucky. The Governor's plane was just stopping down here to refuel; you know he just returned from a tour of *our* South American colonies and I hitched this ride. That's why I wasn't able to meet you, but sent the car instead."

Annette said nothing. Her eyes were on the woman holding a clipboard in her hand, next to the door of the plane. Virginia Dare. A tall metallic blonde with lips painted orange, skin the color of sandalwood, showing pearl molars. As they entered the ship she checked off their names.

The interior of the plane was designed like a conversation pit in a slick townhouse. The color scheme was white on blue in red. It contained a bar, kitchenette, lounge chairs, phones, a three-inch-TV screen, earphones and a bubble gum machine.

The Governor, his two aides—a Mexican and a Cuban—Reverend Afterfacts and his wife, a big Swedish broad with volleyballs for breasts and big fine thighs, sat around in white lounge chairs, all looking very important. Dignified!

Annette cupped a hand over her mouth. The thought occurred to her—from the Gumbo House shithouse to *this*? She cracked up. So this was how the other half, the sedate types, acted. Too much!

Max introduced her around, saying she was an orphan who had not only lost her parents, but also her home. He was taking her to Heaven (that was his metaphor for West Hell) and put her in his Church.

Annette looked at him kind of curiously but said nothing. Her thoughts were into thinking . . . once in the city, the Big City, she was going to cut him loose.

They settled in two lounge chairs opposite Reverend Afterfacts (a tall lean spade preacher with a Castro beard and mod sunglasses) and his wife. Annette squatted near a window. She had a thing about planes. (But this was her first trip, you say? I know, but she still had a thing about 'em.)

She didn't trust 'em. Max got her bag and threw it atop the luggage rack.

"As I was saying," Max settled in his seat and glanced around at the others, "did you see Marie or her mother before you left?"

"No, just Charles," Annette cut him short. Images of Marie in the coffin with black candles flickering rushed through her mind. Outside a priest, inside a thief, attending Voo Doo ceremonies just so he could get a nut. Annette sized him up.

"You know, they're some marvelous people. Simply marvelous."

"Yeah, I know, they turned me on to a whole woop of shit, especially about the way you *mothers* are playing it."

Max let that one slide. Afterfacts grinned but didn't say anything. His wife frowned.

Green neon lights in the front of the plane blinked on:
NO SMOKING FASTEN SEAT BELTS

The big plane taxied up to the runway sounding like a Cecil B. DeMille epic of the Second World War, got take-off instructions from the tower and, like some technological thingamajig about to give birth, it moaned, groaned, revved its four engines—the wings tremblin', rattlin' and shakin' like they were about to break, straining under its own weight like trying to take a constipated shit—and with enough noise to make you think the whole globe had exploded, it started slowly down the runway, gathered momentum and was in the air, circling the city after at least ten minutes of all that bullshit.

Annette unlocked the safety belt. The pilot's voice filled the belly of the jet, sounding as though he were speaking from the plane's substructure or was down in hell, his voice cracking through the metallic walls.

They were flying on Statecraft One and were due to land in Heaven at 0500 hours in the morning. The captain's name was Buck Rogers, his copilot's name was Miles Standish.

And the stewardesses were Susan B. Anthony and Virginia Dare. Flight engineer aboard was Estavanico. Little Stephen to some. The Dap Daddy.

Annette and Reverend Afterfacts exchanged broad grins at the word that a brother from way back was plotting the course. Can you dig it?

His wife pouted. She didn't know what dick was all about. Just that the whole mess was tricky.

Virginia Dare, blonde with blue eyes, and Susan B. Anthony, red hair and green eyes (could have been a stand-in for Rita Hayworth any time) passed out pillows and blankets, leaning over everyone asking if they cared for anything more.

"Max? Do they have any grease on this heap?" Annette snapped. "I'm so hungry I could eat a nation of pigs."

"Sssssh." Max turned red as this page, lips turned blue; he glanced around at everyone present, then looked again at Annette. "Call me father, honey," he pleaded. "Don't let on we're equals."

Annette's eyes popped. She honestly thought he'd lost his marbles. She pointed to herself. "What? Me? Fool! You? Father? Must be nutty as a fruitcake." Then she loud-talked him. "Back at Marie's when you were giving me all that head, you damn near called me mother, you jive-time cracker. I met you as Max, think of you as Max, and I ain't gon' change now, no matter what you ax."

Max's face went through the whole spectrum of colors; from black to blue, green yellow purple white—and tightened up on red.

Everyone in the plane snickered except for Afterfacts. He clapped his hands, pounded his feet, slapped his knees and haw-haw-hawed. Lawd, he couldn't hold it back. "She got you that time, Max. Put all your business in the street."

Max sat there with his eyes downcast. He was feeling so bad, he couldn't help but blush. Then he went into fits of coughing like he was having spasms or something.

Susan B. was standing directly behind his chair. She'd heard the entire conversation. Nervously, with Scotch on her breath, she asked, patting his back, "Do you need a tranquilizer, Father? What is it?"

He felt like he'd been turned inside out. Asshole in his mouth, mouth in his balls, purple blue and red outside.

Rev Afterfacts busted out laughing a second time.

Annette was sitting there clenching her little fists, madder than ten Nixons caught in a nigger trick. Call him *father*, ain't that a blip? And he sucks hind tit.

Max was still coughing, his hand up to his mouth, bent over at the waist, clutching his stomach, his face beet red. A spider slowly crawled down from the side of the plane and dropped down his back. He jumped up and did a fan dance, trying to get it out of his shirt.

Rev Afterfacts cracked, clapping his hands and pounding his feet; he hadn't seen anything so funny since the Irish brothers got fixed and Dago red was caught with the bitch.

Susan B. helped him as best she could. The booze was messing with her head. She stuck her hand down around his behind and pulled his shirt up from the rear while he attacked it from the front. He did a funny kind of jig, real funky, like he had a lot of soul, and dropped his pants to the floor.

"Max. You dun had it." Afterfacts again.

Annette didn't even laugh. Spiders were her thing. And Max? Crazy motherfucker—really, really out of it. She got up and brushed past the two of them strugglin' in the aisle, bumped into Virginia and asked: "Where's the ladies' room, please?"

"Straight ahead, to your right, in the rear. You can't miss it." She half riffed it, half biffed it and half rocked and bopped it, all together in a Laura Nyro voice, her eyes following Annette's behind and thighs, down to her sandalled feet, trying to get a peek through the bells. Ding! Bong! Bong! She really went for the way Annette moved, reminded her of herself when she first got to Heaven and got tied up with the red men, going from one to the other, till she vanished on the train.

Rev Afterfacts, who was all eyes anyway, was watching Virginia watching. He thought he detected a strange look in her eyes. But wasn't sure. He relaxed, rubbed his ol' lady's big fat, fine thigh underneath the table and looked over at Max. He was still coughing and dancing in the aisles, trying to get his britches back up.

Susan B. finally got him to down two Alka-Seltzers and a glass of water. His face had turned grey.

The Governor called him over to have a seat opposite him. He spoke in a nasal voice. "Here, fella, come over here." He was a tall angular man, WASP written all over him, a pirate from the get-go, with manicured nails and sandy hair.

"There's nothing to worry about, Max. I mean, your screwing around with that young doll. At least you're not like Ted. He can't even take a joke—thinks of it as an insult."

"Oh, you talkin' 'bout the way he had that Polish chick to go down on him and give him all that head." Afterfacts jes' had to git into white folks' bizness. I'm telling you, he couldn't let up for a second. He started laughing, "It got so good to him, next thing he was off the bridge and into the water. Then came back and lied to the press about the whole thing. Denied it. That's what he did."

"Right." The Governor really didn't feel up to going into it, not with Afterfacts anyway. "But he's attempting to keep his image clean, no blemishes. That's how it is in this racket. Once they find out you're just as filthy, nasty and dirty as the next one, you wind up off the polls, or the low man thereon. Totem."

Max was feelin' gloomy; hence, he said nothing.

"Reach over in my bag and pull out that pound I brought back with me from Panama, willya, Pancho?" the Governor directed one of his aides. Then to Max, "This will get your head straight."

The Mexican with a fuzzy black mustache, wearing two bandoliers of ammo crisscrossed across his chest, got up and followed the instructions: "Si, Senor. *Excelente.*" He and Afterfacts winked at each other.

"Ya." Afterfacts just couldn't let it go. "All that little jive-assed stud had to do was to get on TV and say: 'Yeah, motherfuckers, I got the pussy and you can believe it was good. She was the best gold digger around. Fact is, I got films of the shit, in case anyone is interested.' That's all he had to say. I mean everybody can get to *that,* can't they?"

No one said a word. After all, it was the Governor's plane.

"Look, I mean with all the noise being made about faggots wanting the world to know they're faggots, lesbians in the same act, why can't those who fuck, suck and ball admit it to each other? Talking 'bout open societies, ever heard of Alex Bennett? My main man and Girodias was on that show in New York, show run by R. Peter, talkin' 'bout good loving and erotic art; next thing you knowed, the dude was offed. I mean, offed. But now he's back. But dun toned his thing down." Afterfacts laughed, but he was the only one who did.

A red bantam rooster escaped out of the Governor's bag—a gift from Poppa Doc. Pancho chased it around the plane.

It headed straight for the ladies' room.

"Get that bird," the Governor shouted, his eyelids fluttering up and down. "Get him." He didn't know himself what he was so nervous about, 'less it was something that Duvalier had dropped on him about white zombies and Voo Doo dolls.

Pancho hustled back towards the ladies' room, caught the bantam rooster by the neck and brought it back to the lounge. It pecked at the table, its eyes darting, staring him dead in the face.

He tried to shoo it away. Nothing was happening. It stood there all proud and arrogant, like it knew the whole

138

score, and stared. Pancho picked it up again and put it on the floor. It tipped around the lounge looking from one to the other.

"That's quite a bird you got there, Max. Where did you pick her up? The girl I mean . . . where did you find her?"

"She found *me*, Rocky. You might say . . . "

"On the floor at Marie's Secret Ceremony. He was down on the ground with his tongue sticking out. Getting wid it." Afterfacts socked it to the Governor, watching the Cardinal blush, slapping his knees and haw-haw-hawing all over the place.

By this time, Max was fuming. But just turned red, like folks do when they ain't got the *power.*

Even the Governor had to grin. "Well, I guess that's better than robbing the cradle in an orphanage."

"I had to tell you something," Max blurted.

The whole plane cracked up behind that one. Even Pancho, who had gotten the bag of reefer and placed it near the Governor's right hand. *"Ici, Señor."* He spoke French-Spanish.

Virginia and Susan B. served drinks all around. Afterfacts had a glass of port with lemon. His wife—gin, on the rocks. Max stuck to coffee and brandy, and the Mexican and Cuban had their own brown bags. Tequila and rum. The Governor had sarsaparilla. He was on the wagon.

Susan B. poured herself four fingers of Scotch with crushed ice and sat on the arm of the Governor's chair. She started rolling joints, licking the papers and passing them around. Bombers.

The Governor dealt the cards, palming aces and spades, sipped his drink and looked at Max.

The Cardinal felt tired, dejected and drugged with the whole set. He wished the Pope would let him have his own plane so he could really go into his act, instead of having to beg, borrow or steal a ride with these clowns, Rocky and Afterfacts.

"I still say that's a nice young piece of ass you got there. What happened, the nuns cut you off?" Rocky grinned, showing rotten black teeth in the back of his mouth. Root canals. "Fella?"

Max gave him the evil eye. (He was part Jewish, you see.) "At least I'm not getting my jollies from checking out *Screw*, *Evergreen* and *Playboy* magazine, or getting the hot towel treatment, like some people I know."

Afterfacts had to let Max have that one. "Lawd! Lawd! Lawd! Go 'head, Max."

"You don't have to get personal, Bishop. After all, I was only joking with you on a friendly basis. Bitch."

(How low can you go?)

This changed the mood of the entire plane. Someone turned on the sound system, images of Sly and the Family Stone appeared on the miniature TV screens, the sound blasted out the walls.

The Governor cut the cards himself. And while Susan B. passed out the smoke, giving one to each of the aides, two to Max and three to Afterfacts (he let his wife have one), and lighting one for herself, the Governor dealt.

Max inhaled on the reefer, his mind still on the conversation which had just gone down. His stomach muscles tightened and his throat contracted as images of eating pussy flashed through his mind. He thought about Annette.

RIFFS: To Be Blown on Meat Flutes or Piped-In Organs

Chorus: Take Four

The big plane soared higher into the black night, climbing past the tropopause into the stratosphere, the whole Earth catalogued in blackness with networks of lights far down below. The plane hummed along at cruising speed as if made of fluid—gone with the wind.

Estavanico sat at the controls in the flight engineer's cabin. He picked up a moving vision on the radar screen. It seemed to be rising from the Equator, south of New Orleans. He took off his sunglasses, dropped the pipe of hashish out of his mouth and put on his earphones. Space-science music on cosmic frequencies echoed through his skull. He took a fresh plug of American-grown marijuana and chewed on it for a while. The spot drifted like some glob, there and not there, all at the same time. Like some giant shadow. He swiveled in his chair, chewing the smoke, pressed a button and picked up Virginia with her tall self, entering the ladies's room where Annette stood before the mirror. First words to run through his mind were: "Who's the fine sister? WOW." He pressed another button and the picture on the screen changed to a view of the lounge.

He laughed to himself when he dug the rooster pecking corn on the floor, jump back on the table and stare Rocky down.

Max. The Governor. Afterfacts and his fat wife. Susan B. soused. And the two aides. He shook his head and grinned again. Actually he was mad about some shit that had gone down centuries before, when the Spaniards had him working as an Indian scout; he'd escaped, caught up with Virginia Dare who was running from the Indians, then when the technology got right, pulled this gig and brought her along. She and Buck, his main man. Zonked. He chewed.

His sonic-visual radar showed a visionary blip about the size of Africa rising with the speed of light somewhere on the left of the screen. He locked his sights. The image danced, sang, rocked back and forth, then became a huge drum. It vibrated like the Earth around the Sun, the Sun around this Galaxy, the whole Universe one pulsating rhythm inside Space. He flashed a message: EVERYTHING IS EVERY*THING*.

Annette listened to the brash metallic sound of the technological monster, the primordial machine as it slid through the darkness which encompassed that part of planet Earth.

Signs: Cornbread 2002, Kilroy killed 1947, moved to the suburbs. War Babies. Liberation! Black. Loves. And So Forth were smudged with red lipstick around the sides of the john. No dirty pictures. Just dirty thoughts. Words!

She slowly undid the handkerchief, wondering about Marie, the changes at her parents' house, the Jive Five—it all seemed like it had happened in some unknown world—and then Max. "What a dip," slipped from her lips. Wondering what they, those she had left behind, would think of her now. She was glad she was gone. In more ways than one.

Inside the red handkerchief was a black cat bone and some goofer dust, taken from a recently made grave. A note was attached on catgut. It read:

BeWare of Snakes no matter what Color.
Signed,
M.L.

Annette was more than a little puzzled. She quickly retied the handkerchief, leaving everything as it was, and was about to drop it down in her purse when she heard a noise at the door.

She quickly wiped her behind; the shit was black. (I don't know what the broad had been eating.) Stood before the mirror pulling up her drawers when in walked Virginia. She strolled in swaying her hips to the movement of the craft, her eyes slits, like she was high behind some good smoke. She eyed Annette's fine round young thighs.

Annette was wise to her eyes. She pulled up the bell-bottoms and tipped as the plane bounced, rocked and shook, moved towards the bowl and began combing her wig.

Virginia gave her a sidelong glance, dropped her drawers, lifted her skirt and sat down on the john. A quick glance told Annette that the bitch had black hair on her pussy and blonde hair on her head. "I've been holding this in since we left the airport. Feel like I'm about to burst." She splattered what sounded like a gallon of water into the commode.

Annette was always shy around people she didn't know. And . . . er . . . white folks, well, to her, let's face it, they smelled. (Of what? She never explained to me.) She gave Virginia a thin-lipped smile and concentrated on the tune going through her mind:

Runnin' thru the city goin' nowhere fast
You're on your own at last

"Man, you sure did tell that Max off, honey." Virginia finished peeing, didn't even wipe herself and pulled up her pink panties. She rubbed her tanned thighs—so unblemished, they looked like mannequin legs sitting in a Surrealist Pop-Art Trash Can. "Served him right, he ain't had no bizness telling that lie on you, honey. Served him right."

Annette glanced at her. Blonde hair on her head? Black hair around a pink-lipped pussy? Annette was having her troubles putting it all together. Virginia looked up and caught her looking at her thighs, then shot a message through her eyes. It hit Annette in the pit of her stomach, dropped to her womb and made her ass feel good. She quickly turned her head and continued to comb her blonde wig. "Damn, I'm hungry. Is there any food on this thing?"

She talked to herself in the mirror.

Virginia acted as though she hadn't heard. She continued with her own line of questioning, dropping her skirt down over her twat. "You from Hoo Doo, right?"

A pain penetrated right above Annette's heart, right between her two lovely breasts. "Huh?"

Annette checked out Virginia's pinkish-brown, red face; the blue eyes and false eyelashes, and the arched eyebrows which had been plucked into crescent moons; the straight nose which might have been hooked in the first generation, and the thin, thin, red, painted-orange lips. Virginia let her tongue roll slowly across her lips as she eyed Annette's hips.

"I was asking if you come from down there? You know, Gumbo?" Virginia moved closer to Annette, Annette could smell the best and worst of American beauty perfumes, colognes and bath oils emanating from her body.

Annette had to get the associations straight in her head before she answered. "Gurt Town. The projects."

The plane humped about ten thousand feet altitude, like flying over a big-titty woman. Annette held onto the wash basin. "Why?"

"Then that means you must know something about the Dark. Er . . . I mean mysteries—Voo Doo, the Occult. But that's what that word means, isn't it? Occult? Dark?"

"Beats me, Bones." Annette couldn't help but laugh, as the image of Marie in the coffin slipped back into her mind, candles burning upside down, black snakes, the eternal, Sun, Moon and children of the night. Infidels. All this ran through her mind along with spirits, natural and supernatural, two heads ha'nts and curses. "Just that they kin put the bad-mouth on you, that's all."

Virginia was originally from the South. But in those days there wasn't such a thing. When she was a little baby, her father had abandoned her little ass and sailed back to England, left her to be attended by the Indians, then the Blacks took her and made her sell pussy; afterwards she went back to her own people and got a permanent position on the Governor's line. This way she didn't have to wash drawers, be humiliated and stuff, just push products instead. Autos, washers, vaginal sprays, cigarettes and Dope.

But she was a firm believer in the dark forces of the Universe, the Indians and Negroes had taught her all that, but when it came to Hoo Doo and root American lore, she was just as dumb as the rest of 'em, believing that everything good came from Europe, and everything that was homegrown was rotten to the core. She'd accept seaweed from China, pearls from Africa and everything from Latin America before she'd buy dis folklore.

144

So when she heard Annette put those two words together, use that syntax, *bad-mouth,* her body started aching, her loins trembled, her box got hot and her tongue was heavy, dripping saliva.

She grabbed Annette from the rear, cupped her breasts and kissed her on the neck.

"Hey, wait a minute, bitch." Annette turned and pushed her off to the side. "I don't play that shit."

Virginia hit the floor and her skirt came up. Red splotches showed on the crotch of her panties. Black hairs sticking out the sides.

Virginia got herself together off the floor and eased up a second time, talking in a low sensuous voice, almost blurring her words. "I think that you are the most beautiful colored girl . . . black . . . I mean *dinge* that I've ever seen. And really . . . "

At this point she placed her arms around Annette's waist; Annette struggled to get free. But Virginia had her in a clinch, breathing hard: "All I want is to suck and tongue-kiss your bad mouth. Is that how you say it? The one between your thighs? Nothing would turn me on more than that, huh?"

Strange creatures. STRANGE. The bitch wanted to play with her poodle but had to call it something else.

Mixed emotions swelled in her chest while Virginia, as best she could, felt her breasts. She smelled like she had been dumped in a vat of perfume with stagnating shit at the bottom. Bull's shit. Suddenly the thought occurred to her, since this was a one-way trip, no coming back this way, not really, suddenly she asked herself, *why not?* And turned, shoving piles of tongue down Virginia's hot mouth.

Virginia held her tightly, rubbing her stomach against Annette's, feeling her breasts with hers, hips crushing against one another. Annette closed her eyes and was still able to see Marie in the coffin. She opened them, looked at the black roots of Virginia's blonde hair, the freckles on her

145

neck, and felt Virginia's wet tongue on her cheeks and in her ears—sending chills down her spine, her core touching her, boxes boxing and rubbing against one another.

Still they clung to one another, Virginia running the palms of her hands over Annette's well-curved hips and fat ass, feeling up her thighs; they swayed in the middle of the floor, listening to their own breathing and the plane's drone.

Annette dropped her hands around Virginia's hips, clutched the flesh of her behind, reached down, pulled up her skirt and felt the soft flesh between her thighs. Virginia opened her eyes, closed them real fast, saw images of nightingales dancing on stairs, then felt Annette's fingers inside the lips of her cunt, working slowly, faster, then slowly, and Annette was staring her in the eyes. They were in utter communication, two bodies moving as one; Virginia continued to rub her legs, thighs and wiggle her hips. The hot gushy liquids flowed slowly down her thighs. She grabbed Annette tightly around the waist, ran her hand up and down her spine, rubbed her shoulders and pulled her even closer to her. Being the taller of the two, Virginia leaned her head down and kissed Annette on the cheeks, the eyelids, all over her face. She whimpered softly in the shorter girl's ear: "Oh, baby, baby, darling, you're so beautiful. I could just love you each and every day. Up here in the airways, down there on the ground, you're the best finger-fucker around."

Quickly Virginia was down on her knees unzipping Annette's bell-bottoms, pulling down her drawers and kissing the pubic hairs of her cunt and the lower half of her stomach, pushing her backwards towards the commode. Annette sat down, and Virginia stuck her head between Annette's thighs.

Annette lifted her thighs slowly and leaned back on the toilet, looking up at the white indirect lighting and listening to the plane, thinking about Marie in the john, Willie at the Gumbo House, watching the golden-headed bitch goddess suck between her legs.

She brushed her hair with the tips of her fingers, held her tightly around the head and wrapped her tanned brown thighs close around Virginia's head.

It was a nutty sight to witness, Annette sitting back on the john like that and Virginia down on her knees, head down, licking the top, sides, bottom of Annette's cunt, feeling her fat round thighs, and trying to get a finger up Annette's ass. It didn't work. She got so carried away, she bent down even further and stuck her tongue up there instead.

Annette let out a sigh that the ground crew could have heard.

(MEANWHILE)

Max and the Governor were deep into their game: five-card stud. The Governor was ahead. Ace-deuce-trey spread.

Susan B. was into her own thing: sipping Scotch, downing them quick and blowing boo like nobody's biz.

Afterfacts sat in the corner reading the Scriptures: trying to get Jezebel's tricks straight with Salome's head. His wife, who was the quiet type, sat playing footsie with Pancho under the table.

While the Cuban aide copped nods: Dreams of future glories, *El Topo*'s gories, raced through his head—a thousand revolutionaries, all white in red.

Estavanico strolled past the card players, the Governor and Max and said, "All systems Go," half winked at Susan B., ignored the others and, like a quarterback returning to the huddle, eased back to the ladies' room.

Either it was the hashish, the American-grown marijuana, or the stogie which he had just dispensed with; whatever it was, it made him think twice. He could have swore that the white-haired mongrel was down between Annette's big thighs instead of Virginia Dare. He felt the black cat bone in his pocket, rubbed his John de Conqueror root around his neck, and clutched a hound dog's tooth in his left palm.

Annette looked up at him and smiled. Her eyes motioned. From just looking in her eyes, he could tell she was fly. Virginia kept reminding him of the bitch of Bucharest for some strange reason, maybe it was because she was down there on her knees, her tongue up Annette's asshole, her two forefingers squishing around in Annette's cunt, her head resting on the fine brown thighs.

Estavanico felt his nuts get tighter; his blood was at the boiling point, his insteps ached, he was so carried away his head began to spin. He walked over to the commode and opened his fly. His joint popped up, bounced, stiffened, aimed at Annette's rosy sexy lips.

Like a pro from the backwoods, Eve in cahoots with the snake, Annette took in five of his ten inches and juiced it around. She moved her head back and forth, kept her eyes closed for a moment dreaming of dill pickles with gristles and cucumbers made of flesh, feeling the head of his member on her tonsils, the foreskin on her tongue and the roof of her mouth, and bit down softly as a hot liquid slowly oozed out.

Estavanico looked down at her little girl's face, a smile on his lips, checked out Virginia who had caused Annette to get one discharge, and rubbed both their heads. He dropped his pants to the ground, leaned in closer to Annette, she still continued to work his johnson and saliva his joint. Virginia dug the action and knelt down behind him. She started licking his asshole, squeezing his balls and fingering her pussy all at the same time.

Estavanico felt like Damballah in the body of the Pope being worked over by nuns who were love machines.

He continued to rub both the broads' heads, pulled Annette's wig off, exposing her naps, and pulling Virginia's stringy hair. *She* looked like a witch. But he was feeling good inside; all down around his knees, he could feel his blood rushing to his temples, drop down around his shoulders and swell in his stomach. A fart escaped from his asshole. Virginia inhaled deeply and swallowed hard, her tongue still up his ass, her hands on his balls. Looking down at Annette's rosy lips, his joint jerked, got hard as a railroad torch, and he came in her mouth.

Annette felt the hot fluids sputtering down her throat, the foreskin on his member become more sensitive as it wiggled like a ramjet—really to her delight. Even Virginia could feel the pressure being released because his asshole tightened, the cheeks of his ass grew taut as the pressure behind the hot blast—which exploded in Annette's little girl's mouth—caused him to drop a one-inch turd, which Virginia swallowed like it was a Hershey.

Max had already lost five games to the Governor and had tired of hearing him telling fuck stories, about this time and that time and how he had turned queer. His thoughts were in the john, as visions of ninety thousand thirteen-year-old pussies floated outside in the sky. The reefer had done its job.

Reverend Afterfacts had drunk so much port and smoked so many reefers he'd fallen asleep with his hands inside his wife's drawers, dreaming of fair-haired, big-titty women and himself with a dick so long and nuts so big that they had to be transported by a dozen freight cars or four Jumbo Jets. Bitches coming to him from all over the world just to have a connaissance and kiss the head of his johnson. Faggots and sissies, lesbians and dykes, sending him poison-pen letters because people now wanted to get straight—forget about makes.

His wife looked over at him; he sat smiling in his sleep. Slowly she removed his hand from her crotch, it smelt of jism and dried-up come. She excused herself from the table and went to see what was happening in the rear of the plane.

Suddenly Afterfacts' dream changed drastically. He was back in Kenya. His Swedish wife lay on the bed, taking on natives one after another. He moaned in his sleep and laid his head down on the table.

The bantam rooster came over and pecked in his ear.

Without really realizing it, he got out his blade and cut the rooster's throat.

Wings fluttered, chicken legs spread, the rooster ran all over the lounge, blood gushing from its neck—crazy, wild, frenzied: a chicken without a head.

Susan B. wasn't really superstitious, but this little act gave her the shits. Her period came on the spot; she rushed to the ladies' room, trying to cover it up.

The Governor had dropped the cards. His dick had gotten hard. He ran around the table, dodged the headless rooster, tackled Susan near the ladies' room and stuck his head between her thighs.

She wasn't wearing any drawers, had gotten that bad habit since living on New York's Lower East Side (where brothers and P.R.s were grabbing broads in the Park), so he had the upper hand.

Her snatch tasted of blood, urine and salt and water. His tongue worked around her thighs, licked her stomach and tickled the edge of her asshole, before he smacked her snatch and caressed her thighs.

The Mexican and the Cuban dug the action, slapped palms and signaled each other. They took off for the cockpit.

Susan B., so drunk, and now fucked around, laid there and moaned.

Afterfacts woke up with a fright, then dug the sight: Susan B. on the floor, the Governor's head between her big fat thighs, her legs around his back and she whimpering. The sight of the rooster almost gave him a fit; its head on the table, eyes condemning him, the rest of the body over near the cockpit door. He dropped his pants, looked around for his wife, charged past Susan B. and her cunt-chaser, running for his life.

Max was too excited to do anything for a minute. He sat, frozen to his seat, smoking a reefer so fast, looked like he was doing a cancer ad. His mind returned to Annette getting up, Estavanico passing through the aisles, Virginia disappearing, then to the preacher's wife's last appearance. Put it all together, something definitely smelled *fishy*.

Action and reaction all around him, but still he hadn't budged. The reefer had him floating. His mind was into digging a trillion young cunts, not a single one a nun—in spite of what the Governor had tried to signify.

Finally he went over to the bubble gum machine, dropped in a couple of slugs, got two jawbreakers and sat chewing the cud.

Back to the john: Virginia lay stretched out on her back, romping and stomping, her shapely tan thighs around Estavanico's behind, his hands caressing her flat ass, squeezing, pushing and pulling like a gorilla gone wild. Annette sat on Virginia's face, moving her bottom slowly back and forth while swapping kisses with Little Stephen, the navigator— Estavanico's monicker.

Virginia felt hot all over: goose pimples broke out on her flesh, chills went up her spine, warm blood surged down around her loins and swelled her head (she had the big head) as she worked her hips slowly up and down. She felt Stevie's ten inches up to the hilt, sloshing around in her hole, working the corners and walls overtime, the head of his member banging against her womb.

She slipped her tongue in and out of Annette's cunt and licked her behind, cleaning out her ass—the chocolate butter—slipped it back inside her cunt and played around her clit, the juices spasmodically discharging all over her mouth. Her arms were wrapped around Annette's big spade ass. It so felt good to Virginia she refused to come up for air.

Annette's eyes were closed. She was still busy swapping spit with Estavanico, feeling the top of his joint rubbing V's clit, while she kissed him in the ears.

The preacher's wife got so excited she almost fell out on the floor. She dropped her skirt and her drawers, took off her blouse and literally crawled on the floor to where the three were working out.

Actually she was strung out on oral sex, being from a cold climate—sweetened in Sweden, if you will—but she didn't know where these people's heads were at, save for what she dug.

She laid her big Nordic body down next to Virginia—her head near V's ass, her ass near V's head. She jackknifed her legs, exposing muscular legs and firm round thighs, then eased them open, and at the same time shoved a hand underneath V's legs. She clutched Stevie's balls and squeezed gently.

He stopped kissing Annette—still working out atop V—long enough to see who it was. He couldn't go for some faggot playing with his balls. He nodded that was all right.

The preacher's wife smiled up at him, showing ruby red lips. She moved her head further under V's thighs while Steve, as best he could, maneuvered V's ass atop the bitch's breasts. V felt thighs next to her shoulders, a leg rubbing against her ears. She continued to work her tongue up in Annette's young but well-greased cunt, and dropped her right hand over to her side. She felt the preacher's wife's big round luscious thighs and got hotter than exploding dynamite. She came in jerks and spasms, while Steve was really working out. He hadn't had a hot pussy like this since Tricia sneaked him up to her quarters. He busted his nuts, feeling the tongue working around the bottom of his member taking care of his johnson while he worked it in and out of V's sloshing cunt.

V was working with her fingers, starting with two, built up to three, inside of the preacher's wife's hole, feeling her big thighs on her arms opening and closing, and still working her tongue inside Annette's box. She felt the fluids.

Virginia's body, without her control, went into tremors. She swished her ass up and down atop the preacher's wife's huge breast, feeling the tongue up her ass and working around her cunt as Steve's dick moved rapidly in, up to the hilt, back out to the lips, over and over and over again constantly, making her discharge in rapid succession. She shoved her thumb up the preachers wife's cunt, her index finger up her asshole. Her whole body felt like it was turning to liquid, melting or something, and she wanted the world to realize and experience her thing too.

The preacher's wife worked, twisted and moved her ass from side to side, shook her hips up and down, down and up, meeting the jabs of V's thumb and finger working in counterpoint in her core and up her ass. Blindly, Virginia's tongue searched and explored every crevice and hidden place inside Annette's cunt, feeling the liquids oozing in her mouth, her nose up Annette's behind, still working out.

Annette wasn't feeling no pain either. You can bet your sweet ass on that, honeychile, sugarpie, whoever you are; she was working with Steve, swapping spit so thick it felt like peach syrup, running her hands up and down the length of his body while he played with her breasts, rubbed her brown thighs and tickled her clit.

By the time the preacher got to the door (the headless rooster following him into the room), they were into a polyrhythmic motion that would cause the most advanced musician to go into retirement.

His wife's head was hidden by Virginia's fine thighs, but he felt like he was bobbing up and down. As her ass moved up, her head moved down; and as Steve Estavanico, who was mounted atop, made his deliveries and came back for strength, Virginia's hips came up to meet his stabs. Annette was moving her ass from side to side, slowly at first, then going round and round.

When the Reverend walked in the door all four of them had spent, but Annette and Steve and his wife were still hot. And Virginia—now that I think of it—felt like a bitch just out of heat. Slowly her legs stretched out on the floor; she maneuvered Annette's ass away from her face and took her thumb and forefinger out of the preacher's wife's crotch. Steve worked her slowly up and down until he was sure her load was spent. She lay sighing, moaning low on the floor.

Rev Afterfacts didn't know whether to get mad, glad, punch someone or laugh the whole thing off. He felt in his pocket, found a snort rag, stuck it to his nose and got a sniff of some coke. He checked out the rag, slowly unbuttoned his grey-striped pants, dropped his frock coat on the floor and crawled on all fours directly to his wife's hole.

He realized that once she had eaten some pussy and sucked a little dick, she was ready to fuck straight up for at least an hour or more. He couldn't understand that part of it, but it was no big thing. He was crazy 'bout her big legs, her big wide hips, the fat firm breasts, in spite of the fact that her face was so ugly. She was worse than just ugly, her face was ruint, and looked like she had been beaten by a ton of bricks. But he loved her just then—some.

Steve got up, his member sticking straight up in the air dripping a little bit, while Annette joined him and rubbed it in her hand. They stood over near the commode. Steve started laughing at the preacher; he looked so funny, crawling across the floor in a white-on-white shirt with frills and a red bowtie. His black ass exposed his johnson, almost touching the floor, stiff as a stick.

Annette got excited. Slowly she was falling in love with Steve. He was such a hoochie-coochie she didn't know what to do. She pulled on his joint and it stiffened and bounced a couple of times; she lifted her legs and tried to climb up on his hips.

Steve helped her. He held her under the knees, put his hands under her buttocks, leaned back against the wall and slipped his dick in her hole. Annette screamed, let out a sigh, moaned a little bit, then worked slowly up and down, feeling it seemingly all the way up in her chest, around her throat and defiantly inside her stomach.

Rev Afterfacts dropped the coke on his ol' lady's pink-lipped, thick pussy, rubbing it slowly around the lips like a mother cleaning off her baby's ass. When he was finished, he bent all the way down and gave it his official salute. This consisted of running his tongue around the lips five times slowly, between the crack of her ass twice and slipping his tongue inside her cunt, working up near the upper part of her cunt four times, the bottom part four times, dead center eight times, making all the changes and slowly taking his tongue out, massaging the cunt with his goatee, slowly, then faster, then kissing it fully on the lips. This accomplished—which took up at least twenty minutes—his wife swooning, sighing softly, crying joyfully to herself, clutching his head and helping him in his ritual, he straddled her body, pulled on his eight inches and dropped two balls of sperm on her stomach. She immediately rubbed it all over the lower half of her body, twisting and shaking her hips, close to a state of delirium as he waited, sticking his big left toe up her cunt and working it around, her thighs closing in around it. He knelt and shoved his joint in her mouth. She sucked it for three minutes, working her head back and forth slowly, then rapidly, while he played with her right breast, leaning forward as best he could and shoving his finger up her ass.

This accomplished, they fucked for the next twenty minutes—the usual way.

She lifted her hole up to the ceiling, come dripping out of it—looking like silver nitrate oozing from a rubber baby doll—her pink lips all red, the flesh all chapped, as he crawled slowly towards it between her big round thighs and slipped it in. It went in so easily Rev Afterfacts knew all body fluids must control the universe, turn the forces around and make changes on the ground. He slipped it slowly in and out, his wife coming forward to meet his thrust, working in counter-motions now, both sighing and hollering, yelling words of good loving in each other's ears. They worked out so good together, not losing their strides, silently and noisily and even and smooth, Virginia got jealous and stomped out of the room. She carried her clothes in her hand.

The headless bantam rooster, not dead yet, followed after her. She almost tripped over Susan B. who was sitting Indian-fashion on the floor, with the Governor's head between her thighs, drinking a glass of Scotch. V wasn't shocked. She knew they constantly got together—anytime either of them were scared, and most of the time they were. Both of 'em were so superstitious, for crying out loud, they got shook if they couldn't find their shadows on an overcast day.

Susan B. rubbed the Governor's head with one hand, sighed a couple of times, grinned and waved at V when she passed, but was quiet mostly. She called the Governor her little ninnie and treated him as such.

The rooster's head still lay on the table, eyes open. A mouse crawled out of a hole in the side of the plane and headed towards the table. Virginia's eyes caught it in her peripheral vision and she thought she was seeing things. She kept going towards the kitchenette; she wanted something to drink. Anything. The mouse, its long tail sticking straight up in the air, jumped out on the table, stood on its hind legs and bared its teeth.

V almost had conniptions. She shrieked. At that instant the plane hit an air pocket and dropped two thousand feet, banked twenty degrees to the left, straightened out, rocked and rose four thousand feet, only to drop down two thousand a second time, straighten out and get back on course. V fell back on her ass, rolled over on her side, grabbed at the table and almost touched the mouse. Her face was an inch from the little creature's paws. Her skin crawled, goose pimples the size of forty-five slugs popped out on her flesh and she almost collapsed from fright.

The mouse did four steps of the new dance in town—called *popcorn*—stepped back and shimmied for a minute, then went over and picked up the bleeding rooster head.

Virginia collapsed and fainted on the floor from sheer exhaustion mixed with fright.

Susan B. had lost her drink during all the commotion. The Governor's head had banged her in the stomach, spilling her drink and knocking her against the wall; she lay spread like a cooked goose on a dining room table—legs jackknifed, head staring at the ceiling and arms outstretched, as the Governor continued to work out between her thighs, beating his own meat.

Reverend Afterfacts and wife, Annette and Steve had rolled with the rocking and the falling of the plane, didn't miss a beat and had busted their nuts.

Annette clung tightly in Estavanico's arms, kissed him on the neck and chin and slobbered on his lips. He worked his joint up and down in her crotch, lowered her to the floor and continued to jab. She rocked up and down, twisted and turned, shouted bloody Marys when her nut came. She started climbing the walls of the ladies' room, her body shaking with convulsions—images of Dip, Willie, the Jive Five. Now this heavy stud, big dick and all, exploded her vagina and gave her womanhood. She lay after a while, panting on the floor, tears of joy running down her face.

Max, who had been left out of the whole episode, was thrown on the floor when the plane lost its balance. His head lay in V's smelly cunt. He grabbed her fine suntanned thigh, stuck his head between her legs and went down after it, his tongue directly aimed. Virginia was exhausted; she had had her share of screwing. She kicked him in the head and on the shoulders and started yelling, "No, Bishop, no! Go on in the ladies' room and get your young friend."

Max was too far gone on the reefer and the liquor. He lay dead on the floor for a few seconds, feeling up her soft thighs anyhow, rubbing her knees and kissing her feet.

Virginia was so tired, she let him have at least that satisfaction.

SUCH A FLIGHT IT WAS!

When Pancho and the *gusano*—who really was a Chicano in disguise—entered the cockpit, Buck was reading a copy of eight-pages about TV's Hugh Downs and Barbara Walters and, instead of pictures about discussions, poverty, pollution and resolutions, they were heavy into orgies. Barbara was down on her knees blowing a male guest, while another was giving it to her up the ass. Hugh was stroking her back and feeling hanky-panky, winking through the cartoon picture at the audience and pulling on his dong. Buck was so excited by what he saw—really, his mind was into nothing since the machine flew itself—his dick in hand, he milked the same.

Miles was looking over the pages while playing with the controls, his head almost all the way down as if to suck Buck's johnson.

The warning light blinked EMERGENCY when Pancho and the Chicano entered, guns drawn, and demanded a change in flight directions.

Miles saw the nozzle of the thirty-eight shoved towards his face, then the mustache and fat face of the Mexican, and almost had a nervous break—he mistook him for Marlon Brando in some strange movie south of the border. It just *had* to be a joke, but he wasn't *that* certain.

Chavez, the Chicano, looked so much like Sirhan Sirhan, Miles could hardly believe his eyes. With a forty-five in one hand and a shiv in the other, someone was gonna have to apologize. And it wasn't gonna be the third world, you kin bet your sweets on that, tootsie.

Miles sounded the buzzer. It went off in Estavanico's quarters. But he wasn't there to get it.

He tried the intercom. Nothing.

The stewardesses: Virginia and Susan B. Where were they?

He didn't know.

Panic-stricken, he pressed the button on the closed-circuit TV. He was shocked out of his wits. Bits and Tits!

Was it real? The reel? Virginia on the floor, the Bishop's head up her cunt. The Governor giving Susan B. some head while in the aisle. And the guests on the plane: the colored girl and the preacher's wife, being screwed something god-awful by two burly black men!

Miles got so mad all he could see for the next five minutes was red. Even the cockpit, the instrument panel, the people in the cockpit, Buck's pink dick—everything was red. Even the black sky outside was a deep, deep maroon. From where Pancho was standing, *he* even looked red, but his lips were white.

Miles' hands began to tremble. His body shook. He was sore down around his asshole and his balls blued. He wanted to get his hands on those two colored fellas in the back fucking those dames. Miles wasn't originally from the South, but had been to the Delta so many times and had heard fantastic tales concerning the size and complications of Smokey's joint; he knew once they (Western man's sex symbol, white proud plastic cellophane!) had had it, it was over for the "white" man. Images of lynching niggers and cutting out their nuts danced inside his head. Which way World? He pondered. Hard!

Suddenly remembering the Mexican and Cuban standing behind him with guns drawn, he quickly unfastened his safety belt and with that constant pain in the ass, he got out of the chair and swung wildly with both fists, knocking them both out his way, and started towards the conversation pit. Mad. With the ass.

Pancho let go a rocket from the thirty-eight; it flew past Miles' head and lodged itself in the doorframe. That stopped him. Miles dropped his hands to his sides, then got up, trying to grab stars.

Buck, who had come out his act when the commotion started, glanced at the closed-circuit TV, got it confused with the eight-pages in his hands, lost his hard-on when he heard the gun report, looked around and saw Miles standing there, red all over.

Chavez hopped into the driver's seat, his gun aimed at Buck Rogers, whose limp joint hung between his thighs, and popped: "You want to blow?"

Buck's eyes bucked and his teeth began to chatter, not because he was afraid of Chicanos but he had a thing about guns. He deuced in a sad, super-sad, high tenor voice: "Please, sir . . . er . . . put that away. I'll suck your dick, kiss your ass, let you fuck me in the ass. Anything."

Chavez checked out Pancho, Pancho checked out Chavez, they slapped palms with their free hands. POW! and cracked.

"Kneel, *yanqui!* Kneel, you artifact, fractured bastard. Come blow my Nixon." Chavez unzipped his fly and a big fat, roly-poly, like-every-girl-who's-ever-been-to-Mexico-knows, reddish-pink carrot popped out.

Sweat popped out on Buck's brow. "You mean your johnson?"

Slap! Pow! Chavez hit him side the head with the back of his hand. "He evicted. Johnson. Evicted. Understand. Nixon I say. Suck."

Ding-dong went the marbles inside Buck's skull. He closed his eyes and the saliva—because of the fear he was enduring and the sight of Chavez's big red dick—thickened in his mouth, his tongue got heavy and his stomach growled. Obediently he got down on his knees, stuck his head

160

between Chavez's legs, grabbed the member in his hand and stroked it a little, then licked all around its head, stuck it in his mouth, felt it buck, jerk and get good to him—a baby bottle's nipple.

Miles Standish was up against the wall, looking into the barrel of Pancho's thirty-eight. "Señor, I would advise you not to try any more funny shit. You might end up pushing daisies sooner than you think."

Smooth as a feather, the big plane flew through the darkness averaging four hundred and eighty knots, with networks of white light far down below, and oceans gleaming gems on their surface as the plane banked, swerved and floated past what seemed to be stars.

Estavanico sensed that the plane had changed directions. But he still had his dick inside Annette. She smiled with delight, hoping there was no end.

Afterfacts and his wife had given the whole thing up. He stepped over to the face bowl to clean himself off.

His wife got up off the floor, grabbed a towel off the rack, wiped between her thighs, then did his face—using the same towel. Afterfacts fell backwards; then suddenly it dawned on him as he grabbed at her body, grinning.

She held him off at arm's length, spreading juicy come all over his face.

He got the word, the reason for her actions. But she didn't have to worry about him trying to get some other broad; *he* was all *hers*. Not other women. Her cunt was big, fat, pink and juicy enough to last him three eternities. He just loved every moment, lying between those big fat thighs.

Afterfacts haw-hawed, washed his face a second time, licking his lips, and said: "Baby, you know I'm *yours*." Put on his grey-striped pants and frock coat.

"I was making sure," his wife answered, twisting into her drawers, the skirt, blouse and coat (gaucho suit), and they pranced—hand in hand—back to the conversation pit.

The Governor was asleep on the floor with his head up Susan B.'s crotch. She lay reading a copy of N.Y. *Screw* about hostesses on American planes who loved to finger-fuck. Balls.

Afterfacts and his wife walked on by . . . The bantam rooster, headless but still alive, stood by the door of the cockpit flapping its wings, trying to shake off sudden death.

Max was still down on the floor with his nose up V's smelly box. He came up for air as Afterfacts and his wife passed, smiled, then went back to work, gnawing and biting like some huge rat. Virginia was totally relaxed—as if he wasn't really there. She looked up at the ceiling and wondered about the Spanish music coming out the speakers. She sensed something had to be *wrong*. Different.

She pressed down on Max's skull, moved her fine luscious thigh to her right, got up, straightening out her mini (she didn't have on any drawers, they were back in the john—lost), and strolled past Afterfacts and his ol' lady, towards the cockpit door.

The Reverend and his wife took seats in the white lounge chairs, their elbows on the table. "Hey, V, as long as you're up, bring us some more port. Two glasses. Haw! Haw! Ha!"

Virginia looked back at him like she was some strange bitch witch, eyes all wide and scary-looking, hair all entangled and stringy, lipstick smeared and clothes on all crooked. A sight! Her eyes caught a glimpse of the mouse doing the *funky chicken* with the rooster's head. She lifted her skirts. Her bare ass showed. Afterfacts cracked.

Immediately, Virginia changed her mind about going into the cockpit (the bantam was still dancing before the doors), and went instead to the bar and got Afterfacts' order.

"Thank you, honey. Haw! Haw!" She placed the tall glasses before them. "Now how about a couple bombers so's I kin relax and contemplate the Scriptures?"

She sat opposite them and silently rolled the joints. But her mind was still in the cockpit. And she remembered that she hadn't seen Pancho and Chavez.

Afterfacts watched her: "Baby, that sure was some other shit yaw'll had going on in the ladies' room." He paused. "Yaw'll do that often? Haw, haw, haw."

Virginia slipped him the joints without saying a word. She sat with her hands on the table, fingers intertwined.

"Wasn't that something, honey?" Afterfacts nudged his wife in the ribs. She smiled but continued to give V the eye.

V's paranoia was slowly getting the best, or what was left, of her. She wanted to go into the cockpit, find out what was happening, but her fears about the headless rooster were keeping her out. "Would you do me a favor?"

"What's that?" Afterfacts' eyes got *biggggg*, he rolled them like Sambo and inhaled deeply on the joint. Signifying.

"Move that fucking rooster out of the way. I think something's wrong in the cockpit."

Afterfacts gave V one of his Dracula smiles. The pot had gone to his head. "For a price."

His black face shined in the neon light. It looked sinister to Virginia, as if he were Satan's double. Price? She'd never heard of such a mess. But decided to play it for what it was worth. "What's the price? Listen, something is definitely wrong inside the cabin. Where are those two *wetbacks?*"

"Your head in my lap." Afterfacts grinned. His wife panned, but still eyed Virginia, her long tan thighs, slender hips, flat ass and all.

Virginia gave him a sneer, as if to say, up yours, and watched Estavanico and Annette dance out of the ladies' room and up the aisle. Annette wore her yellow bell-bottom trousers, the black cat bone on a string around her neck; the goofer dust and note from Marie were still in the red handkerchief which she carried in her left hand, her purse in the right.

Little Stephen was stepping as if there were no tomorrow, dancing through the conversation pit on his way back to the navigator's place. They had their arms around one another and fell out laughing when they spied the Governor on the floor, fast asleep, his head still in the pussy—and Susan B., drunk but trying to read an Olympia book.

Virginia smiled up at Estavanico and winked at Annette, hoping that he would do the trick. As the rule goes, if one blood refuses to work for a white woman, get yourself another. Afterfacts had a price. She popped the question as they passed.

But Estavanico was too busy cracking up over the mouse with the rooster's head, doing the *funky butt*. Suddenly a spider tripped hurriedly across the table and stood on its hind legs, its tongue sticking out at Virginia's face.

She shrieked. Afterfacts cracked. So did Annette. The Governor yawned and shifted his position. Drunk in the hole. Max, his collar off, his black shirt all soiled and pants open, tried to get up off the floor when he heard all the commotion. But he was too stoned to move very far. He grabbed his cock and snored some more—still on the floor looking like Christ's father, the old man in the game.

Virginia stood before them. Latin soul music blared from the speakers. "Stevie, I think something's wrong in there." She pointed towards the cockpit.

Estavanico saw the dead rooster, gave Annette a sly grin and answered: "Naw, baby, in there, everything is everything—under control. Dig?"

Virginia stepped aside, watched them as they disappeared down a flight of stairs, still grinning, and thought about what he had said. Da-Da-Da. Da-Da-Da. Everything is everything. What did it *really* mean?

Annette followed Little Stephen into the navigator's control center. He turned on the audio-visual radar, the closed-circuit TV and dug the action in the cockpit: Miles' hands were tied behind his back and a gag was stuck in his mouth. Buck leaned back in his seat, panting, reading the instrument panel, checking the amount of fuel on board.

Estavanico looked over at Annette. They both smiled, *knowingly.*

In the conversation pit, Afterfacts sat reading the story of David and Goliath to Virginia and his wife. V sat rubbing her hands, listening, but thinking about Da-Da-Da, Da-Da-Da, and watching the black candle flickering on the table.

As drunk as she was, Susan B. had thrown a blanket over the Governor, and moved over to sit next to Max. He wanted to complain about Annette. "Tricked," he said. "Bamboozled."

Susan B. read Max's palm. Telling him like it is: Beware of young foxes from Gumbo, they will trip you up every *trip.*

Estavanico called Chavez on the intercom. "You got it now, baby."

"Got it," Chavez echoed. "A three-sixty turn, heading due north, then south, east and landing in the west. O.K.?"

"That's it, my man." Estavanico checked out the dials on the computerized flight plan, the stars, then added. "We'll be there, in Oo-bla-dee, in less than an hour. Fifty-nine-fifty-nine minutes, seconds. Right off!"

"Whee, baby!" Chavez shouted into the mike, grinning at Pancho. "On time. And on schedule. Straight ahead."

Buck banked the big bird twenty degrees, did a three-sixty, called Oo-bla-dee's tower and got landing instructions: Wind. Temp. Cloud cover. And barometric pressure.

Estavanico pulled out some fried chicken, potato salad, Falstaff beer, sloe gin and vanilla ice cream, and he and Annette scarfed all the way to the set.

OO-BLA-DEE
/
OO-BLA-DA

PAPA DOC JOHN'S BULL-DOG'S BONE

A WHITE-HOT SUN BLAZED DOWN over the seven hills, valleys and cottages which dotted the countryside. The big silver plane, its nose red, the body looking black and blue drenched in the sunlight, circled the Land of Oo-bla-dee four times from an altitude of fifty thousand feet—and swooped down over the Hoo Doo Church.

Brothers on the block who were passing the pluck and telling dark tales, dug the action, commented on the wonders of Stevie, knowing he was a big bad navigator, and improvised lines about what he had brought back this time.

Last time out he had brought back the music which the beast had tried to steal, claim it was his, and placed it in the white-on-white-in-white museum-prison along with the statues of Paul Whiteman, Benny Goodman, Artie Shaw, Barbra Streisand and Janis Joplin.

The time before that he had brought back the dance: Vernon and Irene Castle frozen in the cakewalk, Ginger Rogers and Fred Astaire on celluloid and a whole assortment of beasts, John Hawkins for the brothers, and placed them on thieves' row inside the white museum-prison.

No telling what he might bring back this time, maybe hard-rock blues, long stringy hair and black cat bones. Workin' Mojos.

But the brothers passed the pluck, putting the top back on after each sip, and conjectured anyway.

Foxes young and old sitting on front porches and in backyards along with dogs, cats, chickens and ducks, eating boiled shrimp, chitterlings and drinking java, rare wines and top-shelf booze, swapped lies back and forth as the big red-nosed plane disappeared over the northern part of the town. They were partying already, wasn't even waiting for the big blowout.

They eyed each other shyly but knowingly and told tall tales about his love life, since he was known by all the women about as a coxcomb.

Old blonde hags, blue-eyed monsters, stepped out of soul-sisters' kitchens where they'd been cleaning house, taking care of babies, washing clothes, making beds and cooking food, to catch a glimpse of the big black and blue red-nosed bird, and hear the news of Estavanico's arrival. Wringing their hands, some of them scared to death and already turned into witches—natural-born bitches—afraid that his arrival meant sudden death and evil possessions coming their way. But even this was better than being with the old fay-grey males on this day.

Children on roller skates, bicycles and tricycles, wearing tennis shoes, jumped with glee, kicking their heels, shouted, yelled and made up *nursery* rhymes about Estavanico's antics.

Like the time they told Estavanico to be cool, learn patience, lower his voice and stop all this complaining and stay in his place. Estavanico had got the mother's wife, daughters and granmo' too. Fucked them in the ass, the mouth, the ears, eyes, under armpits all up and down the White House lawn. Twelve o'clock at night. A full moon out. He made them get in line, down on all fours, bark like dogs, crow like roosters, neigh like horses and grunt. Pigs. Then he took his fourteen inches and shoved it down their throats.

"The FBI got pictures of the shit," a nine-year-old told a seven-year-old as he passed the juju.

"And J. Edgar Hoover sold them to *Time* magazine," the seven year-old took a long drag, then snapped back, to show he was in the know.

"And all of them, Hoover and Company and the clowns at *Time,* use them to get their *johnsons* up!" interjected a five-year-old who was jumping rope nearby.

There were no cops, politicians or other lowly creatures in the Land of Oo-bla-dee. Hence, no welcoming commit-tees or ticker-tape parades or speeches at city hall. The people ran their own lives.

Twenty years ago, when John Birks Gillespie was still playing with Charles Parker, commonly know as Yardbird or Bird, he took a breather for a spell and founded Oo-bla-dee. All the hip people got out of Media City and joined in the trip to this crazy retreat— where nothing but princesses and together brothers now come to lay back, relax and T.C.B.

The pimps, shysters, tricksters and would-be police chiefs followed but were put dead in a trick bag. They were all tarred, feathered and kicked out of town, or lynched and hanged as weird ghouls, like they do the colored folks in West Hell.

But the only one who could remember the founding legends of Oo-bla-dee was Doc John, who had made his dust and moved into semiretirement by putting the man's busi-ness in the street, and telling the world about his evils.

He was seated in his pad, a wall-to-wall white bear rug on the floor, red, blue, green and yellow pillows all around,

171

broads of all colors lying back in wraps and panties, smoking, sipping and bullshitting, watching idiots on dull quiz shows via satellite, the sound turned down. That's when the news hit the tubes.

"Hey, baby," Estavanico's voice vibrated from the plane into Pop Doc's sound studio.

"Yeah. What's goin' on?" Doc let a broad grin cover his face. Two broads got up and did a slow snake dance in the middle of the floor.

"We got the mothers, brother. Got um!"

"Solid. That's together. Was there any trouble? I mean, did you have to take any of them out?" Doc leaned back in the leather chair, dick hard, and signaled for Veronica.

A tall redhead with green eyes, freckled soft skin, big boobs, a wide behind and long well-shaped legs pranced over. She bent down, unzipped his fly and mouthed his joint.

Doc John let his fingers run through the flaming hair as a big black bulldog growled in the corner.

"Just Miles Standish. The red-faced pecker is a real cracker. Thinks niggers don't know nothing. Pancho straightened his ass out. He's bound and gagged. I suppose we'll have to put his ass in the Zoo along with Maddox, Wallace and Ian Smith. Barney Rosset's *Evergreen*. Burn his ass in effigy, then scare him to death!"

Doc gave a deep guffaw. He leaned down and rubbed Veronica's soft shoulders and neck, feeling her hips on his knees, watching her head moving slowly back and forth and checking out the contours of her behind.

Estavanico patted Annette's thigh, showed her the manors around on Oo-bla-dee, pointing out various pertinent places. She sucked out the marrow of the chicken bones, then started in on the sloe gin and vanilla ice cream.

Veronica was a Southern belle from down in Alabam', got a bad case of black eyes during the civil rights days. Dude screwed her in the barn, in the haystack and in her mother's bed. She was only fourteen then.

The very next day, she cut out of town. She went to New Orleans and got put in two or three tricks with Voo Doo Dancers, Zulu Kings, and became a blues user's tool.

Cats out cattin' got the word on her ass and would drop by every day, different cats at that, and would take her through the changes, drag her through the paces, then leave her sitting there, pussy all sore, ass all aching and breasts saggy with teeth marks and sweat.

In other words: they ate the bitch's food, drank the bitch's liquor, smoked the bitch's dope, flicked the bitch's hole and took all her gold.

The funny thing about it is she enjoyed every minute of it. When Doc John found her she was wandering around Orleans and North Claiborne—not too far from the House of Blue Lights—crazy as a loon: on the lookout for dudes, hot pants up to her crotch, tits hanging out of her blouse, trying to find any BODY who wanted some ofay pussy. You see, she was brought up in the sort of house that taught her that black men were beasts, hence she was convinced they all wanted her.

Doc John took the broad off the street, cleaned her up and rapped with her for a few nights. He taught her how to shake ass when fuckin', work tongue when suckin', and eventually made her into a doll. Then he put her on duty at the best hotel in the city, pulling dignitaries who came to town for conferences, sent her to world fairs all over the globe, and before you could say WHO, she was bringin' in five G's a week. He set her up in her own bar at Washington and Galvez, then brought her to Oo-bla-dee.

"You still there, Doc?" Estavanico's voice boomed into the room.

"Still here," Doc answered, and added, "We'll fix him," with grim determination, glancing at the parrot who was watching Veronica's actions.

She had her head on his thighs, his joint half in her mouth, saliva all over it, and was fingering his balls. Doc was getting hot.

"Fix *who?*" It was Little Stephen again.

"The cracker. Miles Standish," Doc John answered, rubbing Veronica's shoulders, feeling the veins in his legs cord. His stomach muscles tensed. The bulldog growled.

"How many's in the party?"

"Four of *us.* Pancho, and the other brother Chavez, a cute little chick from down home who I know you're going to dig, and myself." He glanced over the green hills, the valleys and the houses dotting the plains, then glanced at Annette. The sloe gin and ice cream were doing a job. She was *kite-hi.* "Then there's the Governor, Reverend Afterfacts, two strange broads, bulldaggers or something, Virginia Dare and Susan B. Anthony and Reverend Afterfacts' old lady. Nine all told."

Veronica was busy nibbling around the head of his strong big cock, holding it in her right hand. Dock's dickhead was aching; it was getting ready to blast. He motioned for her to take it back into her mouth. Her eyes smiled, the lids went halfway down as she followed his instructions. Gobble. Gobble.

But Doc was still on the case: "Do they know?"

"No one knows but us four. Plus the pilots, of course; they know that something smells *fishy.* Same with Virginia." Then he rapidly gave Papa Doc John a synopsis of what had gone down inside the plane, bringing the case of Max Gordon up, and how Annette was there in the first place, and ending by saying, "And that's how Pancho and Chavez were able to take over the plane. Everyone was fucked."

Doc felt it coming. He reached down and grabbed Veronica under the armpits. She was a big strapping bitch. He slipped his back further down in the seat, sitting on his spine. The bulldog barked, the others watched, smiling. He pulled her up and down and she controlled his johnson till his seeds exploded. "Aaaah. Aaaah. AAAAAAAAAAH. Mercy Good Gawd."

"What was that?" Estavanico popped. Silence on the other end. He reflected for a minute. Watching the controls.

Doc was still trying to catch his breath as Veronica was still sucking on his member, lapping up all that was left. She had a mouthful now. She got it down in one gulp.

Sapphire came over with a bottle of cognac, her big breasts exposed, smiling.

Veronica took a plug. Coughed. Took another. Smiled.

Sapphire picked up a towel and passed it over to Doc John.

But the old man really didn't need it. Veronica had licked him clean, not leaving a single drop on his shirt, fly, pants—nothing. Veronica stood up, smiled in Doc John's face, shook her behind and wiggled her hips on the way to the john.

Doc smiled and zipped up his fly. "Jes' one of my bad habits."

Estavanico caught it. "Yeah. I forgot about you and telephones. Gotta keep yourself busy. Entertained. Huhn? Hahaha! Look, we'll be landing in less than five minutes. Can you get the cars out here?"

Doc stretched, stood up with the phone in his hand, walked over to the bulldog and patted its head. It stuck out its tongue, licked its lips and rolled its eyes.

"Yeah. I'll send Coolout Williams and Steps in one Caddy, and Shitface Turds and Asshole Jerk in the other. Need anything else?" Doc watched the dark brown Siamese cat with emerald eyes arch its back, yawn, walk over near the parrot and sit on its haunches. It stared at the bird. The parrot flapped its wings and yelled: "Git away. Git away from here. You evil sum-bitch. Shoo!"

Doc cracked.

The parrot flew around the room in circles, cussing up a storm, and landed near the Crow's Nest. A sign hung down from the nest which read: *HONEY-HUSH.*

The big black crow raised its eyes, took the cigar out of its mouth, closed them again, then snapped: "Don't you start no shit, sister. Not today. I ain't in no kind of mood."

The parrot got in the wind, swooped down low over the bulldog, passed the cat, then landed on Doc John's head. "Tell that pussy not to be fuckin' with me, Doc."

Doc John busted his sides. He gave it a piece of popcorn, then pointed a finger at the cat. The cat meowed and stretched its paws.

Black Hawk's name exploded in Doc John's brain. He couldn't figure it out. He hadn't thought about that bad-ass dude in over forty years. Black Hawk.

"Jes' the colt. I wanna take this beautiful sister for a ride after we've landed."

"Right." Doc hung up the phone. He went over to where Sapphire was stretched out on the carpet cleaning her nails, rapping with Yoko—a down Japanese chick with long brown legs, silky, wavy blue-black hair, big eyes and a heart-shaped face.

The parrot swan-dived into Yoko's lap and complained to her about the cat. In Japanese, of course.

Bella Duh Zug, a big-boned Jewish chick, looking like she just stepped out of *The Brothers Karamazov* after having given a command performance as Grushenka, the WHORE, strolled into the room. She had dark brown curly hair, a rather pleasing but indifferent look on her face, a nice ass and size-forty breasts. She sat next to Yoko, smiled over at Sapphire and looked up at Doc.

He gave the orders in a cool, relaxed voice. "Get Coolout, Steps, Turds and Jerk from the stables. Tell Asshole to get Estavanico's young colt ready, put it in the trailer and get out to the airport to meet the Jumbo Jet. He's back with a party of nine. Not counting himself. Take two of the cars."

The three girls started smiling joyfully, showing big eyes, gold teeth and excited faces. They got up *off* their asses, and headed for the stables. The parrot shot out of Yoko's arms,

176

cussing in Spanish, and lit atop Doc John's head. "I wanna stay close. Fuck that cat."

Doc cracked, gave the parrot another popcorn and mumbled through smiles. "Don't worry, little lady, Tom ain't tomming on you."

BULLDOG BONE

Veronica walked back into the room buck naked. Her body smelled of Love Potion Number Nine. Indian roses and magnolias. She held a glass of white wine in her right hand, a rose in her left. She stuck the rose between her teeth, looked up at the parrot on Doc John's head and started splitting her sides.

He looked into her eyes, searched her face for any telltale signs, saw a spider crawl out of her left ear, then pulled her to him. Veronica's body seemed to melt in his arms.

She rubbed her cunt slowly over his joint which was stiff in his pants. He slobbered in her ear and kissed her on the cheeks.

The parrot got disgusted and flew back over to the Crow's Nest. "Beat it, Buster," the crow ordered, cigar still in mouth.

The parrot batted her eyelids, commented, "Ain't no peace, no peace in this world." And jumped back in its cage, locked the door and went into a super-sad blues.

The cat meowed, arched its back then lay back down.

Veronica said nothing, but purred and began breathing hard into Doc John's ear. She ran her hands slowly up and down his back, feeling the pressure of his sex against her. Hard.

She dropped down to her knees on the bearskin rug. She was expecting it.

Slowly he took off the Moroccan belt with designs of cobras and rattles all over it. Yawning ever so slightly, and remembering that this was a gig just like the others he had had when in Harlem— having to beat white folks' behinds for them to get a discharge, plus Marine sergeants who were sent to him by the government. *This,* with Veronica, compared to that mess, he thought to himself, was light.

Sambo, the big black bulldog with red eyes, got down off the pedestal, its tongue touching the floor, and stood next to Doc John.

Sambo growled. Doc John patted his head. Suddenly Black Hawk's name startled his thoughts. Still, he didn't get it, assumed he must be getting old. Something.

"Are you gonna do it to me, Daddy?" Veronica was looking up at him, almost pleading. Sambo licked her face.

"Down, Boy. Down, Bo." The dog moved back and circled around Doc John, then sat next to his master. "Yeah, honey, the way you like it."

He looped the belt around his hand, tightened it over his knuckles and snapped it a couple of times. "Put your head down on the floor. Your head forward. Spread you legs a little more. Come on, I ain't got all day." ssssSSSSSMM-MAAACCCCK. He hit her with the belt across the back. Sambo growled, rolled his eyes, bared his fangs. A two-inch welt rose on Veronica's back.

Veronica sucked air through her teeth. She refused to utter a word. He hit her again. Harder than before— sssssSSSSSSSMMMAAAACCCCK!!! A three-inch-wide blue-black and red welt rose from her backside and thighs like varicose veins. Veronica clutched harder at the bear rug and gritted her teeth.

"Come on, *nigger.* Get it over with. Beat me like you mean it. Like you hate me. Come on. Give it to me."

The crow knocked the ashes off its stogie, said: "Sheeeit, the bitch is nuts." Flicked on the set and watched the boob tube. He shook his head, flew over to the bar and got a Lowenbräu on tap. Sat before the set with legs crossed and checked out a talk show. Yawned.

Veronica was already hotter than the preacher's daughter caught in the closet finger-fucking.

Doc raised the belt higher. Sambo gnashed his teeth. The rhinestones and diamonds on its fangs showed. "What? What did you say?" Doc asked.

Through tears, she yelled, "Go, 'head. *Nigger!* Go 'head."

Two alligators spied the action from the pond. They both shook their heads. Said one to the other, "Nigger's a bitch."

Doc thought for a second. He dropped the belt, walked over to the wall near a giant painting of Marie Laveau, Father Divine, Daddy Grace and Bumper Johnson, their eyes met on his eyes following him around the room, smiling really as he got a six-foot-long, ten-ply cord rope and began twisting it in his right hand. He paused at the bar and poured himself a Scotch and water. He poured a bourbon for her, which she could have afterwards. The crow dropped a couple of ice cubes in the glasses for him and made a sign at his ear, signifying that Veronica was out of her skull. Nuts.

"Yeah, I know. John Randolph had the same trouble with Virginia, that's why he went queer." He sipped the Scotch and water, and looked at her welted frame. Still fine. But strange. Blue-black red marks all over.

The crow spoke in deep tones, a whiskey voice. "Really don't know a damn thing about spooks, do she? Callin' you dem names." He puffed on the stogie and took a sip. "Well, back to the idiot box."

"Talking 'bout her mamma and don't know it. That what it's all about." Drink in one hand, rope in the other, Doc John walked back over to Veronica, sipping the Scotch and looking at her body.

Veronica stayed in the same position, eyes closed, while images of a thousand boots and rods yea long scuttled through her brain.

"Bitch, you keep callin' me names, fuckin' wid me, I'll put so much shit on your ass your hair will fall out, your teeth

179

will turn black and fall down your throat and you'll get the piles so bad you'll slide down your own asshole and drown in your own dung. Talkin' 'bout niggers. Shit!"

WWWWOOOOMMMMMP!! He hit her a lick which caused her asshole to tingle.

This time she shrieked. She rolled over on the bear rug and started jerking and rubbing her body like she'd been stung by a nest of yellow jackets. She screamed. Cried. Yelled. Not words, but animal sounds! Grunts. Her eyes all bloodshot, face in such contortions, she looked like some mad dog with a wicked case of rabies. She threw her legs in the air, rolled on her back, exposing her privates—come juice oozing out her hole.

Doc John dropped the rope, patted Sambo's head (the dog barked), sipped the Scotch and stood looking down at her on the floor. Tears rolled down her cheeks. She whimpered, turned over and over on the rug and grabbed her huge breasts with both hands and started squeezing. Agony and ecstasy were written on her face. Doc John smiled to himself. It was time.

Without waiting for Doc's signal, Sambo, with his tongue hanging out, charged the rug, licked Veronica's cunt, then mounted her like some man: his flat ass and short tail down under. Sambo slipped his red dick straight into her hole.

Doc John laughed, shook his head, then thought to himself: I'm gettin too old for this kind of carryin'-on. That's for them jitterbugs to do whose bitches got strange tastes. Shitface Turds and Asshole Jerks. They can have it. He settled back in his swivel chair and read about bloods cussing out Roi Jones because he had issued some kind of edict, tellin' them what to do. No good!

Veronica opened her eyes, smiled into Sambo's bright red eyes, saw the rhinestones and diamonds on his teeth and rubbed Sambo's head while he licked her face. She reached down between her thighs and grabbed his balls. The dog let out a bark, deep down and strong, then growled. But Sambo continued to work at a fast clip, humping away.

She tried to keep up with Sambo's pace, but her back still ached. She hugged the dog for all he was worth, kissed him on the nose, felt the tip of his tongue enter her mouth, saliva dripping all over, and sensed his long dick working out in her hole.

After about five minutes, Veronica turned on her belly and stuck her ass in the air. Now, she was about to find out what dog-fashion was really all about.

Sambo mounted her behind. He rested his paws on her shoulders, licked the back of her neck and slipped his four inches up the crack of her ass.

"OOOO! OooOOOOH!" Veronica screamed. Sambo humped. She smiled, tears flowing down her cheeks. It felt so *good*. Good Gawd. Slippery, warm, hot dog!

Sambo slipped his dick out her asshole, stuck it in her cunt; it got stuck. The pussy was so hot. So was his joint. Veronica stretched her legs. Sambo pulled it out. Breathing hard, his tongue bouncing off her back, Sambo impatiently got it back in, grinning from ear to ear like a mad Emmett Kelly. Clowning on down.

Doc John reached over, grabbed his 16-mm camera and got a few shots of the action. He was thinking about sending them to Veronica's old man. He was a Senator down in Washington, maybe give them to television news teams, for a price. Would cause more racket than the selling of the Pentagon. He played all angles, never missed a trick, nothing got away.

The parrot unlocked the gate to its cage, flew around the room a couple of times, humming a tune called "DOG BONE," then perched itself atop Veronica's head, parroting: "Fuck Bitch! Fuck Bitch! Fuck Bitch!" then landed in the same place. "Fuck Bitch!"

The crow took the stogie out its mouth, leaned back in the chair, shook his head and, with a cynical expression of dejection on his face, mumbled to himself. "I always knew the bitch had gone to the dogs—the day Doc brought her to the house. Old scraggly whore." He recrossed his crow's feet, and watched *The Dating Game* on TV.

Tom Cat, spying the parrot on Veronica's head, still yelling, "Fuck Bitch," blowing a stick of hash and sipping goat's milk, eased over near the two of them and began smelling Sambo's ass.

Sambo tried to kick it away. Tom meowed. Veronica swung again at the parrot; it circled her head, then landed again.

Sambo was working so hard on Veronica's hole, his mind deep inside his drives, he couldn't really pause to kick Tom out of the way. Besides, Veronica's cunt seemed to be getting tighter and tighter, reminding Sambo of that old white-assed bitch of a neighbor's dog he had just fucked yestiddy and left for pregnant. Sambo yelped a couple of times and scratched Veronica's back. She spread her legs. His joint got out.

A vampire bat glued itself to the ceiling and listened to the sighs, moans and panting of Veronica and Sambo down below. Nuts, thought the bat, and vanished in the blackness.

Veronica jerked her head up in the air (the parrot lost its balance, fluttered and flew back to its cage), screamed and cried as the bulldog worked overtime. She got a nut. It flowed from her cunt in jerks and spasms; she was rapidly losing control. Her mind in a daze, her head spinning, her body trembling, Sambo worked out harder, yelping and barking, on her behind—paws clawing at her shoulder blades, scratching her back as his tongue licked at her neck and his squat ass moved back and forth.

Tom yawned, arched its back and went and jumped into Doc John's lap. Doc John laughed to himself, set the movie camera down and rubbed Tom's fur.

Veronica sprawled out on the floor, her big red, freckled thighs spread out on the carpet, her hair all disheveled; she cupped her pussy in her right hand, shoved three fingers up her slit, pulled Sambo towards her face, his red dick dripping (hot and bothered, really going insane with the shit). She blew Sambo's Bulldog Bone.

And what a blow job it was! It really was!

Sambo barked, whined and tried to pull away. But he was getting excessively excited. He worked on her mouth the way he had her asshole and cunt, slipping his red dick between her juicy red lips—come juice all over, blended with saliva. Sambo got a charge. Veronica gulped and swallowed. Her body went into convulsions.

Sambo got up, slipped his dick back inside the skin and tipped to his kennel out in the backyard. Veronica lay panting on the floor, squeezing her breasts and cunt, her eyes rolling.

Sapphire, Yoko and Bella Duh Zug came back into the room. They were shocked, but not surprised when they saw Veronica cringing on the floor. The parrot gave a full report, perched in its cage. "Doc hit. Fuck bitch. Bitch fuck. Dog bit."

Veronica pulled at her stomach, like trying to rip her insides out. She tried to scream but nothing came out.

Sapphire looked at Yoko. Yoko at Bella. Bella at Veronica. No one said a word.

The Black Crow puffed on the cigar, gave them a passing glance, then got caught in the afternoon movie—something about buzzards and crows, jive studs and birds.

The cat purred and walked inside the circle of the three broads. And meowed. Yoko picked it up.

The parrot fluttered in its cage, cussing its fool head off about the essence of being, saying people are crazy, nuts, off their rockers, gone insane.

Veronica's face turned blue, her jaws ballooned and out of her mouth jumped ten black snails, five green lizards, teeny-weeny snakes; behind that, a brown frog jumped out. Veronica lay unconscious on the floor.

Sapphire and Bella got a gallon of vinegar and ammonia and washed her body down. The three of them picked her up and propped her up against some pillars in the corner.

Doc John yawned, drained what was left in his Scotch glass, chewed the rocks, gave Veronica a swift kick in the butt (she didn't even budge) and walked out the room. His mind was into getting Mama Dupre to make some rat soup for the unexpected guests–the crackers.

Sapphire didn't say anything; intuitively she knew Veronica had been fixed. Bella Duh Zug called it a hex. But Yoko knew it was a curse. They sat around on the bear rug eating grapes and smoking joints, discussing the merits of *being* and talking 'bout what they were going to wear to the Big Blowout.

SO IT GOES: Situation Normal, All Fucked Up

COOLOUT WILLIAMS SAT BEHIND the driver's seat of the Cadillac limousine. He had a red patch over his right eye. A mad dog's tooth was on a string around his neck and he carried a John de Conqueror root in his left pant pocket. A thirty-eight special was strapped in a shoulder holster over his right breast. Goofer dust was in the right heel of his green alligator shoe. The brother was ready. He wore a lavender three-button suit, a pink shirt and a robin's egg–blue mod tie. Steps sat next to him armed to the teeth: a double-barrel shotgun and poison arrows, tossing a conjure ball up in the air.

They didn't talk. Just watched the runway.

Shitface Turds and Asshole Jerk stood outside the other Cadillac limousine batting the breeze about broads, who had fucked who, and telling lies about the night before.

"Yeah, the mother was so wasted, Shitface, he fell out on the table, went to sleep in the john and had to be carried home. The nigger was."

"Who? Jerry Roth?" Shitface grinned, then added his two cents. "Man, you shoulda seen *me* last night. I pulled this bitch, you know, one of Hank's bottom whores, took her over to Mama Lorraine's place, fed her some catfish and potato salad, took her home, rubbed some good smack on her cunt, then fell asleep on the booty. Talkin' 'bout somebody who was *mad?* Man, I had the ass so bad, I couldn't say a word. The bitch got up and left. Jes' like that. Put on her clothes and left!"

The big plane taxied down the runway, its engines in reverse, making a whining, piercing sound as it moved towards the parking area, near the two Cadillacs and trailer.

Buck Rogers was at the controls. Pancho sat next to him in Miles Standish's seat eating a fish sandwich and drinking a can of *cerveza.* Chavez leaned over the back of Buck's seat looking back every now and then at Miles Standish who had been tied and gagged and lay exhausted, fast asleep on the floor.

The sign on the airport tower read:

WELCOME TO THE LAND OF OO-BLA-DEE
FOUNDED BY DIZ, WHERE EVERYBODY

KNOWS

It's our *THING* to do what we wanna *DO.*

Annette looked out the side window of the giant air transport, caught a passing glance at the two shiny Cadillacs, Shitface Turds and Asshole Jerk slapping palms, and the horse in the trailer. She had changed to a scarlet miniskirt dress, a tomato-red kerchief around her neck and yellow bikini panties. Sandals on her feet.

"Well, baby, looks like this is *it?*" Estavanico's handsome face smiled, showing gold-filled teeth. An ivory toothpick was stuck in the side of his mouth. He checked out the losers in the conversation pit via closed-circuit TV.

"Home?" Annette smiled, somewhat puzzled, showing little-girl eyes. Her fine smooth thighs looked velvety in the hot yellow summer sun.

Estavanico nodded. He was decked out in black cord gauchos and shirt, shiny black boots with a yellow bandana around his neck. His white ten-gallon Stetson lay next to the boob tube, covering the charts. "Coolout and Asshole are down there with the Caddys and Oo-Shoo-Be-Do-Bee— my horse."

Annette smiled. She was feeling good all over. "That's a blipblopblu name for a horse."

In the conversation pit, Virginia was trying to explain to the Governor what had happened to his aides. "You see they . . . well . . . Rocky, honey, sweetheart, baby, they more or less cocked the pit." But he was too far gone, coming down from his high, imagining that some sort of curse had been put on him in Haiti where he had visited with Poppa Doc—a curse which was to be visited upon the next five unborn generations—because of the President's stupid failure to lay some dust on the Haitians.

Reverend Afterfacts looked out the window, saw the sign, vaguely remembered having heard of the place before, got his stuff together and made ready to depart.

Max wandered around the plane talking to himself, shaking his head to and fro, puzzled about Annette. Had he been duped? And by a fourteen-year-old? "A-Hail A-Mary-Isis' Cherry."

Afterfacts' wife and Susan B. sipped Bloody Marys and exchanged stories about the natives. "From what I hear, all they do is *screw* the women. They don't really harm them."

"But they have stables, don't they? That's the word I got." Susan B.'s eyes got larger as her imagination roamed, thinking about men lined up to get into her saddle—echoes of Mamie Stover's revolt* flashed through her skull. Young bucks. All.

Buck Rogers parked the big plane about twenty-five yards in front of the Cadillacs and the horse trailer. Afterfacts jumped out of his seat and opened the door. The ground seemed to be a thousand feet below.

Shitface, grinning from ear to ear, rolled the moveable steps over near the plane door. He held the forty-five at arm's length and aimed at Afterfacts' chest.

Afterfacts' eyes bulged; he moved back into the plane's interior. "I ain't dun nuttin'. Whacha pointin' that cannon in mah direction for? Ah's innocent. Jes' came along for the ride. That's all." He tried to hide under his wife's skirt. But it was a mini. He shoved his head between her legs and closed his eyes. Fish smells. Swelled. She pushed him to the floor, placed her left foot on the side of his neck. He felt her large calves.

Susan B. and Afterfacts' wife busted their guts. The preacher was such an ass.

The Governor raised his head. Slowly he was coming to life. He figured maybe this was New York after all, and maybe a coup had gone down. Martial law declared. The subway riders had taken over. Stunned, he lay back down.

---

*Mamie Stover was a big-time whore during World War II, living in Hawaii, who was known for her prowess. She took on about forty customers a day. She had a specially built chair, a portable tent which allowed her to be near the G.I.s and she would prop herself up in the chair, and pop 'em off in less than three minutes, douching in between. Forty a day. Ten dollars a head. In other words, it wasn't just the generals and politicians who made money, baby, lots of others with skills between their legs did quite well.

Virginia, who had changed to a white dress, low V-neck at the front with a wide pleated skirt and white silk panties underneath, and high-heeled white pumps, her long blonde hair flowing over her shoulders, stood and started for the cockpit door.

She stopped abruptly when again she saw the mouse with the bantam rooster's head in its mouth, boogalooing near the door. The bantam's body lay near by.

Shitface, followed by Asshole Jerk, mounted the steps in twos and threes and entered the conversation pit. "Women out first," Shitface yelled, his eyes scanning the entire crew. His black ugly face looked mean and evil. Ugly? The man was so ugly, his old lady took him to work with her every morning so she wouldn't have to kiss him good-bye.

"Wait a minute naw, brothers!" Afterfacts got from under his wife's left foot, grabbing her thighs, looking from between her legs. "Wait a minute. I jes' happen to be sky hoppin' wid duh Governor." His wife closed her legs. He held her hips and smelled her behind.

"Shut up, motherfucker! Where's Stevie?" Shitface moved around the conversation pit, not really watching the broads, but his eyes caught sight of the mouse, the headless rooster, and noticed the blood all over the place. He knew there had been a struggle.

Estavanico and Annette stepped into the conversation pit. "Hey, baby. How you been?" They slapped palms, turned and twisted. "You sure didn't waste any time gittin' here."

"Straight up. Doc John sent the broads to tell us that you were back. But we had sensed it from the git-go. What's goin' on?" Shitface spoke as Asshole kept his piece aimed at the crowd.

They slapped palms again and started laughing. Smack! POW! "Ha Ha Ha! Pancho and Chavez are in the cockpit. They got Miles, the crazy cracker, tied up. Buck Rogers brought the bird on home." They all laughed.

Afterfacts' eyes still bucked in his head. He looked around his wife's hips and caught a glimpse of the forty-five, Annette and Estavanico cracking up as if the party had started.

His wife had already started pulling down her drawers and getting out of her dress. Susan B., sipping her third Bloody Mary, was doing the very same thing.

Virginia stared at the brothers, and at Annette. Fuming. Something *had* been wrong in the cockpit. *Shit!*

Susan B. looked at Afterfacts' wife. Afterfacts' wife looked at Virginia. Virginia looked at the brothers, especially Asshole. She noticed the bulge. No one moved.

"Wait a minute, fellas," the Governor started, coming out of his daze and remembering who he was: "This doesn't seem right. After all I'm . . ."

WOP! Asshole Jerk knocked the words back into Rocky's mouth. He thought he was some kind of faggot. He couldn't stand faggots. And that nasal sounding voice—"Wait a minute, fellas"— had really turned him around. The scar on the right side of his face jumped, the muscles in his face twitched. Before you could say Nixon's . . . SOCK! He gave him another backhand jab.

A shudder went through the group. The Governor said in a low murmuring voice, "Oh?" and sank to the floor. Virginia put her hand to her mouth as a thrill shot between her thighs.

"Do as the man says," Asshole Jerk commanded in a sing-song voice. "Wimmens out first."

Max got down on his knees and said twelve Hail Marys and five Lord's Prayers, clasped his hands and looked at Annette with tears streaming down his cheeks, shaking his head, wondering what had gone wrong. "And after all I've dun for you? Wee baby," he sobbed, and grabbed Annette's ankles. The image of Charles and Marie flashed through Annette's schoolgirl brain. She gave him a swift kick in the face.

The women, Susan with a half-filled glass of vodka and tomato juice, followed by Rev Afterfacts' wife, her big ass wiggling, and Virginia Dare, who gave Asshole the eye, cleared the plane.

Afterfacts tried to hide behind the lounge chair. Something was wrong, but he couldn't quite put his finger on it. But was it because he had a thing about the brothers? He didn't know, but he tried to hide anyway. Shitface grabbed him by the arm, stuck the nozzle of the forty-five in his mouth and spoke in gentle terms. "Jes' come on, coon, ain't nobody here but us brothers. Don't be scared. You're one of us, ain'tcha?"

Afterfacts nibbled at the nozzle and shook his head.

Annette and Estavanico followed, passed by the mouse in the bantam rooster's head and descended the steps. The three cracking up.

Coolout Williams stepped lightly out of the Cadillac, stretched his legs, then led the three women to the colt's van. The black, well-groomed colt neighed as he was untied and walked towards the plane.

The three women stood under the hot summer sun, the rays glaring up from the asphalt, and waited, watching Coolout handle the horse.

Steps eyed the three women suspiciously and motioned for them to climb into the van. Hay and horseshit lay on the floor. And brother, did it smell.

"I'm not riding in anything like *that!*" Virginia protested, the slight Southern drawl becoming apparent in her voice.

Steps, always impatient with bitchy women, slapped her side the head, sssSSSMACK! Red blotches shone on the side of her face. She whimpered like a babe.

"Get in there, bitch." He gave her a shove; she stumbled and almost fell on her face, moved forward catching herself and when she looked back, Steps had raised a size-fourteen shoe to put up her ass. She saw that, and without any more hesitation she rushed the van and climbed in.

Meekly, not really knowing what was going on but figuring it was part of the process, Susan B. gulped down what was left of the Bloody Mary, said "Cheers" and climbed into the van after Afterfacts' wife.

Oh . . . but the odor. Horseshit!

Steps then got into the van and told the broads to take off their clothes and "be quick about it!"

Eagerly Susan B. and Afterfacts' wife did just that. Nothing beats exhibitionism. But Virginia had a thing about undressing in public.

Steps pulled out a shiv; it glittered in the sun. He gave her the eye. Signifying. She got the signal. He planned to *cut* the clothes off.

Virginia took off the new white dress and stood in her white silk panties. Her bronzed body looked plastic in the sun. Suntan lotions, creams and rinses had played havoc with her skin; what she needed was a wash-off in lye soap, Steps thought. "The drawers too." He held the knife near her crotch.

"Do I really have to?"

Susan B., who was pretty well stoned about this time, and Afterfacts' wife became impatient with her too. "Take 'em off, bitch, and let the boots see the black hairs around your cunt. Show them you're not prejudiced," Susan B. suggested.

"Yeah, take 'um off, lessen you ashamed or something. What? You got a joint instead of a cunt. Let's see." Steps pulled on the elastic.

Realizing her predicament, Susan B. and Afterfacts' wife gigglin', Virginia thought: "Why not? The kids do it all the time at demonstrations. Why am *I* so *different?*" The joke was over. With everyone still laughing, Virginia got out of her step-ins, the black hairs on the pink lips of her pussy bristling in the sun.

Talking to himself, Steps proceeded to tie their wrists. "This is exactly the way they treated the sisters down in New Orleans on the auction block a few years back. Black, this ain't no news. Blues." He tied the cord to a stake in the middle of the floor. "Dumb, you know. *Niggers.* Ain't got good sense. Nuts." He mumbled to himself, feeling up their breasts, checking their skin for blackheads and skin rash, checked their behinds and rubbed their cunts, then checked their molars to see if they'd had any fillings or if any of the teeth were missing. He made a note of the caps inside Virginia's mouth, the rotten teeth in the back of Susan B.'s head and the pimple on Rev Afterfacts' wife's behind. Really. He was an expert at his job. He was more thorough than the producers who made lewd movies; with them it becomes a *head* thing. Get it?

Annette and Estavanico stood next to his horse. The horse told about life in the stables with Estavanico gone; still talking about what had happened to his ancestors when the Portuguese brought them to these shores. Estavanico agreed, while Annette fed it sugar cubes.

Reverend Afterfacts, Max in his priest outfit and the Governor, who was limping, came down the gangplank led by Shitface. The sun blurred their vision for a minute.

Afterfacts wanted to protest when he saw his wife standing there smiling, looking proud without a stitch of clothing. But he remembered what had happened to the Governor so he kept his trap capped.

The Governor was madder than Daley during the Chicago Massacre. He never thought he'd see the day—white women being treated as slaves. (Of course, he'd forgotten his history, that's all. The importation of white women to fuck and be fucked has always been a big thing in the West. And he knew it. But he was really faking indignation. Dig?) And he didn't say a word for obvious reasons. But took his place in the back of the Caddy, and waited.

Max looked at Annette standing there and cried. That's the God's honest truth. The double-dealing, front-man priest weeped salty tears, saying: "How can you be so cruel?"

Annette gave him the finger. Coolout gave a belly laugh and asked, "Who's the jive-time mother? Berrigan or somebody?" Annette, Estavanico, even the horse, Oo-Shoo-Be-Do-Bee, slapped palms and cracked, "What's goin' on?"

Max whimpered, still saying his prayers, shaking his head, thinking that his days of eating young cunts were numbered. Shitface led him to the car.

Pancho and Chavez were leading Miles Standish down the gangplank, followed by Buck Rogers taking in the glare.

Miles caught a glimpse of Virginia and the other chicks in the horse's trailer and went into a flying rage. Images of cutting brothers' nuts out, pouring gasoline into the sacs and setting them afire swam through his mind. He just couldn't believe it. How could anyone, even colored folks, be so cruel?

Why, the sight of Virginia, her bronze body glittering in the sun, yellow hair falling all over her face and breasts sticking out as if ready to be embraced, her core protruding, the black hairs around her crotch exposed and tiny beads of sweat breaking out all over her skin . . . it was just *too much!*

Arms tied behind his back, gritting his teeth, Miles Standish charged directly towards Coolout.

Coolout, conscious of everything going on around him—the black horse telling tall tales, Virginia crying, the men looking sad in the rear of the Cadillac, their eyes on the action, *Miles* charging towards him—thought first of wasting the mother, shooting him dead in the head, then building a tar fire and burning his ass to cinders. But he let the thoughts fly. Taking the gun slowly out of the holster, he took careful aim and set fire to both of Miles' kneecaps. Pow-Pow! Cracker! Jacks!

Miles sprawled on the ground in the blazing sun and issued what sounded like a death rattle. The pain was so intense, his body immediately assumed a fetus position: pain shooting through his feet, up his legs, his kneecaps numb they hurt so much, his groin and stomach balled up in pain so fierce that his balls ached. His chest heaved and his head felt as though a thousand hydrogen bombs were going off inside his skull. His contorted face was like that of a shaggy-haired dog; he yelped and screamed as his body went into shock. Lights. He passed out.

Coolout blew on the thirty-eight and placed it back in his shoulder holster. He signaled to Shitface and Asshole. They picked up Miles' body and tossed it in the back of the van, cracking up all over.

They loaded the two Cadillacs.

Annette looked up at Estavanico and a smile covered her face. She knew that Little Stevie was on top of it, but had reservations about the others. But after what had gone down with Miles Standish, Coolout and his straight shots, she knew then and there she wasn't dealing with Blue or Dip or no one during that long trip back in New Orleans. Even Sleepy Willie wasn't *that* together. All she could do was to shake her head. Awed.

Estavanico patted her ass, called Oo-Shoo-Be-Do-Bee over and told her to get on, while he held the reins. She mounted the beautiful black colt. Estavanico got on, pulled the bridle and snickered a couple of times.

Oo-Shoo-Be-Do-Bee pranced, tipped and danced down the gold-paved street in the warm yellow sun, the two Cadillacs and the van moving slowly behind them. On their way—*HOME.*

BLOWOUT/ SHOWOUT AND AFTERFACTS' BIT!!

WORD SWEPT OVER OO-BLA-DEE like Black Magic Fire over the land of our ancestors that Estavanico was back, had captured the devil, the three strange witches and was bringing a new girl to town. Sisters and brothers from the four corners of the land rushed to fill the streets and cheer the procession: Annette riding high in the saddle, Estavanico, a smile on his black face, guiding Oo-Shoo-Be-Do-Bee the horse, singing rock rhythms to Motown sounds, the two Cadillacs following, the devil and his disciples huddled in the back seats, and the three strange witches, bitches in disguise, naked but proud, and Miles snoring on the floor cuddled in the hay.

Rumors spread and swept over every nook and cranny in the land, over the graveyards and into the bars about what had gone down inside the plane.

Children danced up and down the street throwing goofer dust in the path of the horse, beating cow skulls, bells, shaking tambourines and bones, blowing mouth organs as the smell of yams, greens, beans, chickens, turkeys, roasting duck, pork and beef filled everyone's nostrils—just the opposite of smells in West Hell's belly: exhaust fumes, dogshit and chemical smoke.

The Governor immediately started vomiting. Steps turned and looked at him. He thought for a moment, but without hesitation told him to swallow it. Rocky turned red, green and blue in the face. Steps took out his forty-five and pointed it at him. Between the eyes. Green at the seams, the Governor reluctantly swallowed. He got his handkerchief out and wiped the scum off his tongue. Said: "Aaaah." His breath stunk the whole place.

His stomach was upset. He had never seen so many smiling, laughing, grinning-from-ear-to-ear black, tan, yellow and brown faces since his trip to Haiti. He'd been to Harlem several times, but each time the people had frowned and tried to spit in his eyes. But these people were all smiles, happy, seeing the joke in the yoke, as if high on some way-out wine—or juju seeds.

Music: the sound of drums beating, guitars twanging, trombones gwan-gawnin' in deep low tones, and saxophones, clarinets and trumpets blaring filled the air of the city, as thousands rushed out of houses and flooded the streets—throwing garlands, yellow and red roses into the air and landing them atop the Cadillacs and the van (getting rid of that smell of horseshit and hay) and irritating Miles' nostrils as he lay unconscious, slobbering all over himself, after his vain attempt to save white womanhood from the hands of *blacks.*

Estavanico led the procession to the yards of the Hoo Doo Church. The crowds followed, singing and dancing all the way. Oo-Shoo-Be-Do-Bee was sent out to pasture. Singing romantic ballads by that famous minstrel man, James A. Blanc, the horse stole the show. But only for a minute.

Hundreds of people—boys, girls, women, young and old men—came and stood in line to kiss Estavanico and Annette on both cheeks and shake hands with Pancho and Chavez.

Chain letters were received and passed around!

It was a happy day in Oo-bla-dee for everyone involved. Estavanico climbed on the dais where Basie's band was playing and interrupted the music to make a short speech. He thanked the people for their welcome, told in brief details about the fucking that had gone down on the plane.

The crowd went wild when he got to the part about Virginia asking Annette about the bad-mouth, flipped and dipped and started snaking all over, slapping palms and feeling behinds when he told them about the Governor falling out, the priest and Susan B., taking it cool, sipping her Scotch.

Estavanico quieted them down. He introduced Pancho and Chavez and had the audience in tears of laughter as he let Pancho describe the takeover.

Too much! A gas! Ball! Wail! Sounds echoed through the audience—their eyes shining, faces bright with happiness and joy.

They cheered, ate barbecue, fried chicken (*Honey—hush!*), chitlins, drank wine, gin, beer and top-shelf Scotch and bourbon. Those who were into it smoked pot or blew coke while others clapped hands, singing and dancing as plates of food stacked a mile high were passed around to all. A real down-home BLOWOUT.

After taking care of the business with Mama Dupre, the deal with the *rat soup,* Doc John showed with his entourage.

Veronica, along with Sambo, who had a thing about greasing on white flesh, paraded before the crowds, along with Yoko, Bella Duh Zug and Sapphire in blue. Oh, yes, and Yvonne. Estavanico, seated at one end, and Annette, at the other, shared Doc John's table with him. He was seated in the middle.

Thousands of kids kept crowding around Annette, giving her follow-me oils, love potions and lodestones.

They ate, drank, exchanged tales and sorrows until way late in the afternoon, embellishing and improvising sounds as they went along. The evening sun, hiding behind grey clouds in the west, sank slowly under reddish-blue, purple-grey skies. The full moon shone.

RITUALISTIC ACTIONS . . . . . TAKE ONE

Virginia Dare, Susan B. Anthony and Reverend Afterfacts' wife were taken to the chamber of maidens where their bodies were washed for at least an hour by big black mammies in a mixture of whiskey, kerosene and black pepper. 'Course Virginia complained. She figured she should be at the party with Estavanico and Annette. She considered herself their *kind* and issued a protest note.

Ma Rainey refused to hear her blues. "Lissen, I'm gitting you ready for the action."

"But what action?" Virginia asked in a soothing voice—the image of the headless rooster clouding her brain.

Ma Rainey applied the mixture between Virginia's black-haired crotch, humming "Go Down, Moses."

Virginia's flesh tingled. Just the touch, the absolute touch of human hands made her want to—really want to! She swooned on the black velvet sheets. *Mercy! Mercy! Mercy!*

Susan B. Anthony and Reverend Afterfacts' wife took the washdown in stride. They had been reading books, watching movies and having conversations on New York's Lower East

Side *and* with Fran and her gang. They knew, intuitively, what the ritual was all about. Remember JEW-MAKE-HER? Souls.

They were then brought back to the barbecue grounds, behind the Hoo Doo Church. And placed upon the stage. Basie's band played on: "Smack Dab in the Middle!!" Young bucks, most of them in their teens, teed on weed, ready for some action, charged the stage and began slobbering all over them. The three women gleamed, screamed and *creamed!*

Virginia took on three. One behind. Another in front. The third with his meat-flute in her trunk.

Susan B. held two joints at arms' distance, a third in her purse.

Afterfacts' wife was cool and collected as she knelt and bowed and let one suck her cunt.

RITUALISTIC ACTIONS . . . . . TAKE TWO

Miles Standish was tied to a yew tree near the stage and was being watched over by a mad hound dog. His wounds had been cleaned out with bottom-shelf whiskey and mud packed into the wounds. He groveled in the dust and cried like a baby. Fear-hate-being, drugged and regusted was written all over his face. Frustration! He too screamed!

RITUALISTIC ACTIONS . . . . . TAKE THREE

Rocky and Max were taken to Doc John's pad, fed Mama Dupre's concoction, rat soup—mixed with carrots, okra, mustard greens and turnips. Then they were given saunas and told to relax.

Three big black dudes, brothers from the South, walked into the room with steaming towels to give them massages. They spoke to one another in the unknown tongue, *shoobedoobin*, boppin' words left and right, rapping to one another about deals that were going down. *OUTSIDE!* Max and the Governor didn't understand a single word. Rocky was trying to explain about the welfare checks, how he planned to up the ante—but the brothers only cracked, split sides and busted guts. The bloods stripped the strangers naked and commenced to give them rubdowns.

The Governor's stubby prick, like that of a character in Diane di Prima's *Memoirs*, stood straight up in the air, stiff as a stick—while big black hands worked over his body.

The masseur grabbed his prick, pulled it for him a couple of times, squeezed his balls and stuck a finger up his rectum. The Governor *got hot*. He shot his load in the air and it landed in a bedpan! Blip! Blop! Then he tried to *kiss* the blood. The brother socked him in the jaw. Rocky collapsed on the floor. Panting.

Max got so excited, he leaped out of the hands of the brother who was working him over, landed on his rump, picked himself up and crawled over to the Governor. He picked up Rocky's limp cock, nursed it with his tongue back into a hard-on and gave him the wildest, frenziedest, freakiest blow job his world had ever seen, while he pounded his own pud.

The bloods stood watching the white folks play, laughing and joking with one another and recalling similar incidents. Max got up on his knees, slapped Rocky on his fanny and moved around to his rear. Rocky opened his eyes, confused, wondering what was going on, saw the puke-green room, the spooks grinning, and felt someone shoving something up his behind. He smelled another's flesh. Rot.

Obediently, without really thinking twice about it—the rat soup having done its job—he got up on his hands and knees while Max mounted him from behind. After a little effort, and recalling the conversation in the plane when the Governor tried to put him down (how low can you go?), Max's prick hit!

The Governor screamed. His face turned red. He reached down and grabbed Max by the balls (they both screamed) moving ass backwards and forwards. A *nut!*

One boot got the tom-tom, the other grabbed a flute. They played seven songs of happiness while Max and the Governor performed.

Max worked around the Guv's fat ass, kissed him on the back of the neck, closed his eyes (inside, images of nuns without cunts blasted his mind!) and drove his dick in and out of that hot asshole, while the Governor cringed, fired, sweat the size of cotton balls dripping off his forehead, enjoying every minute of the bang.

Max got his nut! Let out loud, "AaaaaaAAAAAAH. Ah! Ah . . . Unh . . . unh! . . . Unh . . . hun. Hun-ey, hush!" He tumbled over on his left side, pulling the Governor back down to the floor with him, his joint soft, still up the Governor's bottom. They tongue kissed each other like classic faggots, rubbing their hands over each other's bodies, playing with one another's balls, fingering assholes and ticklin' ears.

Now you *know* the bloods looking on had to crack. And they did. This was the funniest thing since Nix dropped his drawers and mooned in public. Laughing and still talking in loud voices, the boots got the white folks off the floor, saying, "The party's over." They gave them hot and cold showers, slight massages, then called the Zoo to send the glass cage.

The cages arrived in less time than a thought. They loaded the two in the rear, naked as the day they were born, and drove them through the streets.

Hordes of children—throwing peanut shells, popcorn, dead spiders and roaches at the glass cage—followed the procession down the streets, eating cotton candy and playing the dozens about Max and the Governor.

The Governor, his eyes red and bloodshot, his fat flabby stomach drooping over his genitals, his ass all red (a baboon's tail) where max had been fucking him in his behind, tried to hide himself from the crowd. But there was nowhere to hide. Dig?

Max continued to make signs of the cross at the cross-roads, say his prayers backwards and walk in magic circles.

By the time they got to the party grounds, they both were outdone.

Basie's band was into playing some low-down, down, real uptight, outasight blues, a two-beat rhythm made to *Push and Pull* while the dudes waited their turn to take on the three whores. The three strange bitches were propped up on couches in front of the stage. Basie's band blasted from behind.

BUT!!!

Annette laughed and joked and broke up so many times—talking with Doc John, whom she admired, and his friends, and exchanging tales with Estavanico, Pancho and Chavez about her narrow escape and the funny things that had gone down on the plane—her stomach ached, her jaws were sore, and tears filled her eyes. It felt just so *gooood* to be around people who were warm and friendly, not uptight and paranoiac presently, like in New York Bars. Good to be surrounded by love.

She felt herself getting high. The memory of past experiences was somewhat vague in her mind. Like the Gumbo House, Sleepy Willie, Dip, Bertha, and her family seemed like pieces of stories told in monasteries, by monks who had grown cold.

That is, except for the image of Marie; her memory lingered somewhere on the edges of Annette's conscious thoughts. The same with her mother.

The words, the laughter and conversation drifted out into the dark night air, settled on the moon, bounced off

Venus as Mars showed its sign—Aries. Annette's mind floated deep, deep down.

Torches and flares were lit at the periphery of the picnic grounds. Spotlights lit up the stage. The sounds of tambourines, bells, tom-toms, bones and the full force of Basie's band happily blowing the blews away, kept everybody's spirits up—inside a warm glow.

RITUALISTIC ACTIONS . . . . . TAKE FOUR

Afterfacts' bit!

Reverend Afterfacts was so confused when they got to Oo-bla-dee, not really knowing the place existed—thinking he was the only brother *(the one that got away!)*—but believing it to be a mad dream of an author in an outside nightmare, was shocked into insanity and taken to the hospital.

Jock the Rock and Knock the Crock worked him over. He spoke in mumbo jumbo, making clicking noises with his tongue, eyes all in the back of his head—showing only the whites, frothing at the mouth something awful. His thoughts were on his Nordic wife and what to do about her condition.

Knock looked at Rock. Rock left the room. He came back with a white dove, split it open with a butcher knife, placed it atop Reverend Afterfacts' head and let the blood drip down over his face.

Knock walked Rev Afterfacts over to a black face bowl, washed his face with ammonia, dried it with a green face towel and sat him down in a red chair.

Afterfacts felt dazed, exhausted, scared all to hell. He didn't know what was goin' on. But he was too tired, sleepy and drowsy to fight it.

Knock called for a limousine to take him to the lake. Rock picked him up. Mama Dupre's grandson, Lucky, showed up with the Royce. He tooted the horn twice. Chimes-charmed-Bird tunes. Dolphy's flutes.

"That's it," Knock signaled to Rock. They each grabbed an arm, walked Rev to the Rolls, placed him in the rear seat and sat on either side.

Lucky drove.

Afterfacts' head spun.

At the lake, wearing rubber suits, Knock and Rock each grabbed one of his arms and waded in the water until Afterfacts' head was submerged at the "curespot."

Rock held him under for two minutes, submerged him again for a minute, pulled him up and submerged him again for thirty seconds—mumblin' spells in creole, Afro, hip, bop, street, nigger-pimp, musician-mixed-with-*gullah* talk every time he came up.

Meanwhile, Knock got the crock, the towels and what was left of the dove, and flung them further out into the lake.

Lucky stayed in the Royce digging Miles' rendition of Jack Johnson, "Right Off," his mind into his grandfather's thoughts. Black! Magic! Spells!

The pale crescent moon waned, and voices from the dead could be heard floating from the cemetery where souls were being divided. The sounds of singing and dancing mixed with distant laughter came from the picnic grounds.

Afterfacts returned to his senses. He'd forgotten all about the trip on the plane. The tomming he'd performed. And his funny-looking wife who had a thing for chicks anyway.

His mind was with the brothers. It felt good to be black. And *home.*

First words out of his mouth, once he sobered up, were: "Say, baby, yawl got any . . . smoke? I feel like gittin' tree-top high."

Knock looked at Rock. Rock looked at Crock. They cracked up. Sides split. Guts busted.

They put him back in the limousine. Lucky, a bat out of hell, was back at the hospital in no time flat!

Afterfacts was given a mixture of salt and vinegar to drink and put to bed. A book was sent up for him read—*All-Night Visitors.*

But he couldn't concentrate. Something kept bugging him. First he thought it was the mosquitoes. But they were nodding in the corner. Then he assumed it was the roaches and the bedbugs. But they were playing a game—ball. On the walls.

Scratching his skull, wondering just what was the matter, he climbed out of bed and paced the floor. A monkey cockroach cussed out a baboon bedbug. A pop fly broke it up.

Afterfacts looked askance at the black candles burning on the mantelpiece; then he saw his face in the mirror. It was snow-white. His hair had turned red. His eyes blue. He looked down at his hands. They were still black. It was just his mug that had changed.

He charged out of the room, down the long corridor, past nurses, doctors, attendants, stretcher cases and dead souls, and out into the cool night air . . . down, down to the valley where he heard the beating of bones throbbing in his ears.

A strange sensation took possession of his head.

The people! All the people partying back, having their own show-out, set Afterfacts' nerves on edge.

He caught a glimpse of Max and the Governor, naked in their cage, their eyes riveted on the orgy taking place on the stage. At first he didn't recognize them. It seemed that he saw the Governor wink. But he wasn't sure.

And the sight of Miles Standish, asleep under the yew tree, being watched over by wolves and a mad hound dog, gave Afterfacts the jitters. A bowl of *rat soup,* devil's pills and a mojo hand lay untouched at his side.

Creeps. The creeps swept through his body, he thought to himself, And I thought *I* wuz in trouble.

His white smock flaring in the pale moonlight, looking reddish white in the flaring light, Rev Afterfacts ran through the crowds of people up towards the stage, where more people were playing bongos, conga drums, tom-toms, guitars and paper and combs, while others watched the action.

The crowd was more joyful, more spontaneous than even the one up at Woodstock—eons ago: soul-clapping hands, listening to the band, really gitting away, each and everyone into their own thing!

But up on the stage:

Two young bucks had Virginia between them. She went for their game. One was jugging her in the ass, kissing her on the neck; the other had his dick up her hole. Asshole Jerk stood on the side, his pants down around his knees, his ass in the wind. Virginia's left finger was stuck up his crack, whirling around in his asshole. He liked it like that.

Susan B. bent down on the side, blowing Asshole's joint. Her head eased towards his balls, clenching his swipe between the soul-clapping hands of the audience and the movement of Jerk's body as he tugged at her head. Some joker pulling on his mitchell in front of the stage, making vain attempts to fuck some broad through her dress, let fly his approval through jaws of defeat: "Work your thing, baby. Ding! Dong! Ding! Do what you wanna do."

Reverend Afterfacts was having trouble figuring this all out. He got hot and excited watching the broads working out on the stage, the young bucks waiting in line looking at all that fine, fine, luscious without-fear-of-being-lynched white meat on the stage, taking on the brothers. But it left *him* confused.

He looked at his hands. They were tar black. He felt his face. It felt pasty. Dough. His hair. Kinky. Straw. He wondered if his skin was the same color. Black. But he couldn't see himself. He looked around at the crowds, the people standing near the stage, seated at tables.

But no one paid him the slightest bit of attention. They were too busy pulling chicks, chicks pulling cats, folks and animals getting together—this is where it was at. No one had any time to waste looking at some clown with a snow-white face, kinky red straw hair and blue marble eyes.

Inwardly, Afterfacts thought he was losing his mind. Nothing made sense. The whole thing was irrational, superstitious, simply out of touch with scientific reality where logic ruled and people were fools.

But when he caught sight of what was going down on the third couch, he was shocked past far on the other side of Zar, believing the Devil himself had got his mind.

His wife lay propped up on the third couch. A big black cross with a flaming red fire shooting out all about it and a long snake crawling around it was directly behind her. Big Boot, booty-struck, booted it to her from behind, a shit-eating grin on his face. He was slipping his greasy member in and out, like some Faulkner character fucking a calf.

His wife squirmed, funky-butted, grinned and smiled in ecstasy, while clutching the thighs of another brother laying back on the couch. She sucked his balls, fingered his ass, nibbled on his cock, kissed his belly, pulled on his dong, shoved it in her ear and ran it over her eyelids as the band raised the tempo to a fiery pitch. Big Boot booted her harder in the ass and cunt, and she worked more feverishly on the dude on the couch: they all came at once. One big orgasm. Groove! Bang! Pow! Wow!

Afterfacts felt jived around.

Big Boot hit the floor. He got up, held his limp cock in his hand, did a two-beat shuffle, then danced around the stage, waving at the audience. They cheered him on. He took ten bows, five curtain calls, then was swept away.

The other spook jumped up off the couch, grabbed the preacher's wife around the hips before she had time to move, her body still trembling, and went into a sixty-nine that the world ought to be told about.

They worked so good together, real easy and slow, with moans, squishes and squirms . . . that a sudden shock tremored through the crowd, creating a strange sensation of desire surfacing in all who had come to bear witness to the act. Boys turned to girls, old men to young girls, old women to young bucks, as generations reached across ages to get out of time.

Suddenly, Afterfacts senses a throbbing down below. His joint was harder than times on the Lower East Side. He checked out his hands. They had turned *green!* His body shook and trembled; he was rapidly moving past the fifth dimension. He couldn't hold it any longer. None of it!

He jumped up on the stage as the band broke out with "The Tears of a Clown," knocked over microphones, pulled down stuffed lions, tigers, a huge white snake in a box and candles which were burned on the altar, charging past Virginia who lay sprawled out on the couch (taking it in her cunt; some cat who was rocking and swinging, really juicing her down while two members pulled at her nipples, their pipes in their hands, while another gave her a mouthful) brushing Susan B. on the ass. She was bent over backwards, taking dick in her hole, while another two played around her eyes, her ears and nose; she licked heads and tasted come.

Afiterfacts flew over to where white lay under black— his wife and some big strapping brother—clutching one another in a unisex embrace. They were rocking and rolling, mouths going up and down, the spook with his fingers up the cheeks of her ass, his tongue in her snatch, his chin on her clit. His balls lay on her chin, and his tool was slipping slowly in and out of her pouting mouth.

Reverend Afterfacts—with his green hands, white face, red hair and blue eyes, bloodshot around the edges—was so excited he didn't know at first which way to go.

He jumped down atop the pile and his rod popped out. It was poker-hot red! Afterfacts slipped it into the shine's back. Shine jumped up and hollered . . . *screamed* bloody murder! *Yelled* "Good Gawd!" Shouted "Sum' bitch! Sum' bitch!" as if touched by the devil. He took off . . .

He ran off the stage, his ass smoking, down through the crowds of onlookers, pleasure-seekers, girl watchers and men splotchers and submerged his butt in the lake. A wry smile crossed his face. His eyes *rolled!*

Afterfacts tried to sock it to his wife. She took it in her hands, but her hands began to burn. She looked up at his face, got shit-scared, dropped three turds on the couch, her period came, she turned black in the face, her teeth fell out and she scrambled, vanished, ssssSSSWOOOSSSH! as best she could, out of his sight. Like the wind!

Not knowing what was going on, Afterfacts sat in the turds and looked over at the band. They were packing their instruments. The party was over. He looked at the audience, feeling squishy under his ass. Folks were moving every which way, spreading the word that some madman was up on stage—some spaced-out character looking like he'd just returned from Mars.

A dodo bird flapped its wings and did the funky chicken in the middle of the stage, shouting, "AWWW . . . Shee-it! AAAAWWWW . . . SHITTT!" The dodo bird pointed at Afterfacts, shouting, "AAW, shit, he's a masturbatin', 'crastinatin', 'ticipatin', pussy-whipped, jived-around, jackleg preacher. AAW, shit. Aaw . . . Shit."

"The bantam rooster's head? Was that it?" rambled, scrambled, bambled through Afterfacts' skull. The dodo got *gone!*

Afterfacts' gaze fell on Virginia Dare and Susan B. Anthony. The jigaboos who were screwing them quickly pulled up their pants; their faces turned sheet white, then back to black. They got off the stage in cut time, made tracks through the bustling crowd in double time, went home and crawled into bed, trembling and shaking like leaves.

V and S, not knowing what was what, got scared too but didn't know what to do. They stood on the stage, looking from one to the other, watching the band get their stuff together, the crowd slowly disperse, the flares go out, the moon turn blue, as stars fell over Oo-bla-dee.

Then there was Afterfacts. His face white, hair red, eyes blue and dick bright, flaming red, green hands in a white smock sitting atop a bed filled with menstrual blood and turds from his wife, looking around, stark-raving mad. He jumped off the couch and did a buck-and-wing all over the place.

Both the bitches fell out. Virginia and Susan B. It wasn't from sheer exhaustion; 'course that might have had something to do with it but mainly it was Afterfacts' clown dance. They were scared shitless. Legs wide open, pussies quivering and tits bouncing, they lay on the stage hugging one another, afraid of the larceny in Afterfacts' heart. White-fright covering their skin. They blanked out. Drugged.

Afterfacts danced around in circles, head up ass: bucked, winged, pushed, pulled, mashed potatoes, baked tomatoes—cattin', quackin' and beating bones. The cows came home. Pulling himself up by the bootstraps, he barefooted it over to where they lay. He nudged them, budged them, got down on his knees and stuck his tongue up their holes.

His tongue turned black. Ice cold.

That woke 'um up. They scrammed!

FACTS SPLIT / Muddy Water Hollow Log Call!

Annette and group, Doc John and troupe, couldn't believe the stage set was real. Not Afterfacts' scene! They had been sitting there telling tales, swapping lies, laughing and joking, watching the action on stage and talking with the crowd, eating, drinking and smoking dynamite grass (into their own thing!) when this fool with a clown-white face breaks loose, climbs the stage, knocking the altar over, scaring everyone away!

Annette looked across at Estavanico. They shook heads. Estavanico looked at Doc. Doc laughed and felt Veronica's thigh. Sambo barked.

Afterfacts was down on his knees, wondering where the white pussy had gone. His mouth icy, his ass blowing in the wind, he was making vain attempts to get it together.

Sambo broke loose from the table and charged after Afterfacts. He tore a piece out of his behind, reared in the air and growled, chewing the meat.

Afterfacts looked behind him and saw the bulldog's face, felt his ass—*hot butt!* His behind was on fire! Sambo's bite brought him back to his senses. He turned soot black.

He was trying to figure out what he was doing on the stage in the first place, but Sambo was on his case.

Afterfacts backed up, blinking his eyes towards the black flaming cross, searching desperately for his shiv. The smock! A white smock. He wondered where that had come from. His striped pants and frockcoat. Gone!

Sambo went for his throat.

He jumped farther back. No shiv. Fresh out of luck.

Doc John jumped on stage, a red handkerchief filled with goofer dust in his hand—to put a stop to Sambo's act.

Afterfacts caught a glimpse of his not-too-distant past, swore he knew Doc John from the Bayou when he was running games and selling Voo Doo dolls.

Black eyes met. Both sensed the other.

Sambo sensed Doc John's presence and leaped towards his target—Afterfacts' neck.

Afterfacts leaped behind the black cross, deep in the darkness, behind the blazing flames. The snake.

Doc John grabbed Sambo's collar: "Cool it, Bo. I'll nut this crack."

Sambo whimpered, sat on his haunches and watched Doc John work.

Doc followed Afterfacts behind the cross. The snake climbed down from the cross and snaked alongside him. Afterfacts was cornered.

Heart beating digital computers, blood rushing his temples, he stood between two black red-lined coffins, skeletons inside them, trying to decide. Seeing Doc John's eyes sparking in the flames, the snake at his side and Sambo in the background, his brains exploded!

He passed the pressure point.

Without any show of emotion, Doc John watched Afterfacts' body collapse between the coffins, bones falling atop his body.

Sambo rushed backstage and sniffed Afterfacts' feet. Afterfacts' body became ash grey. Doc John pulled Sambo's collar. He patted the snake's head and whispered something in spook slang.

Annette's group and Doc John's troupe circled Afterfacts' body. Doc John solemnly spread goofer dust around the corpse.

Annette's mind went outside. Marie in the coffin filled her inner vision. She fainted in Estavanico's arms. He carried her to a waiting limousine and placed her in the back seat. Coolout was instructed to drive her to the Princess's crib. Estavanico returned to the stage.

The group trooped and sang a Voo Doo Death Mass.

YES, HE RAMBLED

Veronica stripped and danced around Afterfacts' body, while the others—Sapphire, Yoko, Bella Duh Zug, Yvonne and Buck Rogers, who had become a member that day— hummed along and chatted with the rest.

Black candles burned upside down. More goofer dust was spread around the body, and oils and gris-gris were thrown in the four corners. Afterfacts' body turned white. The lips blue. Hair red. Black eyes. Stoned.

Asshole Jerk,

Shitface Turds,

Steps

and Boot lifted Afterfacts onto their shoulders. The women danced around them. Doc John, the black snake in his arms and Sambo barking on his left, led the procession down to the river. A hollow log was split open. They floated the remains down the muddy Miss.

It was *good-bye* Afterfacts. The ghost had given up.

BLA DA: The Princess's Pad

AS THE BIG SHINY LIMOUSINE crept silently up the hill to the Princess's retreat, wolves, jaguars, snakes, lizards and the soft whispering of the wind could be heard coming from the dense black foliage on either side of the black-topped road. It was quiet enough to hear the crab grass grow, breathe and sigh, the same being true for the flowers and trees.

Lightning bugs, dragonflies and green-eyed screech owls; stars, planets and a waning moon above the trees, along with the blue headlights of the Cadillac limousine, illuminated the passageway leading to the house.

Annette woke up suddenly. Darkness enshrouded the purple interior of the car. She shook her head. Her brains rattled. Her body was covered with a thin layer of perspiration. By degrees she was able to focus her eyes and tune in her ears; then felt the soft velvet seat underneath her thighs, saw the silhouette of Coolout Williams in the front seat, smelt the dense, damp swampy forest all around her and was finally able to see the blue yellow green light, the

217

black-topped road, lightning bug and jaguar eyes, stars, planets and the pale half-moon overhead.

It took her a while to recover her senses. To focus her brain. At first she thought she was still on the airplane, being transported to the Burg, and was worried about being attacked by Max. Or was the limousine being driven to the airport to meet the plane and leave Gumbo behind? Then her mind rushed to being picked up by Charles near Holy Ghost Church, driven through the city at the bewitching hour to Marie's Secret Ceremony. Her heart skipped a beat. Marie in the coffin formed an image in her mind. Afterfacts' face. Old. Ugly. On the stage stretched out between two coffins. Skeleton bones covering his body. His body stone.

Sweat popped out on her forehead. Her palms became moist. Her feet got cold. Slowly it all came back to her: the banquet, the barbecue, Estavanico, the house, Doc John, the women on the stage being screwed, Max and the Governor in a glass cage and Miles Standish chained to a tree. It all returned with the suddenness of the universe exploding into bits, then imploding into unity.

She sat back in the seat. Her neck ached. Her shoulder muscles were taut like she'd been asleep on a rockbed. She felt irritable, remembering that she had had some awful dream, a nightmare or something. That's what woke her up—the dream! But she couldn't remember it.

Coolout Williams sat in the driver's seat, the red patch over his right eye and the thirty-eight strapped to his shoulder. The sliding glass partition between the front and rear seats was closed. Basie's "Blee Blop Blues" blasted away on the car's tape deck. Coolout's thoughts were back in Kansas City where he had been a back-door man. That was a long time before he ever got involved with Black Eagle—selling guns to revolutionaries or anyone else who had a bone to pick—then seeking Oo-bla-dee as a final hideaway.

He shrugged his shoulders and looked through the infrared windshield. He could see through the darkness.

Everything appeared green. Over his hands he wore black calfskin gloves, and he handled the short like a space-age cadet in a mock-up. In his lapel was a white rose.

Annette stared at the back of his head, trying desperately to remember the dream, who he was, and where he was taking her. None of it came to her. She spied the intercom, pressed the talk button and popped the question.

Coolout had sensed that she had wakened, so when he heard her low musical voice, sounding like a tulip—if tulips could whisper—ask: "Who are you?" and, "Where are you takin' me?" he was ready with an answer.

"To see the Princess. You blacked out at Afterfacts' death struggle. Coolout's the handle."

Basie's band still blared on the tape-deck. Annette caught snatches of the tune. It sounded like "One O'Clock Jump."

He turned to let her see his face, the red patch covering the right eye. In the dimness Annette could only see the outline of his head, the dashboard's light creating a halo effect.

Strange. Annette shook her head again, thinking she was going under, entering the land of demons. Images of redwhiteblue devils with horns, tails and hooves trampled through her mind.

"Coolout. Coolout Williams," he repeated in the intercom, his voice sounding as if it were speaking in an echo chamber. "I cracked on the cracker." He laughed.

Miles Standish. The whole scene at the airport was crystal clear in her head. She felt somewhat relieved. But the Princess. And then the dream. But she figured Coolout to be a very quiet dude, and decided to let her mind rest for a bit. So much had gone down. Too much.

She settled back in the seat and looked into the darkness all around the car, the blue green yellow pattern of light piercing the blackness out in front, fog patches and low-hanging clouds which the car moved swiftly through.

Just then Coolout stepped down on the gas pedal and cut the limousine sharply to the left. The motor strained a little as he drove up a steep incline.

Somewhere in the darkness hounds began to howl, wolves started to scream and a variety of bitches began barking. A clearing came into view on either side of the road. And Annette noticed two lakes, the half-moon reflecting bluish white in both lakes, like on a sheet of thick blue-black oil, pink and white flamingos were asleep, their heads stuck under their left wings at the lakes' edges.

The car swerved around another bend in the road, through a thick fog patch, exposing red and black smoky brush fires. They illuminated the passageway. The smell of twigs burning filtered into the interior. Memories of hot Southern summer nights stirred in Annette's mind. She wondered where on Earth she was but she kept her thoughts to herself. Still the dream persisted.

The tape deck was off. The only sound was that of the soft murmuring of the big car's engine. Puff, with their thoughts into their own worlds: Coolout's mind into new worlds to discover, leaving the dregs behind, Annette into the whole trip, trying to forget what had gone down.

The car hummed past groups of children seated around fires roasting rabbits, coons and possums or baking yams in coals. (Having eaten her full at the barbecue, the smell made her slightly nauseous. But she held it down.) The children: they looked as though they were merely skin and bones; big-eyed with pig-shaped ears.

Rock sounds splashed in the background.

A dense black cloud covered the sky; the moon and stars and planets disappeared. The air became cool. Coolout pushed the car for all it was worth, traveling in excess of a hundred and twenty. The road was clear of foliage except for bluegrass growing on either side. It rained cats and dogs. Their howling and meowing could be heard for miles around.

Annette caught the apparition of a woman in a long white dress standing beside the road, a white dog at her side, in the pouring rain, as blue, red, white lightning flashed and darted across the heavens—then flicked on a white house with shutters at the very end of the road.

The short took the curves on three and two wheels, the springs giving as the car bounced and rolled as if rolling over dead bodies, bones, buried cities, junk, as Coolout kept it moving at a constant speed, crunching, zooming to the left again, onto a dirt road and out of the sudden rain, which terminated as fast as it had begun.

The full yellow moon reflected the image of a man smoking a pipe, a woman looking on, the skies clear, stars twinkling, communicating, as Coolout parked the car under a large oak tree near the front of the house.

Annette's heart was pounding in her chest, her temples ached and her blood pressure had shot up. Still she tried to relax. *But the dream!*

Coolout Williams got out of his side of the car, walked through the tall grass and mud to her side, and opened the door.

He stood there in the purple suit which looked maroon in the yellow moonlight—black to Annette—and glowing red tie, the red patch still over his eye, the other eye exposed. He beckoned for her to exit.

Annette got herself together as best she could, straightened out the skirt of her red minidress, relaxed her muscles, getting her wits about her. She felt her blonde Afro. It was still in place. Slowly she climbed out the car, clutching the red handkerchief (the black cat bone was tied on a string around her neck) and rattlesnake skin purse, and started up the cobblestone walk towards the house.

Somewhere a dog barked in the distance. The voices and shadows of children played games near the house. She heard their sounds. Saw their shadows. But that was all.

She knocked at the door.

A blonde girl climbed through the waves of the sea, shone in the moonlight, descended back into the water.

Coolout backed the car up and was off down the road, disappearing into the night, the red tail lights becoming dimmer and dimmer before Annette realized what had happened.

Somewhere in the distance, the sound coming from behind the house way below this mountain retreat, Annette heard the breaking of waves against the rocks. Then a woman's voice. The children. The dog. The strange silence. Crickets, cricketing . . . Night flies.

She held her breath for a second. Listened. Chickens. Owls. A coyote? Nothing. An unbearable silence.

She knocked again at the door. Hoping the people inside would hurry.

She looked on the moon. The ole man smiled. He held junk in his arms. Annette was sure of it. Waste.

The door cracked, moved slowly, and suddenly a dog barked behind her. She turned. A frog, green and slimy, looked into her eyes. She screamed. The frog frogged off.

The door squeaked and opened to show the interior of the house. Dark blue light created its own environment. A red glow came from the rear. Annette was able to make out the outlines of a coffin in the middle of the room. (The sounds of the children laughing and playing games behind her grew louder, their shadows danced against the outside of the house.) A skylight let moonlight shine on it. But Annette refused to peer inside it.

Was it the West underneath the mess?

Suddenly the full implication, without remembering the images, came to her!

She cupped her hands over her mouth, felt dizzy, thinking that she was going to faint. An old wrinkled face, hair equally as white with a silver-blue tint and hands that were bony, peeped at her with burning coals for eyes.

Annette copped out on the doorstep.

A Newfoundland sniffed at her prostrate body.

Four dudes in their teens, dressed in red, blue, purple and yellow outfits, matching socks and shoes, lifted her up.

The old woman, a strange smile on her thin lips, held the door open for the foursome.

They took her past the coffin and through the second room—a huge room that served as a temple—up a spiral staircase, to a room painted a light sky blue. Dawn.

They laid her on her back. The bed was the same color as the walls, the chairs, everything. Blue. Sky Blue. Dawn.

The foursome stood looking down at her for a minute. Their thoughts were the same. Their eyes showed it. Annette was just as beautiful asleep, resting peacefully, as when wide awake. It was obvious that her dreams were presently pleasant. The foursome bowed, and backed out of the room.

Annette shifted peacefully in her sleep and slept on her right side, her legs curled up.

Two girls—one dark brown with bright brown eyes, wearing a yellow sarong with multicolored flowers all over it and sandals, the other, obviously a Creole with traces of Indian blood definitely running through her veins, apparent in her facial structure, the eyes and the nose, and wearing a red sarong with multiple flowers and sandals—both the same age as Annette, whispered in soft voices as they took off her clothing.

First they laid a rubber sheet under her body, the flesh still soft and smooth, dampened by moisture due to her recent experience, as she lifted her hands over her head. Her nipples hardened, her stomach muscles relaxed, the V between her thighs slightly protruding. She was back on her back. Her hair was smooth and silky as if combed and brushed. She appeared, in her sleep, ready to make love. Her body had the fragrance of sunflowers kissed by the morning's dew.

Working rapidly and silently, communicating with each other through movements of their hands and their eyes, the

223

two girls washed her body down with garlic, geranium water, dry basil, parsley and saltpeter, turned her over slowly and washed down her shoulders, back, the half-moons of flesh on her buttocks, her fine brown hairless thighs, legs, ankles and feet. The brown-skinned girl removed the blonde Afro from Annette's head and placed it on the brass bedpost. The other girl smiled.

They turned her over again, repeating the process. And then again. A third time.

Slowly Annette stirred in her sleep. She opened her eyes and squinted at the girls. She felt well rested and strong.

The girls exchanged glances and smiled down at her. But they continued with their job. They rubbed her body down with bay rum, verbena essence and jack-honeysuckle. She was given a deep purple robe trimmed in gold. The girls nodded, smiled pleasingly at her, then left the room.

Annette climbed out of bed and felt her body. It was soft and fresh. The dawn blue of the room threw her for a moment. Everything—the carpet, the double bed, the circular walls and three doors, leading somewhere, all were blue.

She put on the robe which the girls had left; it came down to her ankles. But there was no mirror for her to see herself. She paced the room, going in circles, trying to recall her experiences, what she'd let herself be put through, organize the thoughts in her head and put them in *p e r s p e c t i v e !*

Her eyes caught a glimpse of the Afro-blonde wig. She looked at it, remembering the scene at her mother's house, and put it under the mattress. A drag!

Not knowing what to do, Annette opened one of the doors. It opened on a balcony. A full moon shone in her face. Its images reflected far down in the sea below. The mermaid waved, then vanished again in the waves. The waves beating against the rocks sounded mute to her ears. So did a dog barking, somewhere in the night. A skylark sang. Lonesome melodies. *Weltschmerz.* About centuries ago. Dem years.

The brown-skinned girl in the sarong tapped her lightly on the shoulder, and smiled: "The Princess will see you now."

Startled for a moment, Annette turned, nodded and wrapped the robe tightly around her body, tied the gold sash and played with the black cat bone around her neck. It was still there. "And . . . ?"

The girl smiled: "And . . . you're expected."

Annette thought she heard a voice calling from the sea. The Flying Dutchman? Lost? She let her thoughts fly.

But she followed the girl down a thick carpeted stairway, with deep blue mirrors on either side reflecting their images; through a rose-colored empty room and into a brass-gilded elevator. The girl didn't say anything, but stood next to her and pressed a button. The door closed. Blackout.

White light lit a long black corridor. A carved door stood at the end. Out of the elevator, Annette followed the girl towards the door. Black candles, four in number, burned outside it. The fragrance was that of Indian incense. The bas-relief on the door was of snakes intertwined, chains and couples in erotic poses with banana and palm trees in the background.

The girl ran her hand over one of the carvings—a young boy kneeling next to a woman. She glanced at Annette.

The sound of Louis playing "Between the Devil and the Deep Blue Sea" seeped from under the door. The girl pressed a button. Chimes sang songs. Lost loves. Refrains.

A woman's shriek pierced the door.

Annette wanted to run, but she didn't know which way to go. The girl looked at her but said nothing.

The door was flung open. A tall black woman, blue light from inside the room haloing her form, wearing a silver-white robe, stood before her. Deep dark-brown eyes glowing.

She appeared to be at least forty years old, shoulders squared, hair done up in the latest Afro fashion and body poised.

She spoke in deep tones: "At last."

Annette's head felt light, her bones as though they had turned to liquid, to air even. She had the sensation of standing on nothing— a vacuum.

Intuitively, she knew this was her mother!

She sensed the meaning hidden behind the words, eyes and behind her face, which was shadowed from the light.

Her guide vanished down the hall and into the elevator. Blackout.

Annette entered the blue-hued room and found a seat in a chair near a round table with crocheted placemats.

Her mother followed her, sat on the opposite side of the table in a cane rocker, leaned back and crossed her legs. But her eyes were still veiled from the light—the blue-hued light which came from gas jets in the form of candles on the crystal chandelier directly above the table.

Neither spoke for a moment. But let their feelings become one and their minds merge. Annette sensed the presence of someone else in the room—ancient, old and decrepit. Like some spirit from the past.

Her mother lit up a hand-carved pipe, its fragrance like that of American-grown grass. Annette could barely make out the image on the pipe's bowl. It looked like Papa Doc, or was it Papa La Bas? She wasn't sure.

"Marie and her mother only told you part of the story, with a slight mixture of truth."

Annette was amazed at how she began, as if she knew already, that part of the legend had been told before—an interruption made—and she was beginning anew.

"You are *not* the Governor's child. And you were *not* born in Parish Prison." She went on:

Your father was one with Damballah,
Who traveled throughout the land,
Bringing us closer together,

One with ourselves and the others,
Bringing back the Drum;
Speak in signs
and know each other
through Universal vibes.
And as he had come,
He departed back to Haiti into the heart of the Congo,
Where he resides.
But visits me often in the spirit.

Her mother inhaled on the pipe.

Annette was slowly getting the picture, and a contact high!

"Marie and her mother (for actually *I am Marie's black sister*) can't stand me. And never could. They said:

You are too dark
A child of the night god demons.
Restless spirits have possession
of your soul!

"They would hide me from people, even people in my own immediate family, call me Satan's only child and beat me mercilessly for asserting myself.

"But I had already learned their trade, how to practice their irresistible magic that they were pursuing in a dualistic fashion—first to link up with our ancestors for themselves, and second, to do away with the others' evil spirits. I ran away, the same as you, and found a place on the other side of Bayou St. John; in those days, it was mostly swampland. I lived off seafood: turtles, catfish, shrimp, crayfish and boiled pepper grass which grew around the area, plus herbs.

"Your father appeared to me as a natural man—a God, who took the man's form. He took me under the listening of the drums, pounding rhythmically at a distance—where Marie and her mother were holding a ceremony down by the lake—and left me in a family way." As her mother continued to talk, smelling the Indian-African incense which burned on the table, the smell of barbecued chicken, gumbo and fried rice seeping from underneath the black door at her back, and hearing the sounds of drums, congas, toms and traps, marching snares, flutes, piccolos, clarinets and trumpets, guitars, banjos and pianos, electric organs and moogs, male-female voices singing obbligatos in unknown tongues and the pounding of feet far down below—and watching the moon wax and wane, its full face floating silent on its course past the skylight, flap its wings, then disappear into the night—Annette's eyes closed. Was it real? The sensation was so *touching*. Serene. She sensed that her body had lost its form, turned into a spirit and encompassed the entire room.

The image of her mother's story evoked in her mind was that of a little baby, less than two months old, sitting in a banana-leaved cabin deep in the swamps, listening to the sounds of the bullfrogs, the crows, seagulls and skiffs. Drums at a distance. The buzzing of mosquitoes. Smelling the fresh wet grass, trees and flowers, carnations and roses, her mother's breath on her face, and listening as she sang songs and told stories of worlds Annette had never known, while suns, stars and moons, earths even, carried on the joyful festival of life itself.

The tone of her mother's voice changed. Annette opened her eyes. She was back!

"One must never use one's religion for vile purposes. But this was a special case. Yes, I did put a curse on the Governor. But this was when you were two weeks old. He came to me, asking my hand, wanting me to work against my people. He had heard the stories about your father, and knew he had the secret of the city in his hands; everyone depended on him for advice on their lives and the land. But the rational Governor, strung out on Locke, causality and Christian myth, assumed that he was some kind of mystic, a strange Hollywood witch doctor (white folks' fantasies) who performed murder rites. 'Course the fool couldn't see his own scientists in the same kind of vein, atomic physicists, bird-brain plastic men. Men living in one-dimensional space.

"I refused. It's not in my power to condemn or put down, but to act through my veins in the spirit of my ancestors. He called me *raunchy,* whatever that's supposed to mean. Said I was a freak of nature. I put him *out!* I told him:

Let the door hit you
Where the dog hit you,
Get out!

"That night he sent his Archbishop to see me. Max Gordon. He went into his theological bag, deucing that Christianity was nothing more than African Religion disguised, with the Eros omitted. This was something I knew anyway, so it wasn't really news. I yawned, got bored and finally decided that I had had enough!

"He got down on bended knees, yelling: *'Please! Please! Please!'* Grabbed the hem of my dress, said something 'bout *Hail Mary* with hints about gambling—*Dominoes.*

"I put a curse on that cracker's ass which he'll never forget, condemned him to going down on young girls, and ending his days dogging."

Annette got a flash!

"Other folks came by, mostly women, as you probably know. I put all their asses in a bind, telling them to *screw.* Bitches went back to the Governor, told him 'xactly what I had said. That's when they put the chief on my case. They took you away from me. And put me in the slams. But I escaped. That's the secret. None of the Angela crap for me, not your mother, I'm past that stage of the game. Really!"

Her mother paused, tears filled her eyes. Hot angry frustrated tears. From years, ages, memories, spirits of the past ago. She had awakened the Gods, and they were indignant. Let 'um sleep.

The drums became more fiery, the beat even louder. The singing was clearer, words could be distinguished as the notes from the instruments rose, swelled and floated through the room, coming up from the bottom, making the whole room shake!

Annette sat quietly. She was completely turned around by the way her mother performed. But she still felt the presence of someone strange in the room. She was afraid to look around for fear she'd see the past!

"Old Doc John was still in the city," her mother continued. "He heard about what had happened and sent a couple of sisters by.

They fed me a bowl of gumbo that made the state lackeys think I was nuts." She smiled.

"They had me transferred to Parish Prison for a day; there, I told their Freud to go fuck himself. He had me committed." This time she grinned.

"Jung and Laing were just out of the question—tricking whitey with their shit. 'Conscious one, two, three. Fronts.

"But the sisters and the brothers were the attendants. That's the gist. They had learned my legend and agreed with the whole story. They helped me to escape. Sneaking me out of the house in the *dead* of night, they took me *outasight.*

"You heard what happened to the Governor? Marie told you all that. Too bad she had to lie about the rest of it. Poor soul. But it made her *look* good. Oh, yeah, you *were* born with a caul over your face. But lots of 'um is born that way, that don't make 'um any better than the rest. But you been blessed. I saw to that myself. Yeah, you been blessed, child! That's the truth. Your father appeared to me in the form of Damballah, and danced in the circle of fire. Damballah rode your grandfather that night. He was possessed. He picked up the snake and put it in my lap. We partied back, rejoiced and sang, then he disappeared into the night just as he had come! I lifted my dress and showed myself. The men kissed me between the legs.

"Dawn broke. The sun came up bloodred! Orange!

"Blessed you are with the power to see behind the mask, the invisibles, into the future, to tell what's going to happen. That's how you happened here. But, 'course I know you thought it was all incidental.

"Haven't you noticed how stars have been falling?"

Breathlessly, Annette shook her head. Agreeing. Her mother looked so much like Marie, Annette couldn't believe her own eyes. And so much like herself, she had the sensation that she was looking into a mirror of the future. Could it be?

She heard a noise. Suddenly she turned around. There, sitting on a stool behind her was a stooped, wrinkled, looking-like-a-dwarf, white old man. Eyes red, face red, looking off into the distance. Past her.

Fright traveled the length of her body. She couldn't hear her mother's voice any more, the Image was too strong!! She perceived Marie's mother's eyes penetrating through those of the old man. But Marie's mother was blind! She remembered that. This time the eyes had life in them! One winked!

A green-eyed cat jumped down out of the old man's lap. The old man crowed, cackled, bent over and barked.

Annette jumped straight up in the air—the sounds down below grew louder and louder—and rushed over to her mother. She cried like a baby in its cradle.

Her mother caressed her. You've never seen such a sight. She held her child in her arms, cried silently along with her daughter and soothed her mind. All the while, stroking her hair.

She explained that the old man was really her great-great-grand-father who had wanted to convert, become one with them, but didn't know how to change his evil ways. She said that he had intercourse with her great-great-grand-mother, but that a curse had been put on him years ago; he

231

was condemned to live out his years, his children's years, and their offspring's years, seeing them all leave and become blues people, and he would become nothing—cold stone spiritless wrinkled.

"The stars you saw falling was nothing but him and his system of straitjacket, scientific rationality's demise, ailing with its evils. Nothing more."

Annette understood. Intuitively, she understood, in spite of its enigmatic overtones. But she knew he was Satan's disciple, it was in his eyes!

The old man changed forms. He turned into a dog, a white creature, and moved towards the door. But a woman, a white woman in white, stopped him. She entered the room.

Clotted blood and bruises covered her arms and face. The lipstick was smeared across her lips. On closer inspection she looked like Virginia without the artifacts. Plastic. Sheen. Front.

Annette became horrorstruck! Was it real? She didn't know. All she knew was that it was happening. That's all.

The woman's voice cackled when she spoke. "That's what's left of my husband." Her hair was white and pasty, and she walked with a stick.

He left me on the old plantation,
All by myself,
And went out and got the slave women
To turn him on to soul.
All my children were mutants.
Other people's sperm
Stuck up my womb!

Because of that,
Naturally,
I turned into a dyke.

I got hung up on my self.
Strictly hung up!

It was he who got me confused,
As pretty as I used to be,
Sitting there knitting and
Aging,
Seeing myself grow decadent
Before my mirror.
I had nothing to do.
Boredom, without
Nigger titillation,
Fucked me around.

He buried the West with his dealings
With Africans.
He didn't realize he was doing it!

It never once crossed his mind.

His ancestors died,
Because he loved black blood.
And his kinfolks hated him,
Because he loved his brown children.

It was he who changed the reality!

Strangely enough, the womans body collapsed to the floor and turned into a heap of ashes. The dog into the Washington Monument. In miniature, of course. Annette's mother opened the window and let the spirit escape.

The drummers increased the beat. The people downstairs partied! Annette felt faint and confused.

Estavanico entered.

He wore a flaming red shirt, blue pants and a yellow tie. Green shades covered his eyes.

233

Now it was beginning to make sense. They were part of the beginning, same with the end. Wisdom rushed through the windows, and Annette's mother and Estavanico caressed each other and went down on the couch.

Annette excused herself and found herself in a brightly lit room with tons of little boys—all her age, ironically. A TV was running back her story, in color, of course—the entire trip from the Gumbo House to Oo-bla-dee, and showed her sitting in the Princess's pad. The little boys cracked. It was the craziest, funniest, most entertaining story they had seen for days. They hugged and kissed her, saying she was the *star.*

She left the children with their Saturday morning TV shows and walked down the spiral staircase to the front room. Light came in through the front door. Feeling bold, she looked down into the coffin. Immediately she knew what it was all about: There lay history turned on its ass, stone, cold grey, with red, white and blue IDENTITY CRISIS marked across her chest.

Naturally, Annette cracked. Wouldn't you?

NOTE: This manuscript was found under a coffin in St. Louis Cemetery Number 2, which was removed to make room for an Urban Development Program. Centuries ago. Unsigned, but said to have belonged to some mysterious nun—a Da Da Hoo Doo Voo Doo Surreal List #2, of the Seventh Order of the Holy Ghost Church, New Orleans, Louisiana. It fell into my hands as a deal for some reefer. Smoke.*

Steve Cannon
Quasar 285
Somewhere in the Universe
2223 B.C.

*Annette's sign is Libra (O.K.?).

Afterword
by Tracie Morris

She's far too young. That's the first, second and last thing I think about when considering Annette. She's only fourteen. She's reached puberty, her menarche, and is stunning. She's sexually active, a libertine and, what we would call in my youth, a "freak-a-leek." What Annette is looking for is a kind of acceptance in the world that she doesn't get on her terms, but she tries. She doesn't feel shame about expressing her wanton sexuality. She owns it. However, this isn't Rick James's "wild child" teen from his song "17," nor, comparatively, is it Janis Ian's forlorn youngster. When we meet her, Annette is hardly in her teens, and she has been sexually active of her own volition since, we learn, she was much younger.

Later we find out why—how her horrifying home life and her self-awareness as a beautiful young Black girl emerging into womanhood puts her in constant danger, how she sought to take control early in her life, and how bizarre her childhood was before it becomes surrealist later in the book. I see nods to Freudianism and the stories of Alexander Dumas, another outsider in his society who used allegories of race and social trauma to discuss social trauma in a metaphorical way.

More immediately and personally, though, when rereading Annette's story after decades away from this text, I remembered girls her age (when I was close to her age in the book) who were prostitutes, who were mothers, who were subject to incestuous relationships and some whose mothers competed with them for those incestuous relationships. This was not acceptable in our communities but it wasn't unheard of (I grew up in the projects too, in Brooklyn, New York) but it wasn't unheard of. In fact, one or two specific young women come to my mind that I knew back then. So I asked myself, why is Annette so young in this book? Why did Steve make her *that* young? If she was anything like the girls I knew who were considered "wanton" at that age, they were the most vulnerable, the most likely to be destroyed. These are stories I'd heard, people I knew. Steve knew people like this, too:

> Since the Women's Movement was in its inception, I decided to make the main character a fourteen-year-old female who didn't take any crap from anybody, including her parents. At the same time, the specific issue on the Lower East Side was that kids were running away from home due to disillusion with their parents, which is why I made the main character not only a fourteen-year-old female but also a runaway.[1]

* * *

This is not a book for the faint of heart. In what is likely the last interview Steve published in his lifetime, he says that *Groove, Bang and Jive Around* was a novel of its time, combining the libertine tendencies of the Lower East Side

---

1   Steve Cannon, "You're Never Too Old to Blush," *Black Renaissance/Renaissance Noire* 19, no. 1 (Winter/Spring 2019): 53.

with the sexual freedom of the 1960s and '70s. *Groove, Bang* was certainly transgressive when it was first published, but perhaps not as shocking as it is today, when parts of the country and the world are embracing more radically conservative sensibilities toward culture: book banning, anti-diversity efforts and violent misogyny are no longer marginal positions in mainstream discourse.

More affirmatively however, the decline of delicate Jim Crow sensibilities, the full integration of women into higher education, widespread access to birth control, the presence of people with disabilities active in the public commons because of ADA legislation—people who would've previously been hidden as "the sick and shut in"—the accessibility of all kinds of information online and the Pandora's box of micro- and macro-communities being created through instant global connection . . . We've come a long way as a society, both forward and backward, since Steve wrote *Groove, Bang* and sometimes I wonder what he'd say about the topsy-turvy nature of present events besides: "blah, blah, blah" (a favorite term of his).

It's striking how radically different the tone of this book is from that of the person I knew as Steve Cannon. I was, and am, straight-edged, and probably a bit corny by down-town NYC standards, but I don't even recall Steve cussing a whole lot beyond his pointed and moderate heckles from the bar of the Nuyorican Poets' Café when a reading wasn't up to snuff. Steve is as ribald in this book as it is humanly possible to be. Again, *this book is not for a general audience. It really isn't.* It's an explicit, shocking book, but if that's all that it was, there'd be little else to say about it. What I find in revisiting it after Steve's passing is not only his humor but his care and his intricate, multidisciplinary philosophy: the Black bohemian activism that underscored his work and life. As far as I know, this is the only X-rated writing Steve has ever produced.

* * *

Part of the this book's backstory is that certain publishers were looking for specific materials at this time. In this era, we also know that certain subgenres allowed these writers to say more "between the lines."

> Maurice Girodias was a French publisher who arrived here back in the '60s. His family was from Greece and his father, Jack Kahane, was a famous publisher in Paris. He arrived at the scene in the middle of the Sexual Revolution—free love and all that jazz. He put the word out that he was in search of writers on sexual subjects; back in those days, we called it eroticism and not porn. I got word of him from Clarence Major . . . I thought about it for a month, came up with the first chapter, *fictionalizing the story of a young lady from New Orleans—whom I had known when I was a young man twenty years earlier*—wrote it up and took it to Girodias.[2]

The excessive sex and the excesses of sex are unsurprising for an X-rated novel and the framing of sex and desire becomes more and more extreme as the book proceeds. Like François Rabelais, the excess, the grossness, is the point, and affirms a kind of freedom through *addition*. It is worth noting that the book also becomes explicitly *political* as it proceeds, especially in its second half. The utopia of Oo-bla-dee is not sedate, peaceful or sweet. There's love but there's also hard love, a form of balance through comeuppance and retribution. Despite the extremity of the sex and sex acts in the book, the strangest and most surreal parts in the second half are regarding Afterfacts's trajectory. The "jack-leg preacher" was literally *turned out* in the book. His story, a pointed commentary on false prophets and Black turncoats, is so extreme that the author seems to have exhausted the

2   Steve Cannon, "You're Never Too Old to Blush," 54 (emphasis mine).

permutations of the character by book's end. And it is a merciless conclusion.

Afterfact was at a crossroads and took the wrong path. Conversely, and in real life, one might wonder how a blind Black bohemian writer, who hadn't worked regularly for decades because he lost his sight, was able to survive, thrive, create such an impactful cultural institution and land on his feet after being evicted from his home in late age. Maybe he knew a bit more about Papa La Bas and channeled (*ahem*) this trickster in this work. Insatiable sexual appetite is also characteristic of this deity, and Afro-French communities in the New World incorporated this concept/being/metaphysical power into their cultural beliefs, whether traditional or creolized.[3] These references underscore the politically revolutionary undertones of the novel, as these African traditions that permeated Afro-Francophone life were used by Haiti's most famous freedom fighter, Toussaint L'Ouverture, to fight oppression. (To balance things out, Steve also invokes the inverse of the freedom fighter by naming one of the Oo-bla-dee characters "Papa Doc John"—hybrid of Haitian dictator François Duvalier and New Orleans musician Mac Rebennack aka "Dr. John" (both voodoo/hoodoo practitioners—although Dr. John was not of African ancestry).

In this book, however, women are overwhelmingly more spiritually powerful than men, *despite* the patriarchal society, as Steve takes great pains to make clear. Women also seem to have more sexual agency overall (with the exception of Annette's sister who tries and fails to empower herself through her virginity). Creolization, as both a cultural and ethnic identity, as well as in religious practice, is shown in rituals of initiation and baptism throughout the book. "Self-baptized" sexually as a very young person, Annette must go through various stages of initiation to return to her non-judged, loved, young self. This unusual presentation

3   Ina J. Franrich's "Yoruba Influences on Haitian Vodou and New Orleans Voodoo," *Journal of Black Studies* 37, no. 5 (May 2007).

of a return to creolized African American roots in the Blacktopia of Oo-bla-dee evokes the sort of metaphysical and literal journey—that includes child exploitation—later described in Malidoma Patrice Somé's book *Of Water and the Spirit: Ritual, Magic, and Initiation in the Life of an African Shaman*. While Somé seeks his own return to African traditions, Annette's return is to a hybrid of her whole self, rather than a cutting away of the bad parts.

* * *

It's both with the hybrid of the good and the bad, with a bit of poignancy and grief, that I write these notes. Steve is dearly, sorely, greatly missed. Even though he died at the age of eighty-four, it was far too soon for many of us who adored his wit, his kindness and his generosity to younger generations of artists and thinkers, irrespective of their point of view, genre, or status of any kind. He was a fixture, a lighted star, a combo of deep bohemian and hip cat, a great teacher. Reading this novel again, for the first time in about a quarter century, I'm struck by how much I miss Steve. In his exalted state, however, I'm pretty sure we all know where he now resides, holding forth.

Tracie Morris
January 2024

Also from Blank Forms Editions

Anthologies:
01: Magazine
02: Music from the World Tomorrow
03: Freedom is Around the Corner
04: Intelligent Life
05: Aspirations of Madness
06: Organic Music Societies
07: The Cowboy's Dreams of Home
08: Transmissions from the Pleroma
09: Sound Signatures

Ahmed Abdullah, *A Strange Celestial Road: My Time in the Sun Ra Arkestra*
Maryanne Amacher, *Selected Writings and Interviews*
Wesley Brown, *Blue in Green*
Loren Connors, *Autumn's Sun*
The Cricket: Black Music in Evolution, 1968–69, ed. Amiri Baraka, Larry Neal, A. B. Spellman
Curtis Cuffie, ed. Ciarán Finlayson, Scott Portnoy, Robert Snowden
Thulani Davis, *Nothing but the Music*
Catherine Christer Hennix, *Poësy Matters and Other Matters*
Stephen Housewright, *Partners*
Joseph Jarman, *Black Case Volume I & II: Return From Exile*
Tori Kudo, *Ceramics*
Alan Licht, *Common Tones: Selected Interviews with Artists and Musicians, 1995–2020*
Kazuki Tomokawa, *Try Saying You're Alive!: Kazuki Tomokawa in His Own Words*